JENNIFER A. NIELSEN

A NIGHT DIVIDED

SCHOLASTIC INC.

*This story is fictional, but it is based on real events and
the heroism of a remarkable people who lived behind
a concrete wall that stood for twenty-eight years.*

Photographs ©: Ullstein – Sticha/The Image Works:
p. 332 *top*; Popperfoto/Getty Images: p. 332 *bottom*;
p. 333 *top*; Peteri/Shutterstock; p. 333 *bottom*.

For Ilona, who made it out.
And for all those who didn't.

Truly, it is in darkness that one finds the light.

— *Meister Eckhart, German philosopher*

When I want the west to scream, I squeeze on Berlin.
— *Nikita Khrushchev, Soviet Union premier, 1958–1964*

There was no warning the night the wall went up.

I awoke to sirens screaming throughout my city of East Berlin. Instantly, I flew from my bed. Something must be terribly wrong. Why were there so many?

Although it was a warm morning, that wasn't the reason for my sweaty palms or flushed face. My first thought was that it must be an air raid — my parents had described them to me from the Second World War. I pulled my curtains apart, expecting the worst. But when I looked out, my heart slammed into my throat. Not even the darkest part of my imagination could have prepared me for this.

It was Sunday, August 13, 1961, a day I would remember for the rest of my life. When a prison had been built around us as we slept.

Lines of *Grenzers* — our nickname for the border police, the *Grenztruppen* — stood guard along a fence of thorny wire, in some places higher than their heads, and for as far as my eyes could see. They stood like iron statues with stern expressions and long rifles in their hands. It was obvious that anyone who tried to cross would get far worse than a rip in their clothes. Because the Grenzers didn't face the westerners on the other side of the fence. They watched us.

It was very clear who they planned to shoot if there was any trouble.

If only I'd looked out earlier. During the night, I'd heard strange noises. Of hammering, heavy footsteps, and hushed conversations from men with sharp voices. But I rolled over and told myself it was only a dream. Or a nightmare perhaps.

If I had looked, I could have warned my family in time, just as our neighbor Herr Krause tried to warn us.

He knew this was coming. Hadn't he said for years that our government was not to be trusted? That we might salute the flag of East Germany, but that it was really Russia we bowed to? And my father had known.

My father!

As if she had heard my thoughts, from out in the kitchen I heard Mama cry, "Aldous!"

That was his name. And with a final glance out the window, I remembered the reason for Mama's screams.

My father wasn't here. Nor was my brother Dominic. They had been in the west for two nights, and were supposed to have come home later today. With an endless row of guns and soldiers between us, the fence just changed that.

I raced from my room and arrived in the kitchen to see my oldest brother, Fritz, holding my mother in his arms as she sobbed on his shoulder. He eyed me and then cocked his head toward the window in case I hadn't already seen the fence. I only brushed tears from my eyes and wrapped my arms around her back. Maybe she didn't need me, but in that moment I desperately needed her.

She felt me there and put a shaking hand on my arm. "They've done it, Gerta," she said through her tears. "Worse than anyone ever thought."

Mama had been a beautiful woman once, but that was years ago. She had come through too much war and famine and poverty to care about the curl in her hair or neatness of her dress. Her blond hair was already turning gray and her eyes bore early wrinkles in the creases. Sometimes I looked in the mirror and hoped life would not be equally hard on me.

"Why now?" I asked. "Why today?"

I looked up to Fritz for an answer. He was nearly six years older than me and the smartest person I knew, next to my father. If my mother had no answers, then surely he did. But all he could do was shrug and hold her tighter as her sobs grew louder. Besides, I already understood more than I wanted to.

The fence was only the beginning. It had just divided my life in half. And nothing would ever be the same again.

CHAPTER
TWO

You are your only border — throw yourself over it!
— *Hafis, Persian poet, ca. 1325–1389*

I had known something bad was coming ever since the knock on our door Friday evening. Two days before the fence.

We were in the middle of supper. My parents were discussing the day's news, as they always did. Hatred between the east and west was growing, and Berlin seemed caught in the center of what the world described as a cold war, a standoff of loud threats and puffed-out chests. Hopefully, it wouldn't lead to anyone bringing out their guns. Germany still hadn't recovered from the last war. Across the table from me, Fritz and Dominic were debating who should get the last dumpling — the oldest brother, or the hungriest. And I was telling them all to be quiet, that I heard something.

Someone knocked again. This time, everyone went silent.

Papa wiped his mouth with a napkin, and after a warning glance for us to remain calm, he went to answer the door. Though my mother whispered that everything was fine, I was already nervous. Whenever unexpected knocks came, my heart waited to beat again until I knew who it was. Eight years ago, my father had been involved in some worker uprisings in Berlin. He had never been arrested for that, and insisted he'd done nothing to deserve any special attention, but the *Stasi*, our secret police force, seemed to disagree. Every few months, they came to ask him questions, looking at him as if he had already been found guilty of something. I always wondered if they were waiting for a reason to take him away.

This time, however, my father's face widened into a smile, and in a welcoming voice he said, "Herr Krause!" Then he pulled the older man into our apartment with a warm embrace. "Have you eaten supper, my friend?"

"Thank you, but I can't stay."

Herr Krause lived next door with his invalid wife. He was a bit odd, collecting scraps of anything that wasn't nailed down and stuffing them wherever the Stasi might not look. He and my father had known each other for as long as I could remember and had been at that uprising together. Mama once told me he definitely should have been arrested and that we weren't wise to associate with him.

But when he came in, she left her seat and gave him a polite greeting. The more she disliked our company, the nicer Mama was. A lesson learned from our visits with the Stasi.

"How can we help you?" she asked.

Herr Krause kissed her cheek, then dismissed any further pleasantries with a frown at my father. "We need to talk."

Papa invited him to sit down while Mama said, "Children, go to your rooms."

We stood to obey her, but Papa said, "Fritz should stay."

"No, Aldous."

"He's fourteen years old. Fritz should stay."

Mama gave in on that argument, but waved Dominic and me off to our rooms. However, I only went to my bedroom door down the hallway, shut it as if I had gone inside, then crept back to the corner. Dominic watched me with an amused smile, then did the same thing.

"The whispers are growing louder," Herr Krause said. "The government has got to act before East Germany is completely empty."

I already understood that. Our government had closed the border years ago, hoping to stop the flood of people leaving for the brighter lights of the west. But there were always ways through, and trying to keep people in had only made it worse. Another family from our apartment building had left just yesterday, disappearing without a word to anyone. The same thing was happening all over East Germany, especially here in the city.

"So you think they'll begin arresting people who try to leave?" Mama asked.

"No," Herr Krause said. "I think it'll be worse than that. Your family must get over to the west, while you still can."

From around the corner, I nodded in agreement. Why couldn't my mother see what was so obvious to Papa and Herr Krause and so many others who felt trapped here beneath Moscow's thumb?

According to Papa, for the last sixteen years, Germany had been split between the east and the west, our people divided for no reason other than what street they happened to live on. That was part of our punishment for losing the Second World War. Break our country into pieces so we couldn't rise up and threaten the world again, the way Hitler had done.

Now Britain, America, and France controlled the western half of Germany, as well as half of the capital city of Berlin. Russia controlled the east, where my family lived. At first, it didn't matter much to us. Most people shopped, worked, or visited just as we always had, and crossing the border wasn't much more difficult than crossing the street. But Russia's promises of a better life under Communism weren't happening. As the west repaired its war damages, ours remained like unhealed scars. Their shops were full, and ours constantly faced shortages. They were growing stronger, while we leaned on Russia like a crutch, pretending to be every bit as strong.

People had noticed the widening gap between our countries. As more East Berliners left each week, those of us who remained whispered in dark corners about what if we left too. I heard them. I watched as neighbors and friends made their plans to go.

My father was one of those who whispered. Our family would have gone to the west months ago if Mama had let us. She was just as stubborn as he was, I supposed. They argued about it all the time. In whispers, of course. Berlin was a symphony of whispers.

But this was also our home. And Mama couldn't imagine leaving any more than she could think about ceasing to be German.

"Choose to go now," Herr Krause said. "Or soon you will have no choice."

"You want us to leave the life we've built here?" Mama asked. "My widowed mother lives just outside the city; she needs my help. Should I leave her too?"

"Would she ask you to stay here?" Herr Krause asked. "Where it is dangerous to speak, or to act, or even to think?"

"It is only dangerous because you fill my husband's head with ideas he should not have!" Then Mama lowered her voice. This was not the kind of conversation she wanted our neighbors to hear. At least, not the neighbors who might report us to the Stasi. She turned her attention to Papa. "Besides, our children are in school and you have a secure job."

"They have schools in the west," Papa told her. "We can find a new home, and a new job."

"The refugee camps in the west are crowded and don't have enough food to go around." Mama shook her head. After the war, she had gone for months without enough food to eat. Thousands of Germans died of hunger back then, and I knew that memory was never far from her. "We have no family or friends there to take us in, and I won't bring my children into a camp. We're not beggars."

"I'd rather beg there than live here!" I had left my hiding place and spoken even before I remembered I was supposed to be in my room. But it was too late to go back, so I added, "Please, Mama, listen to them."

"You should be in bed, Gerta!"

"What if Aldous goes to the west for a night or two?" Herr Krause suggested. "He can find you a new apartment and ask about jobs."

Papa's voice brightened. "I could leave tonight and be back on Sunday. We don't have to decide anything for sure until I come back."

Mama was silent for a moment, then she said, "Bring one of the children with you so the employers know you have a family to support."

"I'll go," Fritz offered. I knew he would. Last week, Fritz told me he wanted to buy some of the west's magazines and come back here to sell them to his friends.

"You need to help your mother with packing, and Gerta is too young," Papa said. "I'll take Dominic."

Dominic came around the corner now, smiling as if he had won some sort of prize. I glared at him, but the truth was, I thought he had won a prize too. Why couldn't Papa bring me instead?

I asked Papa that very question when he tucked me into bed that night.

He smiled and pulled the blankets up to my chin. "It's going to be difficult getting across the border in the darkness," he said. "Dominic and I will find the way, then return and show it to you in only a few more nights."

"What if you don't come back?"

His eyes became sad, though the smile remained. "I must come back, because nobody else knows our bedtime song."

He got to his feet and started dancing to my favorite song, "The Farmer in March," which described all the chores a farmer must do to get his crops ready. *"They have a lot to do in the home and the garden,"* he sang as he began pantomiming the words. *"They dig and they rake and they sing a song."*

I sang along with him until the very last line, then he kissed my cheek, wished me a good sleep, and closed the door of my room, saying, "I'll see you on Sunday, Gerta."

No, he wouldn't. Because two days later, our city would be surrounded with an endless fence of wire and thorns. As I was about to learn, he would never come back.

Eventually, Mama dried her tears and told me and Fritz to go get dressed, that we ought to see the fence for ourselves.

It was still very early in the morning, and large bulldozers could be heard, already tearing down homes or hundred-year-old trees that were in the way of the fence. Along with most of the people in my neighborhood, I stood on the road, facing the guns that faced us. Mama held one of my hands and Fritz held the other. No one around me cried, and not even the strongest men fought back.

Why didn't we? I looked around, waiting for someone to rush at the officers in a cry for freedom. Then others would join in and fight until we overpowered the guards and showed them we refused to be held in here like criminals.

Or until enough of us were shot. The guards looked prepared to do that, if necessary.

Probably everyone here already understood that, because like me, they only stood and watched. Maybe we were all too empty for tears, and too horrified for words.

When I asked Fritz when Papa and Dominic would be able to come home, he only knelt beside me and shook his head. Quietly, he whispered, "Papa was a part of the Resistance, Gerta, or they think he was. As long as that fence is up, they will never let him come home, and he won't send Dominic back to this place. But don't worry, I'm sure it can't last long."

The people around me had already given a name to this

day: Barbed Wire Sunday. The day that divided a city, and eventually a country. Worst of all, the day that divided my family.

The sun warmed my back as it slowly rose in the east, and I shivered against it. This early morning light had not ended the long, dark night. No.

For us, the dark night had only begun.

It's often safer to be in chains than to be free.
— *Franz Kafka, German author*

It didn't take long for the government to realize that they couldn't guard the fence so heavily forever. Even with the fence and armed soldiers, people were still finding ways out. If things were bad in our city before, they would only get worse now. We all knew that.

Some people made runs in the dark and literally tore their way to freedom. Others tried swimming the canals where the barbed wire couldn't reach. At least one family simply ducked low to avoid gunfire and crashed their car through the fence.

Nobody asked who might try leaving next, but everybody wondered. I kept waiting for Mama to tell us we were leaving too. Surely she would, any day now. But she never did. Maybe she had been a prisoner here long before the fence appeared.

Protests started in West Berlin. They chanted and held signs and aimed their cameras at the Grenzers, who held up mirrors to reflect the sun into the camera lenses and ruin the pictures. Fritz, Mama, and I stood near the fence and looked everywhere among the protestors for Papa and Dominic, but we could never see them.

"Have they forgotten us already?" I asked Fritz.

He smiled, as if I'd told a joke, then reached down and ruffled my hair. "Papa would never forget us, Gerta."

I kept staring, though every time I saw a face that almost was my father, my heart broke a little more. "If he hasn't forgotten, then where is he?"

Fritz turned to Mama and lowered his voice so only the three of us could hear. "There's talk about an apartment nearby that sits right on the border. You can enter the back of the building from the east and walk out the front doors into the west. Go straight through the fence."

Mama shook her head. "The government won't tolerate that for long. I don't want to be there when they come."

And they did. Only a few days later, the government bricked up all the lower exits of that building, thinking that would solve the problem. But then people started jumping from the upper windows, hoping the crowd below on the west side would help to catch them. Fritz was there a week later, watching from a distance when a woman threw down a mattress and all her bedding from the third floor while our police banged on her locked apartment door. When the police got inside, she finally leapt out. But the cushions weren't enough for the hard concrete below.

The morning after, Fritz showed me the newspaper that described her as a deserter and someone with a weak mind who had believed the lies from the west.

I barely breathed as I read the article, but managed to say, "She died trying to get free! Why don't they care?"

Fritz pointed to the final paragraph, which warned the rest of us not to try the same thing. "They care plenty! Because they want everyone to know hers won't be the only death." His warm brown eyes met mine. "Even children, Gerta."

Soon afterward, the police bricked over all the windows and locked up that building, and every other building that stood along the border. Then they made the decision that something more permanent was needed.

The fence began to be replaced with a concrete wall that was taller, thicker, and stronger. Sharp edges of broken glass were cemented into the top to prevent anyone from climbing over it, and watchtowers were built so fewer officers could guard larger areas. With one stacked block of concrete over another, our prison slowly became a fortress. And all we did was watch it happen.

With each brick, my hopes faded until nothing was left. If there had ever been a chance of Dominic and my father returning, then the wall took that too. My schoolteacher taught us a new song that thanked our leaders for building a wall to keep the fascists out. I muted my glares and only mouthed the words when my teacher was looking — I couldn't bear to sing the lies.

After a couple of months, the west sent tanks to watch their side of the border, so Russia sent tanks to our side of the border. The soldiers stared at one another through binoculars, each trying to guess which side would fire first. They all had fingers on their triggers.

"One side has to back down or we'll have a third world war," Mama said over dinner one night.

The tone in her voice sent shudders through me, but I still mumbled, "If the west wins that war, Papa could come home."

Fritz kicked me under the table, but it was too late. Mama looked up with eyes widened by dark memories. "If the west wins again, then there'll be nothing to come back to," she said. Her eyes glazed over, and I knew she was remembering the things she had often described to us from the last war — the nightly bombings, constant hunger, and millions of deaths of both soldiers and civilians. Nobody wanted another war, not even if it brought the wall down.

"We will never be able to leave," Mama said. "The sooner you both accept that, the happier you will be."

I nodded back at her. But I knew I could never again be happy here. And I refused to accept my life inside a prison.

CHAPTER
FOUR

The eye looks, but it is the mind that sees.
— *German proverb*

Mama once said the most wonderful thing about being young is our ability to make things normal. That whatever life does to us, no matter how strange, it isn't long before insanity seems ordinary, as if upside down is the way things should be.

That didn't make sense to me at first, but over the next four years after the wall went up, I saw it happen more and more. Most children barely noticed the wall any longer. They played hoops beneath the eyes of armed border guards in their watchtowers, rolled marbles in the shade of the wall, and learned to do as they were told without asking questions.

I was twelve years old now, and the older I got, the more separate I felt from the other kids my age. Because I always noticed the wall. Always. Over the past four years, I had learned to read the guards high up in the watchtowers and know when they were looking and when they had turned away. I knew when and where the guards did their patrols along the border, and where they didn't often go. And more than anything, I knew that nothing happening to us was normal.

The only one who really understood that was Fritz, who said it was because I had Papa's blood in me. Not a single morning had passed in the last four years when I didn't think of my father and the courage he would expect from me.

My walk to school passed very close to the wall, or as close as we were allowed to get anyway. I usually made the walk alongside my only real friend, Anna, who was as timid and shy as I was bold and outspoken. Where I had blond hair, round eyes, and an athletic body, Anna had darker hair, eyes that nearly disappeared when she smiled, and a thin frame that looked as if she needed to be fed. She worked very hard to stay out of trouble, which made her an ideal friend for me. Unfortunately, my ability to avoid trouble was less skilled. I probably wasn't the perfect friend for her.

Today felt uncommonly cold. I was enduring it and hoping not to arrive at school frostbitten. As usual between us, Anna had made the wiser choice. She was wrapped in scarves until there wasn't much visible except for her eyes and mouth. I'd barely remembered my coat.

"There's a Pioneer meeting today," Anna said through what looked like eighteen layers of wool. "Are you going?"

I groaned. We went to school to study letters and numbers, then stayed at school as members of the Pioneers and learned why freedom was overrated, why individuality was bad, and why we must always avoid the evil influences of the west, such as fancy clothes and Beatles music. I loved the Beatles, but not even Anna knew about that. That secret was only for Fritz and me. He had bought one of their albums smuggled in through the black market, and he and I listened to it very low on nights when the streets were crowded and noisy.

"Of course I'm going," I said. Not attending could bring my mother a visit from the school administrators, and none of us wanted that. Over the last four years, we'd already had too many questions from the school, the police, and even the Stasi about my father.

Nothing in East Germany frightened me more than the Stasi. We always knew they were there, even when we couldn't see them. They existed to protect our country from enemies: either foreign spies trying to get in, or traitors who wanted to get out. My family wasn't either, but that didn't mean we were safe.

After my father left, I had thought there'd be no need for them to visit us anymore, but they obviously disagreed. They had last come almost two years ago, late at night, long after we should have been in bed. I think their timing was meant to make us nervous, and from the looks on my family's faces, it worked. Fritz and I had sat on either side of

Mama on the couch. While she answered their questions, I kept an eye on their weapons. If they'd only come to ask questions, why did they bring guns?

The Stasi officer who had sat in Papa's old chair was on his second cigarette before the hard questions came.

"Has Aldous Lowe returned to East Berlin?"

I was sure I could hear Mama's heart pounding beside me. Or maybe it was mine, because the officer's tone made it clear that he was no friend to my father. Mama shook her head, and if she was trying to answer in a calm voice, it didn't work. "I have not seen my husband since the wall went up."

"Good," the officer said. "We will arrest him if he does return." He took a long drag on his cigarette. "Does he continue to work against the government?"

"He never did," Mama said.

Another man who had stood by the door walked forward with photos that he placed in her hands. I leaned over just enough to see an old picture of my father and Herr Krause, both with stacks of leaflets in their hands. I didn't know what was on them, but from the terse expression on the officer's face, it was obviously something more than party invitations or store coupons.

Mama quickly handed the photos back. "I have no idea what my husband is doing now. He does not involve us in those activities, and never did."

He never involved Mama or me. But Fritz hadn't looked at the pictures, and I wondered if that was because he already knew what my father had been doing.

"Has Aldous Lowe tried to contact you?" the officer asked.

Mama shook her head, but when she paused for too long, I spoke for her. "We have no letters, and you cut the phone lines to the west on Barbed Wire Sunday."

The officer turned his attention to me. His eyes were like ice on my bare skin. "I cut some of them myself, child. Does that anger you?"

Of course it did, but he had the gun, so I only looked down while Mama made humble apologies for my boldness and gripped my wrist like a vise. The Stasi left soon afterward, but even now, two years later, I still felt a chill whenever I thought of them.

Since that night, Mama carefully made sure we did everything that might be expected of a good East German family. We waved our flags at the parades and smiled at the leaders of the GDR — German Democratic Republic — our Communist government. Fritz joined the Free German Youth and made plans to enroll at the university one day. And at the beginning of every school year, I joined the Pioneers. With Anna at my side, I participated in their meetings and activities, chanted the slogan to "Be ready — always ready," and wore the blue scarf and white shirt uniform on every holiday when it was required. If anyone was watching us — and we suspected they were — my family now looked as loyal as the best of them.

"Gerta, stop staring at the wall," Anna whispered to me. "Do you think the soldiers don't notice?"

"I think it's too cold for them to bother with me," I said. "They watch the university students, and the men whose families are on the other side. They don't watch twelve-year-old girls on their way to school."

"Yes, they do," Anna insisted. "Turn away, please. Look at anything else."

"At what?" I gestured around me. "There's nothing else to see. With all of this gray around us, it's hard to remember we live in a world of color!"

We called it Communist Gray. It was the color of our buildings, our markets, our streets. The color of the wall. Even the skies were gray today. Somehow the GDR must have figured out how to bleach that out too.

But because I knew it bothered Anna, I stopped looking, and she and I fell into a conversation about the latest hair fashions. It was the sort of conversation two ordinary girls might have on a perfectly ordinary day, even if one of those girls had her mind on something else entirely, as I almost always did.

I became so distracted by my thoughts, in fact, that I barely noticed when Anna stopped talking. I probably wouldn't have realized she had stopped walking either, if she had not spoken my name.

"Gerta, look."

I stopped and turned back to her. To my surprise, Anna stood directly facing the wall.

"Gerta, is that your brother?"

Several meters away, across the large scar of land that had become forbidden territory, a boy stood alone on a platform behind the wall in West Berlin. I usually tried to ignore the westerners on those platforms because they made me feel like an exhibit in a zoo. I didn't want their looks of pity, or sadness, or especially the occasional homesick expression to return to this lesser half of the city. But the boy on the platform seemed to be staring directly at me, and I squinted to see him better.

It had been four years since I had seen Dominic, and he would be fourteen now. Mama kept a picture of him in the front room, and I mentally compared that with the boy now facing me. His face had lengthened and narrowed, but the hair peeking out from his knitted cap seemed about the right color. I would know him if I saw his eyes, but that was impossible from this distance.

Still, there was something in his posture, the way he held one shoulder higher than the other. Dominic used to do that — I remembered because my mother always reminded him to stand up straight.

It had been a long time since my smile had stretched so wide. "That's him!" I said. "That's my brother!"

He seemed to recognize me too, or at least he waved. I

raised my hand back at him, although such a simple gesture was far too casual for the importance of this moment. For almost four years, neither of us had heard a word about the other, and all we could do now was wave in silence?

"Does something over there interest you?"

I turned to see a border guard standing right behind Anna and me, close enough that I could see the stitching of his black gloves. He was shorter than average, with white-blond hair shaved so close to his head that he almost looked bald. He was several years older than Fritz, but there were a lot of patches on his uniform, so I gathered he was more than a low-level officer. His name, stitched onto the uniform, was Müller, and he stared down as if frightening me entertained him.

Müller had come up so quietly that neither of us heard him, but I should've known. Grenzers often patrolled this area; of course my wave to Dominic would've caught one's attention.

Beside me, Anna had turned to stone, or something like it. She wasn't moving, and possibly wasn't breathing either. Not me. I wanted to look up as far as his eyes, stare him in the face, and tell him there was no crime in looking across the wall. More than anything, I wanted to show him I wasn't afraid.

Except that I was. Müller's rifle hung around his shoulder directly in front of me, and he had one hand on the stock. Maybe it was only my imagination, but I could've sworn that the rifle smelled like blood, as if he had used it on someone before. He lifted it over his head and moved his other hand to the trigger.

"I asked you a question," Müller said. "Who were you waving at?"

I turned back, but Dominic had disappeared by then. So I lowered my eyes and said to the officer, "It was nobody, sir."

"You'd better remember that next time someone over there waves at you." He let the cold metal barrel brush against my cheek, then ran it beneath my chin and pushed my head up to face him. "Because those who get too curious about the other side sometimes get a taste of my bullets. *Verstehst du?*"

I stared into his icy blue eyes and tried not to let any hatred show in mine. "Yes," I whispered, "I understand exactly who you are."

"Then move along. Don't let me catch you stopping here again."

I whispered another thanks to him, which almost immediately began to eat at my sense of justice, then I grabbed Anna's arm. As terrified as I had been, she seemed worse. Her skin was deathly pale and she leaned hard against me as we walked away.

When Officer Müller was out of our sight, Anna released a gasp of air, then said to me, "Promise me you'll never stop there again. No matter who you see on the other side, promise me, Gerta."

Though her reddened eyes begged me to agree with her, I couldn't. Maybe I could promise to be more careful next time I stopped, but that was all. I didn't tell her that — she'd have launched into a fit of hysterics, which would've brought on Müller's attentions again. So I clutched her arm tighter as we continued to walk. My heart was pounding, just as hers surely was, but for an entirely different reason. All I could think was that after four long years, I had finally seen my brother. And I hoped it wasn't for the last time.

CHAPTER
FIVE

The Germans and I no longer speak the same language.
— *Marlene Dietrich, German actress, 1960*

Since both Mama and Fritz worked through the afternoons, it was sometimes my job after school to stop by the market for food. Most things were gone by then, but Mama said that made choosing easier. This was true — often by the time I got there, the choice was between red cabbage or white cabbage. As if I cared which one went into my basket.

Today I wandered the aisles, hoping something more exciting would be available. I could afford it if there was — the government kept the prices of everything we might need very low. It's just that the shelves were always more empty than full, and what was on them looked or tasted as gray as everything else. The good food was called Benders — because if you had something worth trading, the clerk would bend down under the counter to get it for you. But Mama didn't want us bargaining for food. "Just take what is offered on the shelves and come home quickly," she always said.

More than anything, I longed for a banana. We used to have them years ago, and for my twelfth birthday last fall, Fritz had bought one for me off the black market. I still remembered its taste.

Finally, I got some chicken, a few potatoes, and, of course, cabbage. I also picked up a few cans of cola, proudly made in East German factories. Fritz thought it left a bitter aftertaste and said one day he'd smuggle in some "real" western cola for us.

"After that," he said, "you'll never want our cola again."

"If that's true, then don't get it," I had responded. "It'll be one less thing that I can buy."

Once in line, I stared at the people ahead of me, watching them watch nothing at all because it was safer that way. Mama described us as practical, durable people, which I think she meant as a compliment, though I never took it that way. Our strength came from the collective; every school-teacher I'd ever had said that until it played in my head like a skipping record. Individuality was a weakness, a sickness of the west. So we all walked in step, eyes ahead, and with conversations at a minimum. We all smiled, but not much, and frowned but rarely cried. Nobody could succeed here, but most people around me seemed to be okay with that. It meant they wouldn't fail either.

I didn't want to be like them. And at the same time, I was beginning to forget how to be different, how to be my own self. It was the feeling of being swallowed up, and I hated it. That was all I thought about as I hurried home with my groceries.

We lived on the fourth floor of a drab apartment building that looked more or less like all the other apartment buildings. That wasn't an accident. Beautiful things were signs of individuality. Wherever possible, Mama had tried to provide some beauty inside the apartment, but still, our furnishings were spare and simple.

With little to look at inside, I went to my room and stared down to the small garden space below. I had buried the peel from Fritz's banana there, hoping it would sprout into a tree this spring. I knew it was impossible, but I still looked every day.

And when the tree wasn't there, I always turned my attention to the wall. If I got the angle just right, I could see into West Berlin.

"There's nothing but greed and selfishness on the other side," my schoolteacher often told us. "If you try to look, it shows nothing but greed and selfishness in your own heart."

Well, I was greedy and selfish, then, because I could never help but to look. I couldn't see much, but it somehow seemed brighter across the wall, as if the sun gave more of its light to the west. Maybe the people there *were* more selfish, I thought. Because we needed that sunlight far more than they did.

Then some movement at the wall caught my attention, and when I saw what it was, I laughed. A rabbit had become trapped in the Death Strip — they often did. But it was always amusing to see the Grenzers come running to try chasing it away. They didn't like the prints the rabbits left behind in their perfectly smooth dirt.

Over the past four years, what started as a simple barbed-wire fence had evolved into an entire system designed to stop, capture, or kill anyone who tried to get through. In most places in East Germany, even before reaching the wall there was an open border area that nobody would dare get close to unless they had a death wish. People who encountered the Grenzers there on patrol often disappeared, sometimes for days. Sometimes forever.

Behind it was the Backland Wall, which I passed each day. It was a simple concrete wall that surrounded West Berlin, making that free half of the city an island within Communist East Germany. What I knew of the area behind the Backland Wall came only from the glimpses I saw from my window, or occasionally from Anna's bedroom if she didn't catch me looking, and from what Fritz told me he had seen while out on bricklaying jobs. Beyond the Backland Wall was another barbed-wire fence that might have been electrified, which I figured was bad enough, but Fritz thought it was something else. He believed touching that wire sent a signal to the guards in the watchtowers. If it was true, that would be worse.

Past that was what we called the Death Strip. The government hadn't given it that name, but they didn't discourage its use either. Soldiers and fierce dogs often patrolled it, barriers and deep trenches were set up to stop any vehicles that tried to crash through, and the dirt was left smooth so on the rare chance that someone did get that far, it would be easy to follow him.

Soldiers were ordered to shoot on sight, and shoot to kill — they never hid that fact. And they had done it before. Western television broadcast the pictures of border guards carrying dead bodies out of the Death Strip or pulling them from the water. I'd seen it myself, at least when we could catch the television signal here. Our government would then respond with ridiculous excuses such as heart failure or a swimming day gone bad. Well, heart failure didn't cause bleeding wounds ripped through a person's gut, and nobody ever swam the Spree River for fun. They had tried to escape, and had failed, reminders of our own fate should we try it too. There were some successes, no doubt, though we didn't hear about them as often. Those who escaped usually kept quiet about it. They didn't want their loved ones left behind in the east to be punished.

Eventually, the rabbit hopped away, or perhaps someone I couldn't see chased it off. I never could figure out how the rabbits got inside in the first place. Since they couldn't pass through solid concrete, they would've had to dig a tunnel underneath. Even the animals wanted to leave East Berlin, I supposed.

I would've kept watching for the rabbit, but Mama called me in to supper. I came in and plunked down beside Fritz, but right away it was clear his mind was somewhere else. He picked at the food until Mama finally set down her spoon and said, "You're quiet tonight. What's wrong?"

He shrugged. "Just a hard day, that's all."

No, that wasn't all. I knew it, even if she didn't. Since the wall had gone up, Fritz never told Mama anything that made her more worried or sad than she already was. So if he went as far as admitting it had been a hard day, that meant something awful had happened, or would soon.

Fritz met my eyes and offered a grim smile, but he looked away when Mama turned to me and asked, "What about your day, Gerta? You had a Pioneer meeting?"

"Yes." I reached for another slice of bread. "They had an announcement. A few days ago, the first person ever to do a space walk was outside the spacecraft for over twelve minutes. He's Russian. They want us to be proud of that, though I don't see how it has anything to do with Germany."

"They want us to be proud because it means the east beat the west. Nothing more." Fritz's tone was more biting than usual. Something was definitely bothering him.

I decided to leave it alone. After all, sometimes I didn't want to talk either.

"Where's the butter?" he asked.

I shrugged. "Food shortages." Butter never lasted long on the shelves.

Trying to distract us both, Mama asked, "Did anything else happen today, Gerta?"

Immediately, I thought of having seen Dominic. Ever since that moment, I had debated whether to tell them. Would Mama be happy that I had seen him? Or sad because she had not?

I didn't know the answer to those questions, but I was certain of one thing: If either Mama or Fritz had been the one to see Dominic, I would want them to tell me.

I hesitated a moment, then in only a whisper, I said, "I saw Dom this morning."

The room became as still as the grave, and I almost wondered if Mama thought that's where I said he was. Shouldn't she be asking how he looked, whether Papa was with him, and how I had felt in that moment?

But with a stiff voice, she only asked, "Where?"

"On my way to school, on one of the platforms in the west. I think he was waiting for me. He knew I would be there."

Mama frowned and the lines in her face deepened. "We've talked about this before. You shouldn't be looking over the wall. If the Grenzers caught you —"

One had — I still got a pit in my stomach when I thought about Müller's rifle against my cheek — but I certainly couldn't tell her that. Instead, I faced her scolding with my own anger. "We wouldn't have to worry about the Grenzers if you'd let us leave with Papa that night!" It wasn't the first time we'd had this fight.

"We all want to be together again." Mama's voice was tired. "But it's not possible. You know that."

Yes, I did. Some days, all I thought about was ways to get my father back here, or how we might get over to him and Dominic, but never once could I come up with an answer. The wall was larger, stronger, and far more deadly than anyone my age could challenge. I hated that wall, and resented my mother every time she tried to make me accept it.

"Did you hear me?" I almost shouted now, but that was better than tears. "I saw Dom today! Your son!"

Fritz tried to calm me. "Gerta, you don't —"

But it was too late. I slammed my fork back on the table and ran to my room. My father would've understood why I waved at Dominic, but Mama didn't. Sometimes I thought she was just like everyone else here: blind to the fact that there was an entire world out there beyond the wall. Maybe Mama no longer cared about Papa and Dominic, or had forgotten them entirely. I never would.

The Wall will be standing in fifty and even in one hundred years if the reasons for it are not removed. — *Erich Honecker, first secretary of East Germany, 1971–1989*

It was a Beatles night.

Fritz lay on his bed, staring at the ceiling, while I sat cross-legged on the floor with a book I had given up on reading. In the background, John Lennon harmonized with Paul McCartney as they sang philosophies of love in a language I barely understood. If it weren't for the Beatles, I wouldn't have known any English at all.

"For me, it's the lyrics." Fritz had taken an English course in school and spoke it much better than I did. "The things they write could never be played here."

"Of course not," I said with a smile. "It'd corrupt us."

Personally, I preferred the tunes, although mostly I liked the Beatles simply because we weren't supposed to like them, or for that matter, even know about them. But all the kids did, Fritz's friends especially. The boys smuggled in albums we weren't supposed to have and pictures of shiny Ford Mustangs we'd never own, and the girls got fashion magazines, and colorful beaded necklaces to hide under their mattresses.

Even though she never stopped Fritz and wouldn't turn anyone in, Mama disapproved. She wanted us to buy the censored albums instead, but that missed the whole point of rock and roll. Nobody wanted "approved music."

I wondered if maybe Mama wasn't angry that I had seen Dominic. Maybe it made her sad. Because nothing she could do would bring him home again. I never should've told her about Dom at supper, and never should've yelled.

Fritz must've been thinking about that too. "Mama loves them as much as you do, Gerta. She misses them so much it hurts her to talk about them. You can't be angry with her that Father is gone."

He was right, of course. I didn't want to be angry, but sometimes it was the only emotion I understood. I missed my father singing to me at bedtime and the earthy smell of his coat before he left for work each morning. Sometimes, he snuck a kiss from my mother when he thought no one was looking and it always made me giggle. I even missed Dominic. The way he used to tease me and hide my dolls and jump out from behind corners to scare me — those were good memories now.

Our family was like a house of cards in a stiff wind. And when it became too much to feel the pain of our collapse, all I could do was become angry.

"We need to get to the west, to be with them," I said. "There's got to be a way through that wall."

"Of course there is. But the only way to know for sure is to try, and there's a high price for being wrong. Are you so certain there's a way through that you'd risk dying for it?"

I wanted to say yes. More than anything, I wanted to be the kind of person who dared to say yes. Papa would take the risk, maybe Fritz too. But I wasn't sure about myself.

"If I knew we'd make it, then yeah, I'd try to cross." Then I added, "But that's all the bravery inside me."

"That's not how bravery works," Fritz said. "Courage isn't knowing you can do something; it's only being willing to try . . ."

His voice trailed to silence and the record player spat out static in the gap before the next song began. The needle on the player was going dull. It would be a long time before Fritz lucked into finding another one. Shortages. Always shortages.

Once the music began again, Fritz rolled over to face me and rested his chin on his hands.

"I gotta tell you something," he said. "I wasn't going to, but if you really believe there's a way through the wall, you ought to hear this."

I leaned forward, certain this was the secret he had kept from Mama at suppertime.

"Do you know Peter Warner? Anna's older brother?"

"Sure." I didn't know him well because he was so much older. He was away at the university, but I saw him occasionally on weekends. As the first in his family to attend a university, Peter made their parents very proud, and they talked about him all the time.

"Peter is going to the west tonight. Nobody knows about it but me."

I sat up straight. "Not even his family? They'll be furious."

"He hopes they'll understand, and maybe even be happy for him."

I paused, letting that sink in. Then I asked, "How is he getting out?"

"Some students in the west got a pass to come to East Berlin for a museum tour. They're going to smuggle him out in their car — it was specially designed just for that reason."

I shook my head. "It sounds dangerous."

"It is. But where we live, walking can be dangerous. Talking is dangerous. For you and me, being the children of Aldous Lowe is dangerous — that's why he never sends letters. Just because of who our father is, they probably watch you from the moment you step out of this apartment until you get inside again. If the chance came for me to leave the same way Peter is leaving, I'd take it."

I felt a pinch in my chest. It was one thing to think about Anna's brother leaving, but I couldn't imagine if Fritz left too. Would he just disappear, like Peter?

I was about to ask when a knock came to our door. Fritz looked over at me and with a stern voice said, "Don't say a word about this. Don't make Mother responsible for knowing." When I agreed, he got up and opened the door.

Mama pushed past him and turned the volume down on the record player. "They'll hear you on the streets."

"Not with the windows closed," Fritz said irritably. "Besides, the police have better things to do than confiscate teenage music."

"And how do you know that? Only because they haven't come here yet to do it, that's all."

Fritz nodded and then switched off the player. Neither of us was enjoying it now anyway.

"Off to bed, Gerta," Mama told me. "You too, Fritz."

I got up off the floor and gave Fritz a long look before leaving. Mama stopped me in the doorway and put her hands on my shoulders.

"I'm sorry I became upset before," she said. "I was only worried that you might've been caught by one of the border guards. Can you understand that?"

Yes, *that* I understood.

"I am glad you saw Dominic," she said. "I wish I could've seen him too."

"He looked good," I said. "He's as tall as Fritz is now, and he looked healthy."

"Did he seem happy?" she asked.

I didn't know how to answer that. He must've ached

about the divide in our family, just as all of us here did. But he was also free, and I wasn't sure he would give that up, even to be back with us again. So I only shrugged the question away, which seemed enough for her.

She kissed my forehead, then said, "Now, good night and sleep well."

I wished her a good night too, but I knew there was no chance of sleeping well. Sometime in the next few hours, the brother of my best friend would vanish into the west. I whispered a prayer that God would see him there safely, and then carry his family through the storm that was sure to follow his disappearance.

SEVEN

*There are no dangerous thoughts; thinking itself is
dangerous.* — Hannah Arendt, *German political theorist*

Anna said nothing about her brother on the walk to school
the next morning. I didn't think she would — he lived at
the university and it would probably be a while before anyone in her family knew he'd left. I wondered if Peter had left
behind a note of explanation, or if he would send word to
them once he was free. I wondered how they'd feel afterward:
proud of his courage, or ashamed that he'd abandoned them?
And I wanted to know if Peter would ever look back with
regret for what he had done. Would I, if it were me who left?

I glanced at Anna's cheerful expression and felt a rash of
guilt for knowing what she did not.

"It's just as cold today," she said. "Hopefully it will begin
to feel like spring soon."

The weather was trivial. So were the books in her hands,
and her annoyance with the boy who pulled her hair when
the teacher wasn't looking. Anna wasn't even thinking about

her brother today. And all I could think about was whether he was still alive.

"Are you feeling okay, Gerta?" Anna often preferred to interpret my moodiness as illness. It was the way she tried to understand me.

"Springtime. Sure."

Was that even what she'd asked? My mind was at Checkpoint Charlie, where Peter would have crossed into the west. Fritz said the car had been specially designed to hide him, but the border guards always searched carefully, and they had dogs, and maybe other detection devices as well. I tried to picture Peter sitting in a coffee shop with the other students right now, laughing at how easy it had all been.

But I couldn't laugh. Not yet.

"What if you had the chance to go to the west?" I suddenly asked Anna. "Would you?"

Anna stopped and glanced around to see if anyone was nearby. When she was sure we were alone she started walking again, then said, "Don't ask questions like that. Don't even *think* questions like that."

It was wise advice, though I never could stop my thoughts from coming. They just did, all the time. Maybe I wasn't trying hard enough to stop them. I knew I wasn't.

As we approached the same area where I had seen Dominic yesterday, I looked around for any border police. At least for now, the street was empty. Then I turned toward the platform on the west, but nobody was there. Still, I shuffled my feet and walked slower, just in case.

Anna seemed to know what I was doing and grabbed my arm. "Please don't, Gerta. He won't come back after seeing you get in trouble yesterday."

Maybe not. But I still had to hope. "Help me keep an eye out for guards and we won't get in trouble," I said.

Anna huffed, but she began looking around.

We couldn't walk as slowly as I wanted. Other students were on our heels, trying to get to school before this cold rain turned to snow. I kept my head down, except for the occasional peek to my right. There was nothing, and then nothing again. And then just before we passed by, Dominic's blond head rose into sight.

I stopped but didn't wave. Anna gasped and told me not to look.

I ignored that and replied, "He's my brother. I'll bet Officer Müller has family on the other side too. You can't split a city in half and not divide everyone in some way."

Dom didn't wave this time. Instead, he motioned at someone below him to come up. I barely breathed as I anticipated who it must be.

My father.

His head rose higher with every step up the platform ladder. He wore glasses now and his light brown hair seemed thinner. It seemed odd to finally see him, looking much as I remembered him, yet it had been so long I felt I scarcely knew him anymore.

He waved only once and wiped a tear from his eyes with the back of his hand. I think I needed to see that, to know he missed me as desperately as I missed him. But then he did something I didn't expect.

He danced.

Not the formal dances the adults knew, but the silly dance he used to do for me all those years ago, the one from "The Farmer in March." He started by pantomiming the farmer's wife telling the maids to get back to work. His movements were from the song's second verse. We had sung this so many times together when I was younger that the lyrics and actions were etched into my brain. It still ran through my head sometimes at night, when he wasn't there to tuck me in.

"They have a lot to do in the home and the garden," the song went. *"They dig and they rake and they sing a song."* My mouth formed the words even as he performed, and the cheery tune rang in my mind.

With that second line, my father pretended to hold a shovel and dig, but when he should've moved to the rake, he only continued the digging motions, looking up at me very deliberately, and then made a silly bow, just as he had when we used to do the song together years earlier.

I smiled and acted out an applause, just as I used to do, then he motioned that I should leave and keep on walking. I nodded obediently, faced forward again, and then Anna and I walked away.

"You could've gotten us arrested just now," she scolded me. "And for what? A silly dance?"

"Papa was playful like that. It used to be my favorite song."

But Anna shook her head. "He wouldn't have you take that risk just to show you a dance."

No, he wouldn't. It took me the whole school day to think about it. While the others dutifully studied geometry, Russian vocabulary, and whatever else we learned that day, I considered Anna's suggestion that perhaps there had been a message in his words. Why had Papa chosen to pantomime from the middle of the song? If he had wanted me to think about this time of year — March — then the beginning of the song would've made more sense. And if he had danced just to bring up the fun memories, the final verse was the silliest to perform. So why choose the middle?

I figured it out during reading time that afternoon, forty-five minutes in which I could not recall a single word I'd read. It came down to the mistake Papa had made in his performance. Where he should've changed from a shovel to a rake, he only kept digging. And that was the end of his dance.

He was digging.

Papa wanted me to dig.

But why?

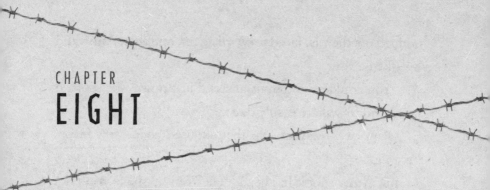

*Fear . . . was the most powerful weapon possessed by the
Stasi.* — David Cook, British author

Years ago, Mama and some other women in our building
used to garden in a small patch of dirt behind our apartment. They enjoyed the work, and the food from the garden
was very good. But one year, the food shortages had been
particularly fierce, and the harvest disappeared into the
hands of those who walked by it each day. Mama never gar-
dened again. Said it wasn't worth the bother.

I found the shovel after school, right where she had left
it. It was tucked in a forgotten corner of the basement along
with the things other families in our building had no room
for upstairs. There were many boxes and crates, and dusty
surplus tins left over from the war that probably weren't
even edible anymore. Nobody ever went down here, though.
The corners always stayed dark, and every time I came, it
felt like the roof and dirt floor were closer to each other than
the time before.

Although my instinct was to leave the basement as soon as possible, I forced myself to stay and stare at the shovel, as if another hard look would somehow help me understand what Papa wanted me to do.

Perhaps he wanted me to encourage Mama to start gardening again, or for me to plant one myself.

No, I didn't think so. He had pantomimed the lyrics for digging, not for planting.

Digging.

Maybe before he left, he had buried some sort of treasure nearby. Papa must be worried about our family, and of course he would want to take care of us.

Well, he didn't need to worry. Fritz's after-school bricklaying job helped us with money. Sure, we didn't have a television, but Anna did if there was anything I really wanted to watch. Most of our entertainment came from Fritz's record player, which was good enough most of the time. And we had no Trabant like other families, but it was okay to walk where we needed to go, and besides, they were ugly cars anyway.

Still, if Papa had some sort of treasure buried in the area, I wanted to find it. I hoped to see him again at the viewing platform soon so I could try to figure out where to dig.

Fritz didn't get home that night by supper, which was unusual. But sometimes his bricklaying required extra time at work, and so Mama and I didn't think much of going ahead without him. He would probably get back before supper was finished.

"This is better anyway." Mama's shoulders seemed heavier than usual, and just seeing them made mine feel heavy too. "I had some very sad news at work today, and wanted to share it with you in private."

I set down my fork and looked over at her. I couldn't imagine what must have happened, and already a pit was forming in my stomach.

"Your friend, Anna, has an older brother, doesn't she? A boy named Peter?"

If she had not spoken another word, I would have already known how Mama's story was going to end. I wanted to press my hands over my ears, pretending if I couldn't hear it, then it didn't happen. But life never works that way, and all I could do was close my eyes and pray that I was wrong.

"Anna's parents got a visit from the Stasi this afternoon. Peter attempted an escape last night, hidden in a special panel of a car from the west. He was discovered before reaching the border and tried to make a run to the west, but they shot him in the back. In all the confusion, the students driving the car were able to escape, but Peter didn't make it." Mama grabbed my hand and gave it a squeeze. "Anna probably got the news once she came home from school. The family has been allowed a day home tomorrow to mourn his loss, but this will be a terrible time for them. I thought you should know. It's a reminder to us all of what happens to those who try to escape."

They die.

Tears rolled from my cheeks, but I didn't care if Mama saw. I couldn't begin to imagine the pain that Anna and her family must be feeling right now. She loved her brother just as much as I loved both of mine. Losing one of them would feel like my whole world was coming to an end. Fritz would feel awful too. He'd feel guilty for knowing Peter's plans and not stopping him.

Wait . . . Fritz had known. And he still wasn't home!

"Why isn't Fritz back from work?" I tried not to sound as worried as I was — after all, he had been late before. But not often, and Fritz had said nobody knew Peter's secret but him.

What if Fritz had tried to escape too?

Although she had only the smallest understanding of why my face was suddenly flushed and hands were shaking, Mama said she knew I was upset and asked if I needed some time alone.

I left the table and practically ran into Fritz's room. I had half expected to see a note on his pillow too, some words of apology and explanation for his own escape attempt. There was nothing, so maybe it was just my imagination. But every minute that passed sharpened my worries. Fritz was never this late.

I reappeared in the kitchen, where my mother was finishing cleaning up, except for a plate she had left out for Fritz.

"Can we go to his job site and look for him?" I asked. "Please, Mama, can we go and find him?"

Mama pressed her eyebrows together. "Gerta, I know the news about Anna's brother upset you, but —"

"Fritz and Peter were friends," I said. "Fritz knew about the escape."

Without another word, Mama set down her dishrag and hurried to get a coat. Minutes later, we were outside, pressing through the busy city streets, deeper into East Berlin where Fritz had been hired to help lay brick for a new building.

So much of Berlin had been destroyed in the war, and even now, twenty years later, piles of rubble were still strewn about the city. The government was rebuilding as quickly as they could, but it took a lot of resources to maintain the wall. Their second priority was rebuilding public places, or areas near the border that were meant to show the world how superior our system was. It was behind the glossy scenes that everything remained in ruins.

Every day after school, Fritz had been working on one of those high-profile buildings, and they were in a hurry because of some visitors coming from Moscow. A few men were still on the job site when Mama and I got there, but Fritz was clearly not one of them. She told me to stay back while she talked to the job foreman. I hated being left behind, but a man in his position wouldn't want me in the conversation. So I waited where I could see their faces as my stomach twisted into knots.

In response to Mama's question, the foreman shook his head and his mouth was turned in a distinct frown. He checked his watch and then spoke to her some more. Even from here, I could tell that nothing he had to say was good. *Where was Fritz?* I wanted to scream. Why were they just standing there, talking?

Finally, Mama's back stiffened and she clutched at a handkerchief in her fist. But she only nodded, looking as if she wanted to scream too.

The foreman reached out a hand as if he might try to comfort her, but Mama stepped back, said a few more words, and then turned. Without speaking, she grabbed my hand and yanked me into a walk so fast that to keep up with her, I almost had to jog along.

"Where is he?" I asked. "Mama, where —"

"Hush. Wait until we get home."

The walk to the job site had taken less than a half hour, and though we were moving much faster now, it seemed like hours before we finally entered the safety of the apartment building. I asked again what the foreman had said, but by then it took all Mama's effort just to hold her emotions together.

She didn't say a word until we were inside our own apartment and her trembling fingers had locked the door behind us. Then she collapsed onto the ground and sobs poured out of her.

"The Stasi came to get him today," she said through choked breaths. "They believe he was involved in Peter's escape attempt. They took him away."

"What will they do to him?" I once overheard Papa telling my mother that he wasn't afraid of anything, except our secret police. He said that if he were ever arrested, no matter what they did to him, his life would be over.

I didn't know a lot about what happened to people after the Stasi got them. The only people who knew for sure were either the agents, or people subjected to their interrogations or tortures. They rarely talked about what had happened to them, *if* they ever returned.

Even the locations of Stasi prisons were secret, so I knew Mama couldn't answer any of my questions. But Fritz was her son! Even if it was only based on instinct, she had to have some answers, some way to make this better.

Except I had learned long ago that there were some things even a mother couldn't fix. She couldn't bring Papa and Dom back, or bring us to them. She couldn't keep me from missing them every single day. And nobody I knew could bring down that wall.

All my mother said was, "They told Fritz it was only for questioning, but the foreman doesn't know if that's true." Then she turned to me. "Are you sure Fritz knew about Peter's escape?"

"He told me last night."

"And you waited this long to say anything?"

"By the time Fritz told me, Peter had already left. I'm sorry, Mama."

She closed her eyes and the tears ran beneath her lashes like the steady leak of a pipe. I put my arms around her, hoping to comfort her a little.

"Go to bed, Gerta."

I didn't want to. It wasn't my bedtime yet, and I wanted more than anything to stay awake until Fritz came home . . . *if* he came home.

"I'm going to Herr Krause's apartment next door," Mama said. "He will know if there's anything we can do."

We didn't see Herr Krause as often as we used to, not since Papa left. Mama had brought him dinners after his wife died last year, but she also felt it was dangerous for the Stasi to believe that we were anything more than casual neighbors. If she wanted to see him now, then I knew how frightened she was for Fritz.

"Let me come too," I said.

"You've done enough!" Mama snapped. Then her eyes softened. "I didn't mean that. Please, go to bed."

I kissed her cheek, though I'm sure she didn't feel it. And apologized again, though I wasn't exactly sure what I'd done wrong.

On the way to my bedroom, I passed Fritz's room. The door was closed tight, which I found odd because it hadn't been when we left. Maybe he'd come home while we were out.

I turned the handle and darted in, fully expecting to see Fritz lying on his bed with his Beatles album turned low.

I saw that record first, smashed on his floor like someone had crushed it beneath his boot. Fritz had a poster of Ann-Margret on his wall, supposedly a popular actress in America, but that had been ripped down and nothing but the tacked-in corners remained. The rest of his room was in disarray, with drawers pulled out and books thrown onto his bed, but nothing else seemed to be damaged. The Stasi had been here. They had stood right where I now did, and maybe gone through our entire apartment too. Although it should have shocked me more, somehow this too seemed normal.

"I told you to go to bed," Mama called from the front room.

I almost asked her to come and see what had happened, but a voice inside me warned it would be too much for her tonight. I planned to get up extra early in the morning and clean it for her. Then, when Fritz came home — and I had to believe he would — everything would be okay again.

Whether that was true or not, I chose to believe. I made myself believe it, or the worry would drive me insane.

The penalties for being an accessory to the attempt to flee the [GDR] were greater than the crime of trying to flee itself. — Anna Funder, Australian author

A cold rain was falling early the next morning, making it hard to leave my bed. It didn't help that I had barely slept, and whatever sleep I got was filled with nightmares about Fritz. When I finally did drag myself into the front room, I was surprised to see him seated closely beside Mama on the couch. He looked exhausted and had a dark bruise on his cheek where someone must have hit him. From what I'd heard about the Stasi's brutal methods of questioning, he was lucky if that's all they had done.

Mama and Fritz were sitting in silence, and at first, neither said anything to me when I walked in. I called his name and ran toward him, but he put a finger to his lips to quiet me and shook his head in warning.

"Oh good, you're awake, Gerta." Mother spoke deliberately and her words were far too cheerful to fit the situation.

"We should have a nice breakfast to celebrate Fritz coming home."

Celebrate his coming home? The Stasi had arrested him and obviously questioned him by force. Maybe we were grateful, but to call this a celebration sounded like a word they would want us to use. To hear it from my mother's mouth felt strained and unnatural.

"It's a cold morning." Fritz wasn't quite as cheery as Mama had sounded, but his tone also didn't match his bruise or the heavy bags under his eyes. "Maybe I'll build us a fire while you cook. Help me with it, Gerta."

Anna's apartment was newer than ours and had central heating, which was considered a great luxury. I envied her every winter when we had to collect wood to burn for our heat, which never reached all the way into my small bedroom.

But except for the rain, I didn't think this morning was particularly cold. We wouldn't normally use up valuable wood to warm an apartment we'd all be leaving for the day. Which meant something more was going on.

Fritz stacked a few sticks of wood in our fireplace and grabbed a handful of papers to use as kindling.

He picked up the first paper and I saw his handwriting on it, which said, Be careful what you say. The apartment is bugged.

Bugged? A thousand questions instantly leapt into my

mind. Where were the microphones? How long had they been here? Who was listening to them?

He knew I'd read it because my eyes were wide with fear. Then he crumpled up the paper and stuffed it into the middle of the wood stack.

The next paper had already been written out for Mama. It said, The Stasi knew about a private conversation between me and Gerta the other night. They listen to every word we say in here.

My mouth went dry. I remembered listening to the Beatles and I was sure we had complained about the GDR, because we usually did at night. That same conversation in Fritz's bedroom was where I had told Mama the details about seeing Dominic. She had come in unexpectedly, cutting off our conversation about Peter.

Fritz said Peter had told no one else about his escape. And Fritz had told nobody about it but me.

We were the reason they had caught him. The reason he was killed.

Tears filled my eyes and I shook my head, horrified at what all of this meant. But Fritz had a paper for that too. He rummaged through a few in his stack until he found one that said, We didn't know. But we do now and we'll be more careful. We must sound happy.

We'd gone too long without speaking, and Fritz called out, "Gerta and I will have this fire going soon. Then I'll shower and we can get to school. Maybe since Anna won't be at school today, I can walk Gerta there."

"That's a good idea," Mama said. "Although we'll both be at work after school, Gerta. I expect you to come straight home today."

"Yes, Mama." I croaked the words out, and it felt as though I were speaking them directly into a microphone, which I supposed I was. Everything around me felt forced, and I didn't see how Mama and Fritz were just carrying on like normal.

No, it wasn't normal. We never talked like this. Mama didn't make celebratory meals, and we wouldn't have celebrated his release from the Stasi anyway. And Fritz never walked me to school whether Anna was with me or not.

But there we were an hour later, with Fritz walking beside me within throwing distance of the wall. I used to think this was the last place we could talk freely, but now it seemed like the only place. Beneath a shared umbrella, our conversation was as private as it possibly could be. Still, we kept our voices low.

"I heard about Peter's death yesterday while at school," Fritz said. "A friend told me the Stasi was interviewing his parents, and that they might be arrested too."

"For what crime?" I asked. "Peter tried to escape, not them!"

"The Stasi view escape on the same level as treason. So

they'll embarrass and shame Peter's family now. They'll have to work extra hard to prove their loyalty to the state."

An older couple was passing by us, so Fritz and I fell silent. When we were alone again, Fritz said, "When I heard about Peter's death, I knew the only thing I could do was keep my head down and hope nobody remembered that we were friends. I got through the end of school, but Stasi officers were waiting for me the minute I arrived at work. They said it was only for a few questions, but I knew otherwise."

"What did they do to you?"

Fritz lowered his head. Clearly he didn't want to answer that question, not even for me.

By then, we were passing the platform where I had seen Dominic and Papa yesterday, but they weren't there this time. I had been so sure they would come — after all, if Papa was trying to send me a message, then why wouldn't he be here? Especially today, of all days.

Maybe it was for the best. Even from the distance between us, Papa might have been able to see the dark bruise under Fritz's eye. It would worry him.

"There's something more I have to tell you," Fritz said. "And Mother doesn't know about this part so don't say a word to her about it."

"I won't." It wasn't the first secret we'd kept from her.

"They showed me a huge file they're still keeping on Father. Before he left, the Stasi documented everything about him: where he went after work, who his friends were, even what newspapers he brought back from the west when he visited there. They never found anything serious he had done, but were sure it was just a matter of time before they had a reason to arrest him."

This wasn't a surprise. Papa had told me the same thing himself, and we'd had the visits from Stasi agents to our apartment. Papa knew he was being tracked because of his part in the uprising, and because he continued to speak to others who wanted more uprisings in the future. But he never committed any crimes or incited anyone to violence. Papa wasn't a violent man, just a thoughtful one.

Fritz continued, "Then they showed me another file, one with my name on it."

I stopped walking to stare at him. "Why? What have you done?"

"Nothing! Or at least, I didn't think I had. But they know Papa is in the west now and so they're watching to see if he contacts me, or if his friends do. Maybe one day I'll happen to bump into someone who used to know him. If anyone even asks about Father, someone is bound to hear it and then that report will go into my file."

"Well, if you haven't done anything wrong, then they can make your file as big as they want. If you obey all the rules, everything will be fine, right?" I looked over, hoping to see him agree with me. "Isn't that right, Fritz?"

But he shook his head and lowered his voice to almost a whisper. "They told me what the file means. I've been branded a potential enemy of the state. It doesn't matter to them if I've done anything wrong. They just figure I will, one day. With that file, I won't be allowed to go to a university, or to get a good job. By the end of June, I'll be old enough for the military, and before they put a gun in my hand, that file means I'll get special training until they're sure I believe the way they do. Once I wear their uniform, I'll get the most dangerous assignments, the ones few people survive. That file means I have no chance in life, none. They've already determined that I will fail."

"All because of Papa?" I asked. "None of that's your fault!"

"I'm not blaming him," Fritz said. "I smuggled in that Beatles record and that banana on your birthday, and other stuff you don't know about. Nothing bad, but nothing I'd want to get caught with either. They must've heard me complain about the government every night on their microphones, and I've never made it any secret that I don't want to join the military. My file might've started because of Father, but I'm the one who's been filling it."

"Well, I won't let you fail," I said stubbornly. "If you can't get a job, then you'll live with me. If they brainwash you, then I'll talk you out of it when you come home. Whatever they do to you, Mama and I will be there to help."

Fritz rubbed the top of my head with his hand. Usually, I hated that, but not this time. It was his way of showing affection, and I wanted that comfort from him now. Then he sighed and said, "You don't understand how bad it is, Gerta. They have a file on you too."

CHAPTER
TEN

A thought, even a possibility, can shatter and transform us. — *Friedrich Nietzsche, German philosopher*

To my surprise, Anna was at school that day, but her eyes were red and she made a point of keeping herself apart from everyone. I tried to talk with her at lunch, but she asked me to go away. When I looked back, she was crying again.

Inside, I felt just as awful, but for more reasons than I could count. It broke my heart to look at Anna and know how she must be collapsing inside. The other kids whispered about her until I threatened them. Even if it cost me a detention to protect her, I would follow through on my threats if necessary. Besides, what did I care? The Stasi already had a file on me. What did it matter if disorderly conduct in school was added to the list of my supposed crimes?

Other than the threats to Anna's gossipers, I spent every free minute of that day reviewing details of my life that might somehow qualify for a file. What had I done?

Every time we walked home, my eyes did inevitably wander to the wall in the west. The Grenzer had used his rifle to warn me of the consequences for that. But was it a crime to see what the rest of East Berlin so effectively ignored?

I was a member of the Pioneers, but not an enthusiastic one. I wore the uniform when it was required, but mine was never as crisp or smooth as the other kids', nor did I want it to be. That was it, then — wrinkled clothes. My secret rebellion.

Then at night when we listened to Beatles music, Fritz spoke of his frustrations with our lives, and I always joined in. Often it was just jokes about the daily inconveniences of living in such a closed-off world, and the way the government paraded its few successes around like fine art hung in a crumbling room. Sometimes we weren't joking, though. Sometimes we genuinely resented the life we were forced into. I could admit that.

But was it a crime to feel that way? Everyone complained now and then. Surely I had done nothing all that wrong.

In fact, the only crime I could be sure of having committed was having been born the daughter of Aldous Lowe. If Papa had once created trouble for the government, then apparently that was enough to convict me as well. For my file proved there had a been a trial of my loyalty to the GDR, and at twelve years old, I was already found guilty.

After school, Anna left so quickly that I wondered if she

had somehow snuck out early. So I gathered my books and coat and flew out the door behind her.

I caught up to her as she hurried along the sidewalk, marching home as if the devil were at her back, with her head down and shoulders slumped over. Even from here, I felt the pain she was experiencing, as real as if I could touch it. Seeing her ache made me hurt too. I couldn't help but think of what I'd be going through if Fritz had not returned home last night either.

"I'm so sorry, Anna," I said. "It must —"

"Don't you dare apologize!" She swerved on me with a rage I'd never before seen in her. Her eyes blazed and her mouth was curled in an ugly snarl. "Your family knew what Peter was going to do. Why didn't you stop him? Why didn't you tell me?"

I stepped back, caught off guard by her words. "We — I — he'd already left when I found out," I stammered. "And he didn't want you to know because he didn't want you to be in trouble afterward."

"Well, we are, and you could've at least warned us!" she said. "My parents told us to stay away from you and your family. They knew how you are. But Peter and I always insisted you were good people, that you didn't cause problems like your father did. We were wrong. You're just as bad as he was!"

"Don't speak about my father!" I snapped. "If Peter tried to leave, that was his doing and no one else's. My father had nothing to do with that, and neither did anyone else in my family."

She stiffened as if I had slapped her. "They told us people would lie about their involvement, to save themselves. Peter broke the law when he left, Gerta, just as your father did when he left. You ought to be ashamed of him, just as I have to be ashamed of Peter now."

"My father loves Germany, and he hates what's happened to us. I'm not ashamed to feel the same way. Why are you listening to the Stasi?"

"I have to." Tears filled her eyes. "They could take my parents away for this, Gerta. Throw them in prison, or worse. What would happen to me then?"

I wanted to hug her and take the pain away, but I only stood there, feeling useless yet again. No, the state hadn't taken my father, but they were certainly the reason he couldn't come home. At least I still had my mother.

"No matter what, I would always help you," I said. "The state can't take our friendship away."

"Yes, they can." Anna bit on her lip a moment before she continued. "To stay out of prison, we must prove our loyalty, and your family is . . . well, your father anyway . . . Gerta, we can't be friends anymore."

And she ran off down the street, on a road that led the long way to her home. That's how eager she was to get away from me.

I felt like a disease. Just as my father had infected me, I could now infect others. But with what? Courage to speak out? To act? To think and question and believe what I wanted to believe? Somehow I lived in a world where these were bad things.

A little way farther down the road, I happened to look up to the platform in the west. And although he had not been there that morning, my father was there now. He stood up straight as if he had been waiting for a while, knowing I would eventually pass by. When he saw he had my attention, he started into his dance again and then went back to the motions of shoveling.

I turned away from him down another street, on a road that was the long way to my home too. Away from the disease.

ELEVEN

*Wherever they burn books they will also, in the end, burn
human beings.* — Heinrich Heine, German poet

Over a week later, Anna still wasn't speaking to me. "She blames us for what Peter did," I said to Fritz as we walked to school. "It's like we're not even friends anymore."

"You're not." Fritz spoke sharply at first, then drew in a deeper breath. "Just be patient, Gerta. Their family is in a lot of trouble."

"But that's not my fault!"

"You don't know what it's like to face the . . . Stasi." Even after a week, he hesitated before naming them, and I wondered if the bruise they'd given him was nothing compared to other wounds that maybe couldn't be seen. "Anna understands it now. If they told her to avoid our family, then that's what she's going to do. It's her only choice, really."

"If they told you to avoid me, would you?" I asked him.

Fritz just chuckled and rubbed my head. "Avoid you?

Don't be silly. You and Mama are the only reasons I'm still here!"

I laughed along with him, but not really. I knew a part of him had meant exactly what he said.

In the days since coming back from the Stasi, something about Fritz had changed. He was working fewer hours, or maybe not even working at all, I wasn't sure. He blamed his mood on the rainy spring weather, but I felt certain there was more to it. He was spending more evenings at the youth clubs, playing table tennis, and had gone to the theater on a couple of nights with his friends, even though he admitted the movies weren't much for entertainment. I did notice him combing his hair more carefully before he went out. Maybe he had a girlfriend. I hoped she liked moodiness, because that was also part of the new Fritz.

Since I didn't have Anna for company, and since I figured making friends with anyone else would just infect them too, I took up reading and went through books so quickly that the librarian said she wondered if I would end up reading all the books the library contained.

I doubted that. I made it a point to avoid the books that sounded too preachy, although I did check them out now and then in case the Stasi wanted to add my book choices to their secret files. And there weren't many books I really wanted to read anyway — a lot of shelves that had once been filled were empty now. Because books make people think. The GDR wanted to be sure it was their kind of thinking.

Mama seemed to like the idea of me reading, since she knew I would be safe at home while she was at work. And she definitely liked Fritz doing more with his friends. She thought it meant we would eventually become more settled into our lives here. Mama still didn't know anything about the files — both Fritz and I had decided that wouldn't do her any good. Nor did she understand that I had too much of my father in me to ever be settled in my life here.

I was so much like him, in fact, that I hoped he would understand why I avoided the route to and from school that would take me past the platform. I figured if the Stasi were watching us, the worst thing was for them to see my father up there dancing out the lyrics to a song while I tried to figure out what it meant.

I wasn't even sure if I wanted to figure it out. Whatever secret he buried before he left, I doubted it was worth the risk of digging it up. Our family didn't need any more trouble, and that was all we'd get if I did understand his dance.

By mid-May, the whispers of summer were growing. School would be out soon, we'd have time to run and play like children should, and the weather was becoming so perfect that it felt like torture to be inside.

Which was exactly my attitude late one afternoon as the temperature in the apartment became unbearably warm. I had opened the windows, and the breeze was perfect enough that I put on my shoes to go outside. Mama didn't like me to wander alone on the streets while she was gone, but this was the middle of the day. I felt perfectly safe.

I had just finished buckling up my shoes when I heard a scuffle going on in Herr Krause's apartment next door. He wasn't alone. Something was wrong.

Through the thin walls of our apartments, I heard him cry out for help and I darted into the hallway. I wasn't exactly sure what I should do, but there were always people down on the street. Perhaps I could run downstairs and bring someone back to help him.

He cried out again and then something crashed against the door. "Hold on," I yelled. "I'll get the police!"

His door opened and Herr Krause collapsed onto the floor in the hallway. His head was bleeding and he was groaning. Two men followed him through the doorway and grabbed him by the shoulders.

"We are the police," one of them snarled at me. "Go back inside."

No, they were Stasi. Their greenish-gray uniforms and the square-and-compass emblem on their hats were dead giveaways to their identity. The question was *why* they had come for our neighbor.

"What has he done?" The question fell from my mouth before I could think better of it. Surely they had made a mistake. Herr Krause wouldn't swat a fly without feeling guilt. But they began dragging him away without answering.

Two more Stasi left his apartment next. The smaller of them pushed past me to clear the way for his companion, who was carrying an armful of books, papers, and what appeared to be rubber stamps. It was a child's play set — I used to have one just like it, in fact — so I couldn't think of any reason Herr Krause should have it, or why the Stasi would be interested if he did.

Unless . . . it wasn't being used for play.

A gust of wind came from my open apartment door and blew into the hallway. It caught a few papers from the officer's hands and scattered them on the ground. Without thinking, I reached down to help pick them up. Sure enough, the printing on them was stamped with a message that looked as if it had been hand carved into the stamp.

IF I CANNOT SPEAK WHAT I THINK, THEN IT'S A CRIME JUST TO BE ME!

Despite its promises of a free press, the state controlled all printing machines and wrote the stories for the newspapers to publish. No citizen was allowed to write his own ideas if they differed from the state message, and certainly it was against the law to distribute those writings.

But that's exactly what Herr Krause had done. He had carved a political message into children's toy stamps and in so doing had risked years of imprisonment. From what I knew of Stasi prisons, there would be no public trial and he would have no opportunity to defend himself. His interrogators would stop at nothing before he signed a confession for whatever crimes they decided he had committed.

In effect, Herr Krause's life was already over.

"Give me that paper," the shorter officer ordered me. Something about him seemed familiar, though I couldn't quite place him.

"Let her read it!" Herr Krause shouted from the end of the hallway. "Why is the GDR so afraid of letting its people think?"

But the officer shoved me against the wall, and in the moment when our eyes met, I whispered, "I know you." He was a friend of Fritz's, or used to be years ago. When I was very young he used to ride me around on his back like a pony. Didn't he remember that? Didn't he know me too?

He reached for the paper, but for some reason I clutched it to my chest. He raised a hand and slapped me hard across the cheek. I gasped as it knocked the breath from me too, then someone shouted, "That's my sister. Please stop!"

Suddenly, Fritz was at my side. He apologized to the officers, then grabbed the paper from my hand. When Fritz went to give it to the officer holding me, his eyes widened. "Viktor?"

That was his name, I remembered it now. Viktor clearly recognized my brother too. But in an instant, his expression hardened again and his grip on my shoulder tightened.

Fritz reached out a hand to me but Viktor wasn't loosening his hold. I shuddered inside. Was I going to be arrested too?

Fritz's voice remained calm. "Viktor, let her go . . . for the sake of our friendship."

"Finish with the girl and come!" Viktor's companion called.

After a final squeeze on my shoulder, he shoved me toward Fritz and said, "The Stasi have no friends. You'll be joining us soon. You'll find out."

Once they left, Fritz hauled me into our apartment and locked the door behind us.

"What were you thinking?" he yelled.

"I heard Herr Krause calling for help! Printing a paper can't be such a bad crime, is it?"

"It's not up to us to determine his crimes, or to help him." Fritz slumped onto the couch, closed his eyes, and massaged his temples as if a sudden headache had come on. In a quieter voice, he said, "Viktor and I used to be friends. He was a good guy . . . once."

I sat beside Fritz, feeling as exhausted as he looked. "Is that what'll happen to you, after you go to the military?"

Fritz only sat up and stared blankly back at me. "Yes. I think it's exactly what will happen."

Do not rejoice in luck, do not hesitate in the storm.
— *German proverb*

Fritz and I agreed we shouldn't tell Mama about Herr Krause's arrest and the trouble I'd nearly gotten into there. She seemed happier lately, and neither of us wanted to ruin it for her.

"We're in a routine again," Mama often said at dinner. "That is good."

But the routine was starting to wear on me. And something about reading the stamped message from Herr Krause made me want to see my father again. It seemed like something Papa would've said if he were here.

The next morning, I looked for him as I approached the crowded platform — it was a Saturday, only a half day of school for us, but my least favorite day to walk there because of the western tourists who often came to the wall on the weekends. They took pictures, brought their binoculars, and stared into our world as if we either needed or wanted their pity. I hated that they watched helplessly but did nothing for us.

Then I stopped, as if I had just seen myself in a mirror for the very first time. Who was I to complain about them? Wasn't I guilty of the same thing? Of staring helplessly and doing nothing about my own problems?

The tourists couldn't do anything for me. Not even the powerful governments of the west could break through what they called the Iron Curtain. And everyone inside East Germany with any sort of influence stood shoulder to shoulder with Russia.

No, there was only one person who could change my situation. Me.

A couple of Grenzers were patrolling the wall this morning, but I didn't have their attention yet. Nor did I care. I knew down to my toes that my father would be on the platform, and I wanted to see him.

I didn't at first. But then as I kept walking forward, Dominic pushed to the front of the crowd and pointed to me. He gave a whoop I thought I could hear from where I stood, and then called down. Almost instantly, my father was on the platform too. He started into his dance with the digging, but the platform was far too crowded.

And he didn't need to do it. I understood what he wanted, just not where. So I counted out three long and deliberate paces. Then with only a peek his way, I knelt on the ground and drew a small X.

X marks the spot.

My father nodded back at me and I hoped he understood what I wanted to know. The problem was that even if he did, how could he possibly communicate to me something as complicated as where I should be digging, or what sort of treasure I might be looking for?

It had been risky enough for me to draw the X, and though I quickly brushed it out with my foot afterward, I still drew the attention of a couple of guards in the tower, who shouted down for me to walk on. I quickly obeyed, and hurried away with my heart pounding. But it wasn't from fear. It was excitement for what my father might do next.

Only a few days later, I found out.

On most school days, our teacher allowed us some time in the afternoon to quietly study with one another. And since it was near the end of the school year, there were some important tests coming up, so she gave us more study time than usual.

Although Anna had successfully avoided being anywhere near me for weeks, this time the teacher assigned her to join my group, and the only spare seat was right next to me. I glanced sideways at her, but she did a good job of pretending not to notice.

"Anna," I whispered. "Can we talk?"

She answered by raising the book in front of her face so that no one, especially me, could see her.

A sour-faced boy across from us snorted. "Since when did she become too good for the rest of us?"

I kicked him in the shins. Hard. When he started to complain, I slouched like I was preparing to kick him again. And I would have, if necessary. From the corner of my eye, I noticed Anna lower her book just a little, and I was pretty sure I caught the barest hint of a smile.

Nearing the end of group time, we were discussing the causes of America's Great Depression when Anna silently slipped a folded paper into my hand. All schoolkids know how to secretly pass notes, but this one surprised me.

I wanted to thank her. No, I wanted to grab her shoulders and pull her into the tightest hug ever. But I didn't do either. Instead, I slipped the note between the pages of my folder and began counting the minutes until school ended.

Once we were dismissed, I quickly found a quiet spot under a tree, and only then did I dare to unfold the paper. At first what I saw made no sense.

It was just a pencil drawing of an old building. Square and made entirely of brick, there were two long windows in the front, but with no glass in them except for jagged pieces in the corners. An old chimney ran up the side of the building, but the bricks were shaded darker, suggesting it was an addition to the original place. There were three ground-level window openings too, but no door, so I might've been looking at the back of the building. That frustrated me. As hard as it would be to find any building in East Berlin, it would be nearly impossible to see the backs of them without wandering from yard to yard. Anna couldn't draw a circle, much less a building, so I knew this hadn't come from her. But there was no letter, no artist's signature, and no explanation of why I should have received it.

Anna walked past me a minute later. I stuffed the picture into my folder and then caught up to her.

"Nothing's changed," she said. "Please go away."

"I will. I mean, I will in a minute. Just tell me about that picture."

"I don't know anything about it."

But she had to know something! So I touched her arm and said, "Please, Anna. Then I'll leave."

She stopped and I saw tears in her eyes. She looked around us and then, in a voice so low I barely heard it, said, "We have family in West Berlin. Someone told them about Peter's death and they sent us a letter of consolation. This picture was in that letter with your first name on it, but I don't know why or where it came from."

It was from my father, I was sure of that. And while I was less certain, I thought Dominic might have done the drawing. He used to be artistic, though I had no way of knowing if he still was.

I started to tell her so, but she shook her head to cut me off and said, "Don't say anything else, please. You don't want me to know why you got that."

"*I* don't even know!" She started to leave, but I added, "Anna, I want us to be friends."

I thought I saw her soften just for a minute, then her face became stone again until I barely recognized her as the girl I had once known so well. "I hid the picture before my parents saw it," she said, "but you and I both know it means something. I can't do any more favors for you, Gerta. Next time, I will tell someone."

I backed away to let her leave. If she suddenly pulled a mask from her face revealing a Stasi officer in disguise, I wouldn't have been any more surprised than I already was. Because that's who it felt like I was talking to. And who knew? Maybe I was.

I looked at the drawing one more time before setting off for home. Well, not *directly* home. Somewhere in East Berlin this building was waiting for me. I needed to find it, and that's where I would dig.

CHAPTER
THIRTEEN

In the middle of difficulty lies opportunity.
— Albert Einstein, German physicist and intellectual

Three days of searching turned up nothing. So many places came close, but something was always different from the picture — it had the wrong type of roof, or different windows, or no chimney at all.

It seemed like everything built since the war looked alike, and the building in the drawing appeared older than that. About a half mile east of my school was a street of older homes, but I didn't see the one from the drawing among them. I was beginning to wonder if this building really existed, at least in East Berlin.

The fourth day was another Saturday, a week since I had last seen Papa. Mama sent me to school with a loaf of bread to give to Anna's family. It wasn't much, but it was all we had to spare. And Mama wouldn't have dared offer more anyway. Anna's family was still being shamed for what Peter had done. Mama didn't want it to look like our families were that close.

But Anna wasn't in school that day, and the teacher said she had complained the day before of not feeling well. So I decided to deliver the bread on my way home that afternoon. At least it gave me the opportunity to walk a different neighborhood of Berlin, and a part of me hoped that as her sorrows healed, so would our friendship.

Anna met me at the door, and although she looked as healthy as anyone else, I didn't question her. If I could get away with faking sickness to skip school, I'd do it every day and not feel a hint of guilt.

Before Anna slammed the door, I shoved the loaf of bread at her. "This is from my mother," I said lamely. "She thought your family might want it."

She didn't seem too enthusiastic about accepting it. And though I wanted to believe the Stasi couldn't find anything wrong with my mother's simple gift, I wasn't that naïve, not anymore. But whether she wanted it or not, the bread was in Anna's hands now and the only way she could refuse it would be to drop it on the floor or hurl it back at me. If she did, I wouldn't have much cared. All Mama had asked was that I give her the bread, not force her to keep it.

Finally, Anna mumbled, "Thank you." She started to close the door, but I put a foot on the jamb to block it.

"I'm sorry Peter's gone, but you shouldn't be ashamed of what he tried to do." Though I hadn't planned to say that, the words poured out of me. The thoughts had swirled in my head for so long, it was a relief to speak them, and at least I was careful to keep my voice low. "He wanted a better life, a *free* life. You can't blame him for that. Or at least, I don't."

"We have a good life here," Anna said. "Why wasn't it enough for him?"

I explained it to her the way Fritz explained it to me long ago. "You've seen the sun, Anna. Now that you have, could you ever be content with just the stars for light? Would that be enough for you?"

Anna bit her lip and her eyes darted both ways along the hallway. If anyone had been there, she'd already have shut her door on me. When she was sure that we were alone, she whispered, "The night he tried . . . escaping, Peter left a letter for us on his bed. The Stasi have it now, but his roommate at the university found it first and told us what it said. The final line was, 'If I don't stand for freedom, then I must sit in chains.' Is that what you believe too, Gerta?"

Of course I did. We were in chains, even if she couldn't see them. I spent six days a week in a school that taught me freedom was a lie, and every minute in public pretending I believed it. She knew the consequences for speaking out just as I did. Why else was Herr Krause arrested?

And, there was the wall. If life was so terrible beyond it, then why force us to stay here?

But I couldn't say any of this to her, not anymore.

Anna seemed to already have the answer for her question. Her gaze hardened. "I told my parents the real people in chains are those who break our laws. They must know they're going to be caught sooner or later."

Suddenly, our simple conversation began to sound like an accusation. I wasn't sure why. As far as I knew, I wasn't breaking any laws. None of the big ones anyway.

A door opened down the hallway and I turned to see who was coming. In that instant, Anna slammed her door shut, and I became a disease again.

I marched from her apartment with a few unkind phrases in mind that I wished I had said while I had the chance. She was practically quoting the state's propaganda, no better than a puppet on their string. Besides, I had only brought bread — not smuggled goods or revolutionary pamphlets. No secret messages were baked inside and we asked for nothing in return. It was only bread, and yet she had treated me like I'd brought the plague.

No, she believed something worse, that wherever I went, the Stasi would eventually follow. That was a ridiculous idea.

Wasn't it?

I decided to take a shortcut home, which sent me down a narrow alley that I usually avoided because of the leftover rubble from the bombings at the end of the last war. But this time, all I wanted was to get home and slam my bedroom door behind me and try to forget I had ever been friends with Anna.

Except where I should've turned back onto the main road, I looked farther down the alley and saw it led to the back of some other older buildings. I'd never been on this abandoned street before, yet it still felt familiar.

Walking faster to keep pace with my racing heartbeat, I took in the details of one particular building. It was old and square and made of brick and looked like it would crumble if hit by a strong enough wind. Two long windows ran up the back and a chimney going up the side was made of a darker-colored brick. The three square windows at ground level were boarded up, and once I left the alley it was easy to see why.

The building now served as part of the Berlin Wall. Tall cinder-block rows butted up directly against the old building, and the barbed wire emerged from the wall all the way up and over the top of the building. I could only assume the front of the building was inside the Death Strip, and that it was sealed up too. Two more old buildings connected in a row to the building in front of me, then the wall continued on from there.

The ground where I now stood looked like a small patch of forgotten farmland. It was infested with weeds, some that were almost as tall as me. Halfway to the road, a deep irrigation ditch supplied a small pond.

Far to the left and behind the wall was a watchtower, which I knew from all my previous observations was always staffed with Grenzers, who constantly looked out for anyone getting too near the wall. But they'd need binoculars to see me well, and there didn't appear to be a border zone here, or at least, nothing was marked to keep us away from the wall, and the tire tracks from the Grenzer patrols didn't look too recent.

My eyes flicked back to the building in front of me as my heart pounded with possibilities. This was the place my father had wanted me to find, and something was buried inside it. I didn't know what, but the first chance I got to return with Mama's shovel, I intended to find out.

CHAPTER
FOURTEEN

Who wagers nothing, he wins nothing. — German proverb

My opportunity came the following morning. It was Sunday and Mama had plans to go to church. She never invited us along — not because she didn't want us there but because she knew the state frowned on religion. They wouldn't punish her for being in church — not directly anyway — but she thought it might somehow affect Fritz and me. Another stain in our files.

Fritz said he had plans to meet up with some friends, which I think included a girl named Claudia. The only things I knew about her was she sold bicycles and wore her hair in the bouffant style like young women did in the west. I overheard Fritz's friends teasing him about her, and by his reaction it was obvious that he liked Claudia a lot. The minute he left, I hurried down to the basement of our apartment, grabbed our shovel, and left for that old building in Papa's picture.

I had hoped for an uneventful walk there, but a young girl hauling a big shovel through the city is hardly inconspicuous. I hadn't even left my own block when Frau Eberhart, a woman who lived in our apartment building, greeted me and asked, "Where are you going with that? Does your mother know what you're up to?"

Frau Eberhart always looked to me like the human version of a turkey, minus the feathers. She collected gossip like other women might collect buttons or teacups. In the west, she'd have been dismissed as a simple busybody or snooping neighbor. But behind the wall, we all knew the neighborhood tattler was as dangerous as fire. Stasi informants were paid well.

"I, um, want to surprise my mother," I stammered. "I found an area for a garden, just a few streets away." Inwardly, I kicked myself for the way my voice had trembled as I lied, for looking anywhere but at her. No, I was supposed to be smarter than this. Papa expected more of me. Somehow, knowing he would want me to lie made it easier.

Frau Eberhart's beak of a mouth pursed together as if she wasn't quite sure whether I had told the truth. I was sure she could read the deceit that was almost certainly written all over my face. But this wouldn't be my last lie. Mama often warned me that the Stasi had blanketed the country with informants. It might be a bus driver, or a coworker, or even a family member. And it wouldn't have surprised me in the least if the woman I was facing ran off to the Stasi to tattle on me, if she guessed the real reason for my shovel.

Finally, she smiled. "A garden is a delightful surprise for any mother. But if you want me to keep your secret, then I'll expect some of your harvest."

Maybe that was just polite conversation and was totally meaningless. Or maybe she wanted a bribe for her silence. I really didn't know. Either way, it presented a problem since there wasn't going to be any harvest. All I could do was avoid bumping into her again for a long time. Forever, if I could arrange it.

Once I spotted the building, I did a careful check for any officers in the area. This time, fresh tire tracks ran through the crusty dirt, so I knew they had come through only last night. Hopefully that meant they wouldn't feel the need to come back around anytime soon. I got as close to the Berlin Wall as I dared, but not because I was challenging the Grenzers. Just the opposite, in fact. I knew if any eyes looked down on this area, then the closer I stood to the wall, the better chance I would have of slipping past them unnoticed. For my own safety, I would use their barricade against them.

My heart was locked in my throat as I crossed to the building, but nothing suggested that anyone had seen me. No sirens, or barking dogs, or soldiers shouting orders. After a tense moment, I finally allowed myself to breathe again. Like all the others around it, this building looked like an old shop that had been abandoned for longer than I'd been alive, and there was no reason for anyone to come to this out-of-the-way street. I crouched beside each of the ground-level windows and pressed at the boards, hoping for one that seemed loose.

The first two windows were still boarded up tight, but the third seemed to have some give. I had to use the shovel to pry the boards loose, but I finally managed to open up a small gap, then slide through it.

Once inside, I had a short jump onto a hard dirt floor. It smelled of mold and rotting wood from the floorboards above me, and the standing water in the corners probably still hadn't dried out from winter. The only light came in slivers between the wood boards across the windows and painted creepy, dusty shadows. It gave me a shiver, though I couldn't be sure if that was because the room was chilly or because I was afraid. No matter how eerie this room was, I also knew full well that the boundary for the Berlin Wall ran straight through this building. If I touched the brick on the far end of this room, I would be standing within the line of the Death Strip. In fact, I thought the Grenzers would probably consider this entire building inside that forbidden zone. If so, then *I* was in the Death Strip now.

I wanted to leave, to just climb back out the window and run to the safety of my bedroom. I never had to tell anyone about this place, and the next time I saw my father, I could just shrug at him as if I had never gotten that picture. He could go forward with his life, and I would go forward with mine.

But now that I was here, I knew I couldn't do that. Papa wanted me to find this building, and he wanted me to dig here. I wasn't sure why he had chosen this place, but it was important enough to let me take the risk of standing here. It had to be good, an entire chest full of money or better yet, fake passports that would allow us an easy slide across the border. Or something better than I could dream of. Something he believed was worth the risk to my life.

A crumbling stone stairway led to the main floor above me. I poked my head up there, and printed in old paint on the wall was a faded sign that simply said, *Willkommen*. In that moment, I named this place in my mind, the Welcome Building.

The main floor was empty except for piles of old brick. The same brick filled every window and door opening facing onto the Death Strip. There was enough brick so they could've scaled up all the back openings too — maybe they'd given up before they finished. Another stairway went to an upper level, an attic maybe. But nothing would ever get me up there where I was even more exposed. I crept back downstairs on the hunt for Papa's treasure.

After choosing my starting place, I raised the shovel, stuck the tip of the blade into the dirt, and crunched my foot down on the blade's shoulder. But in the hard earth, it didn't even go down a full centimeter. I tried again, pushing harder, and even jumped up on it, using all my weight to force the blade into the ground. But nothing I did made any difference. It was like digging through concrete with a spoon.

I moved the shovel to a different spot and tried again, but still with no success. The same thing happened in another corner. It was quickly becoming obvious that my father hadn't buried a single thing in this basement, not unless he had done it thirty years ago, because I was convinced this hard ground hadn't been disturbed for at least that long.

I tried in still another place, right in the center of the room. This time my blade struck something metal. It rattled enough that I quickly fell to my knees to quiet the echoing vibrations. I dropped the shovel and ran my fingers along the ground, feeling for the edges of the metal. Whatever it was, it lay nearly at the surface with only a thick layer of dust to cover it.

If my father was going to bury something to be kept secret from the Stasi, he could've done better than putting it right at the surface. Anyone might find it this way. Then my heart dropped as I realized another possibility. Maybe his treasure had already been discovered, and only the empty container remained.

I had found the edges now, some sort of metal plank wide enough to stand on. When I brushed off the dirt, I saw grooves cut into one side and hinges on the other. This wasn't a plank. It was a door, buried in the earth.

Curiosity was mounting inside my chest, so much that I almost couldn't stand it. I pried the door up with the shovel and then pulled it the rest of the way open. The door was heavier than I had imagined, but I was certain that something inside it would make all the risk and effort worth it.

With some effort, I got the door open. I peered down, but it led to a hole too deep to see the bottom, with a rusty metal ladder on the side that I didn't entirely trust to hold my weight. Nor did I have any interest in diving into some unknown darkness without knowing whether I could get back up again, and with nobody in the world aware of where I was. I wished I had a flashlight.

I walked around it to try to get a better sense of what was down there, then happened to notice dim writing stamped onto the underneath side of the door: *Luftschutzraum*. An air-raid shelter.

There were hundreds of them all over Berlin, places built underground during the Second World War when the Allies began bombing the city. There was nothing special about them — we had one under my own apartment building in fact, and so did Anna. So there was no reason, none at all, why my father would go to the trouble of putting anything special inside this one, so far from home.

I closed up the door and even scattered dirt across it again, then did my best to erase any evidence that I had been here. Obviously, I had misunderstood my father's instructions.

Whatever his meaning was with the silly dances and the picture, I couldn't understand it.

Maybe there was no meaning. Maybe his dance was only a dance, and this picture was only a picture. It might not even be from him at all! If I was reading secret messages into it, that was only a sign of my boredom and desire to find some lost connection to my father.

I climbed out of the basement, pulled the boards that had blocked the window back into place, and stashed the shovel beneath some rubble in the alleyway so I wouldn't have to answer any questions about it on the way home.

I hadn't lost hope, no, that wasn't the right word for it. It wasn't lost because I didn't intend to try finding it again. As I walked home that morning, I simply accepted the reality that it was wrong for me to ever have had hope in the first place.

CHAPTER
FIFTEEN

Who shows courage, encourages others. — Adolph Kolping,
German priest and social reformer

The following Wednesday, two letters came to our door.
The first was from Oma Gertrude — my mother's mother
and the woman for whom I'd been named. For as far back as
I could remember, Oma Gertrude had always been old, but
over the last year she had also begun to have some health
problems.

The state was usually very cooperative about giving my
mother time off from work to take care of Oma's needs, but
Mama seemed worried this time. "She's fallen and broken
her leg," Mama said. "I'll have to stay with her for a while.
Perhaps the state will give me work near her home."

"What about us?" I asked. Our family was separated
enough, I didn't want Mama leaving too.

"We can take care of ourselves," Fritz offered. "School is
almost out for the summer, and I've got to stay here in Berlin
and work. Gerta can take care of things around the house."

"I'll come home as soon as I can." Then Mama frowned, second-guessing herself. "You should both come with me."

"No!" Fritz and I were in agreement about that. Aside from whatever work he could find, Fritz had a girlfriend here now. And I didn't want to stay with Oma. Her house smelled like fish and there was nothing to do.

So against my mother's better judgment, it was decided that we would stay in Berlin while she went to the country-side to help Oma Gertrude. None of us seemed particularly happy about the idea, but we all agreed it was our best option.

The second letter was for Fritz. It was from the military, reminding him that he would turn eighteen in June. By the end of that month, he would be expected to enroll for a year and a half of service. Refusing to serve, the letter clearly stated, would have serious consequences. Well, of course it would. Everything had serious consequences.

Fritz's eyebrows pressed together as he read it, and I could tell that he was bothered. But even if he was, he clearly remembered — as we always did now — that the ears of the Stasi were hidden somewhere in our apartment, and so he couldn't say anything when he finished other than "This is a great opportunity. I can hardly wait."

Fritz wasn't as good a liar as I was, probably because he had a genuinely good heart, or a better heart than mine anyway. His attempt to sound positive came out sounding sarcastic and brittle. So I countered by saying, "I know you're excited. But we'll miss you." It sounded believable, though my sympathetic expression to him said otherwise.

He smiled a thanks in return. Mama didn't appear to have noticed any difference in him, or any particular strangeness in the tone of his words, but neither of us blamed her for that. She looked more tired every day, and now with the news of Oma needing care and the reminder of Fritz's military duty, I was sure Mama's mind was full of all the worries it could possibly hold.

She left early to go into work and speak with her supervisor. Fritz said because of that we had some extra time too and did I want him to walk me to school? I should've refused his offer — after all, I was plenty old enough to get myself to school. But I missed walking with Anna and it would give us a chance to talk in private.

It was a busy morning, with the street full of Trabants, the bulky, inexpensive eastern cars that were about as reliable as snow in July. The common joke said that the best feature of any Trabant was the heater in back, which would warm your hands as you pushed it home.

As we left the building, a white truck pulled up directly in front of our apartment. It looked like a delivery truck but had no markings on it at all. That alone was odd. Our building rarely received deliveries.

A door opened and a man was pushed out onto the street. He fell on his hands and knees, and the second I recognized our neighbor I darted over to help him up.

"Herr Krause?"

I glanced up only long enough to see Viktor — Fritz's former friend — standing in the doorway of the truck. He frowned at me and then eyed Fritz. Neither of them said a word, and Viktor's expression was so cold I thought maybe he had been turned to ice. Then he shut the door and the truck drove away.

Herr Krause had heavy bags under his eyes and his hands were shaking.

"Are you all right?" I asked him. "Can we send for a doctor?"

He put his hands on either side of my face and tears streamed down his cheeks. "I never should have printed those papers," he said. "Do you hear me? I was wrong."

By then, another woman in our apartment had seen Herr Krause. She darted forward and used her shoulders to prop him up.

Fritz held out a hand and said, "I can carry him in."

"No!" The woman pushed his hand away as if he had offered poison rather than help. "It's better for everyone if you go to school." Her eyes darted around the street. "Please just go."

"It's getting worse," Fritz said to me when we were alone. "People are more suspicious of us, and they keep their distance. Word is getting out that I was arrested."

"Anna barely looks at me anymore." Then I shrugged. "School is out at the end of this week, though, so at least during the summer I won't have to watch her ignore me all day."

Fritz stopped walking and shoved his hands in his pockets. "There's this girl I like."

"Claudia?"

He smiled at first, hearing her name, but it quickly faded away. "Yeah. We've known each other for a long time but just started dating a few weeks ago. I like her a lot, actually, and even asked if she'd wait for me until I got my release from the military. She said she would . . . until last night. Her father doesn't want us dating anymore."

"Why not?"

Fritz kicked at the ground with his foot. "The Stasi showed him my file. They suggested it wouldn't be good for Claudia to continue dating me."

"I'm sorry, Fritz." My sympathy wouldn't make him feel any better, I knew that, but I felt his hurt and frustration like it was my own.

He only sucked in a whistle of air and then blew it out again. "Ever since I was arrested a couple of months ago, I've tried, Gerta. Honestly, I have. I've tried to say the right things and do the right things and be whatever it is they want of me. But the more I try to do what they want, the more I understand that my life has been put on this track to failure. From now on, wherever I go, they will stand in my way. I can't win against them."

"You can get Claudia back. I'm sure you can."

"Maybe, but that's not why I told you." He smiled, but it was so sad and hopeless I'd rather have seen him frown. "The same thing is coming for you too."

Even though he spoke quietly, his words echoed like thunder in my ears. Watching Fritz was like looking at pictures of my own life five years down the road. When I would be seventeen and hoping to get into a university, only to be rejected. Needing to get a good job, or any job for that matter, only to be turned down. Trying to find someone I could love, only to have him pulled away from me for reasons I would never fully understand. I knew it would happen to me, because it was already happening to Fritz.

"This all started when Father participated in that uprising twelve years ago," Fritz said, and now his tone grew bitter. "He thought because he wasn't arrested that he got away with it, but he didn't. And then he spent every year since then talking to people about ideas that are considered dangerous here. He thought he got away with that too because they were only ideas. But look at where we are now."

I started walking again and Fritz followed along at my side. "You and I have ideas too," I told him. "And I don't want to become like *them*." I stared up at him. "That's not me, Fritz, and I don't think it's you either."

"No, it's not," he said. "In fact . . . never mind."

"In fact, what?" Fritz was avoiding my eyes now, so I moved in front of him, forcing him to look at me. "Tell me!"

He opened his mouth, then clamped it shut and walked past me. A new worry sprouted in my chest as I hurried to catch up to him. Fritz had been keeping secrets from Mama for years, just to protect her. But something had changed. Now he had started keeping them from me as well.

CHAPTER
SIXTEEN

Freedom lies in being bold. — Robert Frost, American poet

After school, I returned to the Welcome Building. Every minute since the last time I was here had nagged at me. I'd left too quickly before. My father wanted me in that air-raid shelter, and today I intended to get down there. I didn't bring the shovel in from the alley, but I did have a flashlight that I had snuck into my bag and kept hidden throughout the day.

I stood in the alley and kept an eye on the guards in the nearest tower. The instant they turned their backs, I ran for the building, watching them the entire time. I didn't anticipate the irrigation ditch being as full of water as it was. I almost made the jump across, but still landed in mud, which slowed my run afterward. I must've made it to the building before they saw me, or else sirens would be headed my way already. But it was still too close, and even running so fast would've looked suspicious. If I was going to be on this property, I could never be stupid like that again. From now on, I would approach from the side, in the shadow of the wall.

After I reached the building, it wasn't hard to squeeze between the pried-up boards, drop onto the dirt floor, and then push the boards shut. There were fresh tire tracks from Grenzers on patrol, and more could be laid before nightfall. I needed to hurry.

I grabbed the flashlight from my bag, stuffed it into the waistband of my skirt, and pulled open the heavy metal door to the air-raid shelter. Then I lay on my stomach and angled the flashlight downward to get an idea of what might be inside. I didn't expect ghosts or monsters to leap out at me, but at the same time, I wasn't fully ruling out that possibility either.

The ladder was covered in spiderwebs and felt damp to the touch, but I gritted my teeth in some effort to feel more courageous, brushed off what I could reach, and then climbed down.

The room below was colder than I had expected, but then I realized that unlike some shelters, it wasn't surrounded in metal. This was really only a deep hole with a metal lid, and some crates at the bottom that probably had once held emergency supplies. There was a bench at the far end and a couple of pipes that seemed to carry in fresh air from somewhere outside.

The building above me was still standing . . . mostly, so I wondered if this room had ever been used during a raid. Probably it had, even if the Allied bombs had never landed here. Papa had been around my age during the war, and described staying awake all night in the shelters, being too tired to stand but too nervous to sit. There he would wait with whatever group had gathered in the shelter, hearing the airplane engines coming and then the incredible explosions as the bombs found their targets.

Most of the bombings happened late in the war, and Germany's eventual defeat was certain by then. However, the Führer, Adolf Hitler, wasn't ready to surrender, and seemed content to let Germany be entirely destroyed for his stubbornness. By that time, the Allies didn't seem to care where their bombs fell. They blanketed Germany, and particularly Berlin, with destruction. My schoolteacher said that by the end of the war, nearly all of East Berlin had been completely destroyed.

Mama said the reason East Berliners didn't fight the wall was because so many citizens considered it God's punishment for Germany's crimes in the Second World War. Maybe that was so, but God didn't seem to be punishing the west equally, and besides, the war was the crime of my grandparents' generation. I didn't see why I should be forced to share in their penance. I was too busy with my own crime anyway, that of standing in this air-raid shelter.

It quickly became obvious that there was no treasure in this room. If anything had ever been here, it was stolen away long ago. But Papa should've expected that. He wouldn't have sent me here for something that could so easily be taken. Besides, whatever was here, he wanted me to dig for it.

The east side of the room was crowded with crates and the bench, and the dirt behind it was buffered with large rocks. So I wandered to the west side and pulled at the dirt, which crumbled in cakes in my hand. Maybe Papa had buried something inside the walls.

It made sense. If the ground above me was so hard, Papa couldn't have dug there to bury anything. But he could've put something down here, just buried behind a thin wall of dirt.

The wall.

The Berlin Wall had to be nearly over my head right now. And I realized that even if Papa had wanted me to find something buried in this dirt, it was far too dangerous for me to dig. Because every centimeter I clawed in there put me one step farther inside the Death Strip. If I went too far, I'd —

If I went too far, I'd end up in the west.

The truth crashed into me like I'd just tumbled through waves of the ocean.

I had been wrong before. There was no treasure buried in this air-raid shelter. No, the shelter itself *was* the treasure.

Papa must've known about this shelter because maybe he had stood in this very room as a child. This was where Papa wanted me to start digging.

He wanted me to tunnel into the west. To freedom. To him.

CHAPTER
SEVENTEEN

Forge the iron while it is hot. — *German proverb*

I dug a little deeper with my hands, but didn't get very far before I realized this wasn't a smart way to start a tunnel. At the least, I needed the shovel and more light than what came from this small flashlight. And I couldn't walk out of here with my entire body as filthy as my hands already were — that would get me noticed by every Stasi officer in Berlin, not to mention the border guards, informants, and probably the great majority of nosy neighbors within a square kilometer of this place. Before I dug any farther, I had to have a plan.

I also had to ask myself exactly how serious I was about escaping. Now that I knew what Papa wanted, I better understood just how dangerous it was for me to be standing here. I didn't have to dig or tunnel or do anything but *be* inside this air-raid shelter to give them enough reason to arrest me, or worse. And if I started, I would have to finish, because a half-dug tunnel was no different to the Stasi than a failed escape attempt, and my punishment would be no less severe. If I started, I was committing myself to literally do it, or die. And my odds weren't exactly on the side of success.

My legs were shaking when I climbed out, and I took extra time to make sure the wood boards across the window looked exactly as they did the first time I'd found them. I'd been angry when I left here before and might've been more careless with the boards than I should've been. My footprints showed clearly in the softer part of the dirt, and Frau Eberhart had already seen me with a shovel. I hadn't even started digging yet, and already my mistakes were mounting.

I brushed over my tracks and then stuck to the hard soil instead, but I couldn't work up the nerve to dart across the empty field and into the alley. The best I could do was to slink along the edge of the wall and hope if anyone saw me that I looked casual enough to escape any further attention. But it was nearly impossible to pretend that my senses weren't focused on every detail around me. If the watchtower guards had binoculars, they might look at my hands and wonder how they'd gotten so dirty. I wished I had pockets like boys did for their pants, but my skirt didn't have any. So I hid my muddy fingers within the folds of my skirt and hoped that wouldn't look as strange or obvious to anyone else as it did to me.

Every person I passed on the way home seemed to be watching me closer than usual, and the expression on my face must have invited questions. But nobody said a word. Perhaps God still granted miracles to those behind the Iron Curtain.

The first thing I did after getting home was to scrub my hands until long after the water had run clean. Or, maybe, until they had stopped shaking. When I finished, I found a note from Mama on the counter. She hoped to be at Oma Gertrude's only until Sunday, and thought that if we were careful, there should be plenty of food in the house to last Fritz and me until then. And she was very clear that we weren't to get into any trouble or break any rules. Considering where I'd just come from, her note had come too late for me.

I paced the apartment for the rest of the afternoon, debating whether to tell Fritz about the tunnel. I knew I shouldn't. Tunneling under the Death Strip was probably impossible, and even if it wasn't, we'd still have to get through the tunnel without being shot like Anna's brother. Despite that, I couldn't stop thinking about the possibilities if I were to succeed.

What would it take to build a tunnel? Lots of digging, obviously. Was I capable of all that on my own? Maybe, with enough time, but there was so much I didn't know. How would I know if I was going straight, or that I was deep enough? How would I know when it was safe to tunnel back up to the surface? That'd be my luck, to tunnel straight up into the center of the Death Strip. Considering the limits of my own abilities, I knew I needed help.

But Fritz was trying hard to be a model citizen, probably to get Claudia back, so I couldn't involve him, and there was no one else I trusted. If I was going to be smart about this — and it was about time I did something smart — then there was really only one option: let the tunnel be a good idea that wasn't meant to happen.

By the time Fritz came home, I had decided for certain not to tell him. And I knew that was the right thing to do once I saw the slump of his shoulders and frown on his face. He looked worse than sad — it was like he'd simply accepted what the state was doing to his life. He'd given up.

Maybe he had good reason to look the way he did, but it was worse because I was helpless to cheer him up. Even if I could, there was nothing encouraging I dared say to him in our bugged apartment.

He mumbled a hello and said he was going to his room. I offered to make dinner, which really only meant I was going to warm up Mama's leftovers from last night. It wasn't much, but it was something.

When dinner was ready I called him to the table, but there was no answer. Even if he was seriously depressed, Fritz was never one to ignore a chance to eat. Thinking he must have fallen asleep, I went to his bedroom and opened the door to tell him to come. But he wasn't sleeping. Fritz was at his desk, writing on a paper, and when his door opened, he turned it over in a blink. I didn't know hands could move that fast.

My eyes narrowed. "What are you doing?"

"Nothing!" Which was obviously a lie. Then his eyes darted around the room, as if the Stasi's secret bugs would be that easy to find. "Just a little extra homework, that's all."

"Oh right." My voice might've sounded like I agreed with him, but the expression on my face made it perfectly clear I knew something more was going on. "Food's ready."

We shared the usual meaningless chatter over dinner. We talked about school, about how long Mama might be at Oma Gertrude's, and about our plans for the summer. I didn't care about any of it and neither did he.

Fritz did let one piece of actual news slip into the conversation, something I had suspected for a while but never dared ask about. He had been fired from the bricklaying job, and we both knew why.

"I've tried to find other work for this summer, but nothing's turned up yet." His voice was hopeful, but his eyes were dead.

"Does Mama know?" Without Papa here, we counted on the money from Fritz's after-school job to get us through each year.

"Mama doesn't need any more worries."

I thought again about the tunnel I could build. With his bricklaying skills, he could easily get a job in West Germany, and their money was worth five times the value of ours.

After supper, Fritz returned to his room with strict instructions that I wasn't allowed to enter without knocking. He'd never done that before, confirming my suspicions that he had some big secrets. I would've snuck in and peeked at his papers if he left his room. But he never did. Not once.

I didn't find out anything until breakfast the following morning. He came out of his room with the papers in his hand. He commented on how cold it was and that he wanted a fire. It was actually a perfect spring morning, one in which we'd never build a fire. Not unless we needed to burn Fritz's papers, of course.

I told him I'd help with the fire, and after it was started, he let me see the papers. I had figured it must be some way of getting back together with Claudia, but it wasn't. What he had written was so much worse.

Page 1: There's no future here for me. I'm leaving East Berlin tonight.

My eyes widened and I drew in a sharp breath. He shook his head as a warning for me to keep quiet, and then crumpled that page and threw it in the fire.

Page 2: I found a place near the Spree that isn't well guarded. I can run for the water and swim across before I'm seen.

I shook my head as violently as I dared. The Spree was a powerful river, and the Berlin Wall ran along much of its wide banks. Large, heavy boats navigated that river, and everyone knew the current was stronger than it looked on the surface. Even for an experienced swimmer, it was dangerous. For Fritz, it would mean death.

Remembering the microphones, he commented that the fire should get us warm soon. I was too stunned and angry to make any response. Then he raised his pages again.

Page 3: I wanted you to know so you can explain to Mama. It's not fair, but it's the best I can do.

No! I continued shaking my head and tears stung my eyes. He wasn't the first to try escaping through the Spree, and so many people had died in the attempt. Either they drowned on the way or else were shot in the back by Grenzers as they swam. Even on the small chance that Fritz got as far as jumping into the water, he wasn't likely to get out again.

Page 4: I will not join their military. Eventually, I'll think like they do. And I will not let them ruin my life. You must understand, Gerta.

His eyes pled with me to accept his decision, but I couldn't. Yes, I understood the desire to leave, and his frustrations over feeling that there was no hope for him here. I felt just as boxed in as he did, maybe even more. There probably wasn't much hope for me either, and it would only get worse if he left me behind. I wanted to leave just as much as he did. But not in this way.

Page 5: *You can't stop me. My mind is made up. I am going to leave.*

He started to crumple up that page and toss it in the fire with the others, but this time I grabbed it and ran for a pencil. While making a lame comment to the microphones about breakfast, I smoothed the paper out again. On the back, I drew a map to the building I'd found near the wall, and then pulled out the picture Papa had sent to me. On his paper, I wrote, *Meet me here after school. Be careful.*

Fritz looked up at me, his eyes burning with curiosity. I wrote one more word: *Tunnel.*

Once I was sure he knew where to go, I crumpled up his paper and tossed it into the fire.

CHAPTER
EIGHTEEN

Start with what is right rather than what is acceptable.
— *Franz Kafka, German author*

I arrived at the building first, and despite how anxious I was to get down into the shelter and begin digging, I forced myself to wait in the basement to be sure Fritz got in safely.

He approached the building the same way I had, using the shadow of the wall to hide him. I waved him in through the window, and after he slid inside, we shut the boards up again. Fritz was bigger than me, so he had separated the boards even wider and the nails were bent. If someone really looked at this window, they might notice that the boards didn't shut tight anymore. That made me nervous, but there wasn't much we could do about it.

He started to talk, but I'd already opened the heavy metal door into the air-raid shelter and quietly motioned for him to follow me. The shovel was down there too, ready to begin.

Without saying a word, Fritz stood in the shelter, inspecting it just as I had a day earlier. He opened the crates, patted at the walls, and dug into the dirt to test it. His eyes ran along the ceiling, no doubt questioning where the line for the Berlin Wall should be. If we weren't beneath it already, then it couldn't be more than a meter away.

"How did you find this place?" he asked.

In a whispered voice, I told him everything. About seeing Dominic and Papa, the dance Papa did on the platform, and getting the picture from Anna. I fully expected his excitement to grow at the prospect of tunneling to freedom, to see his eyes widen the way mine had when I first realized the possibilities down here. If he planned to swim the Spree anyway, this was a much safer plan. And this offered the chance for all of us to get to the west.

But instead of showing any enthusiasm, it was just the opposite. With every new revelation, his shoulders slumped further, and the light dimmed in his face.

"You were young when Father left, so you didn't know him as well." The tone in Fritz's voice was sympathetic, as if my innocence deserved his pity. "You must've misunderstood his message, if there even was a message. Father never would've asked us to put ourselves in this much danger. Never."

"But he did, Fritz! I saw him and you didn't."

"You saw him doing a children's dance and read meaning into it."

"Then why did he send that picture?"

"How do you know it's from him?" In frustration, Fritz turned from me and ran a hand through his hair. "How do you know it's not some test from the Stasi to get us here and then have a legitimate reason to arrest us?"

"They don't play games like that!"

"They do, Gerta. They do that all the time! If they believe our family has some sort of rebellious streak, do you really think they'll sit back and wait for us to commit a crime when they could just trap us now? Or maybe Anna's family drew this picture to lure us here so they can turn us in to the Stasi and get forgiven for what Peter did."

"Anna's family wouldn't —"

"Yes they would, and if you want to stay naïve about how dangerous this tunneling idea is, then you have no business even thinking about it! Our friends could betray us, family members could betray us. Some stranger on the street could report us and we'd never know who it was. There is nobody we can trust!"

But he had said "us." Fritz and me, together. Fritz would never betray me, and even if the Stasi locked me up for a century and did their worst, I would never betray him.

I picked up the shovel and pushed it into the dirt wall. "Look at the way it crumbles, Fritz. This is soft dirt!"

He put his hand to it, and more dirt fell. "Where's the boundary for the Death Strip?"

I pointed to his feet. "You're standing on it now."

He stood back and watched me, which was something. At least he wasn't leaving and dragging me away with him.

"We could never do something this big," Fritz said. "I don't know a thing about tunneling."

"We can figure it out as we go," I said. "All we have to do is keep moving forward and make sure the ground above us doesn't cave in. A couple of weeks of digging, and then we're out on the other side."

"They sweep the Death Strip with sound sensors," he said. "But thanks to this shelter, we're already pretty deep. If only we knew how wide the Death Strip is here." Now his mind was working. "And we would have to make sure this tunnel came out into a safe place on the other side, inside another building or something. How can we find that exit when we can't see over there?"

"We can figure that out too," I said. "And Anna's apartment isn't far away. I can see the Death Strip from her bedroom and figure out how wide it is from there."

"How will you get inside? She isn't speaking to you."

I shrugged. First I had to get him to agree to this plan. Details like getting into an ex-friend's home could be worked out afterward.

Fritz took the shovel and dug at the dirt, trying it for himself. Within a few minutes, he already had a gap wide enough that he could stand inside it. Then he turned around. "What would we do with all the dirt? There's going to be a lot of it."

"We can leave it in the room right above us. Nobody looks in there, so it won't be noticed."

"Yes, but we would be. It'll take a long time to dig this. Someone will see us coming and going from here and start to wonder why. And we'll be dirty, with no way to wash off until we get home."

I'd already thought about that too. "On my way to bringing the shovel here, Frau Eberhart asked where I was going. I told her the shovel was for a garden. What if we did plant one, right outside the building? It's only dirt out there, and nobody appears to be using it. We could garden in the day while people are watching, and then tunnel when they aren't."

He dug at the tunnel again, his way of thinking it over. "I dunno, Gerta."

I grabbed his arm. "This is better than trying to swim the Spree. You'll die if you go that way, and whether you make it to the other side or not, what will the Stasi do to Mama and me afterward? We know they've terrified Anna's family. Do you want them to come after us that way?"

"No," he mumbled. "No, of course not."

"If you are going to escape, then we need a way for all of us to escape. We're a family, Fritz. Half of us are already on the other side. If we're going to cross, to be together, it has to be all of us."

Fritz stared at me a moment, then crouched down to stare at the dirt wall in front of him. "You're right," he finally said.

My heart leapt. "Then we're building a tunnel?"

"No." Fritz drew himself back to his full height. "No, you're right about the danger. Mama will be home on Sunday, and she'll never agree to this plan. I don't know what message Papa intended to send you, but he wouldn't want us to dig either. If anyone could make such a crazy idea work, it's you, but it's not worth the risk to our family."

This was a good plan, and it was slipping through my fingers like water. "Listen to me, please! If we just —"

"It's over, Gerta." Then he rubbed my head with his hand, something I didn't appreciate at all this time.

We climbed back up the ladder into the basement and pulled the boards closed as best we could. Never to return there again.

CHAPTER NINETEEN

There are none so blind as those that will not see.
— *German proverb*

The night before the last day of school was a long one. I wasn't sleeping well anyway because of my excitement to begin summer break, so when I heard the sounds in the apartment next door, I easily woke up.

Someone was crying in the neighboring apartment, but not just anyone. It was Herr Krause. I couldn't understand that at first. Herr Krause was a strong man who'd come through two world wars and hunger and the death of his wife. I wouldn't have thought anything could affect him so greatly now. Maybe even though he had been released from his arrest, the Stasi had done something that was still torturing him.

Because he clearly was crying, which made me hurt too. In the week before the wall went up, at almost the same time he had warned my own family to leave, he had sent his children and their families across the border. If his wife had been well enough to travel, I knew he would've gone with them. Now he was alone, surrounded by a crowded apartment of assorted tools, car parts, and trinkets that would do nothing to comfort him.

The crying bothered me enough that I got out of bed and walked into the kitchen for a drink of water. I was surprised to see Fritz there. "Herr Krause woke you up too?" he asked.

I nodded, and Fritz turned on the water tap and then a small radio that Mama kept on the counter. While it blared out some all-night dance music, he motioned for me to lean toward him.

He whispered directly into my ear, "He's done that every night since he came home. It was his crying that finally made me decide to swim the Spree."

"I thought you weren't —"

"I won't. You were right before, about the risks of trying to escape that way. But I've been awake all night listening to Herr Krause and wondering what happened to make him cry like that. Then I wondered if that could become me or you or Mama one day. My mind was already made up to leave, Gerta. I just wasn't sure about how." He drew in a breath and then said, "Papa might not want us to dig, and Mama would never give us permission, but it doesn't matter anymore. We're going to build that tunnel."

I felt so happy that I nearly cried out, but Fritz made some excuse to the microphones about the water not warming up and maybe we could try in the morning instead. Then he winked at me and leaned closer to mouth the words, "Tomorrow we begin."

It was a lucky thing that this was the last day of school, because I barely heard anything my teacher said in class. We had some tests that I undoubtedly flunked, and in any other situation that would be a serious problem. But what did I care now? I wouldn't be here when the next school year began.

The one detail I did have to pay attention to was Anna. As our relationship stood right now, I wouldn't get inside her apartment for a simple drink of water, much less the chance to see the Death Strip, but I hoped to plant the idea of maybe letting me visit one day soon.

So at lunchtime I sat next to her as casually as possible. Her mouth started to drop open and then pinched closed. For the past two months, I'd eaten alone, just as she had. With my brother's arrest and her brother's death, we were equally tainted. While I picked up my sandwich, she began studying hers as if cheese and sauerkraut were suddenly too fascinating for her to be bothered with me.

My plan was to act as if everything was normal between us. It wasn't so many weeks ago when I'd never have sat anywhere for lunch other than right beside Anna, and when she'd have saved the seat for me. Why not just pretend this was one of those days?

"I'm sure excited about summer," I said enthusiastically. "Do you have any plans?"

Anna ignored me. Or pretended to. I knew she was listening.

I continued on. "Mama left to take care of my grandmother, and Fritz isn't working, so he had a great idea. We found this patch of dirt that looks completely abandoned. We might try planting a garden there. Neither of us knows much about gardening, though. Do you?" I didn't really wait for her to answer — there wasn't any point when she was still working so hard to pretend I didn't exist.

So I reached for my dessert, a fruit crumble that was actually quite good, and kept speaking while I ate it. "The dirt patch isn't far from your apartment, just down an alley to the west. Maybe if I'm working one day and it gets too hot, I could come by for a glass of water?"

By this point, I was getting frustrated. Talking to Anna wasn't much different than talking to a stone. And I figured the stone would be friendlier.

"We'll plant corn, I think. Maybe some other stuff too, or whatever we can get seeds for. We're going to start on it today, when school is over. We probably can't sell the harvest, I'm sure the state wouldn't allow that. But we could give it away. It's too bad we can't sell it. I bet our corn will be so good, so juicy and sweet, that every family in Berlin will want some. We could make ourselves rich!"

"Stop it!" Anna slammed down her sandwich hard enough she nearly smashed it in her fist. She turned to me and hissed, "Why do you have to talk that way? Why do you have to think that way? You'll probably get in trouble for growing it, and even if you don't, why do you have to care about getting rich? I know you admire the west, Gerta, with all their rich people. But there are also many poor people too. Nobody has everything here, but at least everyone has something. Why can't that be enough for you?"

I was so taken aback by her words that I only sat there in shock. It wasn't *things* I longed for. What I wanted was far simpler. And somehow, much more complicated.

I wanted books that weren't censored. I wanted to see places that were now only pictures in the smuggled magazines that had passed through my hands. Places like the canals of Venice, or the beaches in the South of France, or maybe even one day the Statue of Liberty in the United States.

I wanted a home without hidden microphones, and friends and neighbors I could talk to without wondering if they would report me to the secret police.

And I wanted control over my own life, the chance to succeed. Maybe I would fail, but if I did, it shouldn't be because some Stasi official holding my file had made that decision for me.

None of that involved my interest in *things*, and I was angry with Anna for accusing me of caring about anything so trivial.

"If you don't want the corn we grow, then that's fine!" I said. "I wouldn't share it with you now anyway!"

Then I stood up and marched away. Only then did I realize the strange irony in my words to her. Of course I wouldn't
share our corn with her. I couldn't. There was only one reason for us to be on that land and it had nothing to do with
a garden.

CHAPTER

TWENTY

What is not started today is never finished tomorrow.
— *Johann Wolfgang von Goethe, German writer and statesman*

The tunnel was under way by the time I got into the shelter after school. Fritz had been let out earlier than me and was already hard at work. Where he could have barely fit his body inside the gap yesterday, now he had carved out a small cove about two meters deep. It looked beautiful

I couldn't keep my smile from spreading. "If you work that fast every day, we'll have supper with Papa and Dominic next week!"

"Not in time for supper perhaps, but we'll share their dessert!" Fritz laughed, and pulled from his pocket a letter from Mama. Before I could read it, he said, "Oma Gertrude was worse than she thought. She sent a little money for groceries and expects to be there for at least another few weeks. This is the time we need, Gerta! I think we should try to have the tunnel built by then."

There was a downside to his news, though. Fritz was wearing a new outfit, worker's overalls, and he had a set for me. "Yours might be a little large, but it was the smallest size they had. I had to use Mama's grocery money to buy them."

"But why?" Mine was brownish-gray and the material was scratchy. I would have to stuff my skirt into the pant legs, which would make it even more uncomfortable.

"Even the hardest-working farmer would never come home as dirty as we're going to get. These clothes need to stay in this room and we'll put them on over our other clothes to work. That way, even if our hands get dirty, we won't draw nearly as much attention. And don't worry, we won't get hungry. Mama has some food saved up in the cupboards. If we're careful, we'll have what we need until she sends us more money."

I'd looked in the cupboards that morning, and there wasn't as much as he made it sound like. But this tunnel was my idea, so I couldn't very well start complaining about it. I slipped the outfit on over my school clothes and zipped it up.

"It feels like I'm playing dress-up in Papa's old clothes," I said as I tried to roll the pant legs higher.

Fritz laughed again and helped me with the sleeves, then went back to work. He pointed behind us to a bucket with a handle. "Your job will be to get rid of this dirt the best you can. The bucket will get heavy if you fill it too full, so just scoop in as much dirt as you can carry, dump it out in the basement above us, and come back for more."

Again, I wasn't too excited about that idea, but he was right. Fritz would dig much faster than I could, and someone did have to remove this dirt. Without complaining, I set to work at my end of the job.

A lot of dirt was already piled up in the shelter, so I tipped the bucket to its side, pushed dirt in until it was half-way full, and then hooked the handle over my arm to walk up the ladder. Once at the basement level, I peered around to be sure we were alone, then climbed the rest of the way up. I emptied the dirt into the farthest corner — a lot more dirt was going to fill this room and it was better to use the space wisely. Then back down I went.

By the time I did all that, Fritz had loaded five or six times that amount of dirt into the room. I needed to work faster. So I did, but it didn't take many more trips up and down the ladder to realize I'd never be able to keep up with him, and I was already getting tired.

Maybe Fritz's job required more muscle, but I became convinced that mine was harder. I filled the bucket with as much dirt as I could possibly lift, and then had to balance that while climbing a ladder. After only an hour, my arms were beyond tired and my legs were worse. I became thirsty and the overalls were so warm, I wondered how long it would take before I baked in them.

Fritz eventually noticed me slowing down and told me just to stay up top and empty the bucket for a while. He would do the work of filling it and climbing the ladder. His buckets were more full than mine had been, so after only a few trips, he doubled the size of our dirt pile in the room.

After an hour of this, he handed me another bucket and said, "Most of the dirt that I dug out is emptied. Do you think we should —"

"Quit for the night? Yes!" If he was going to end his sentence any other way, I wasn't interested.

"Come back down into the shelter, Gerta. You need to see how far we've gotten."

The hopeful tone of his voice gave new strength to my legs, and I hurried back down the ladder. As tired as I was, I still thought it was the most fabulous thing I'd ever seen.

We were probably at least as far as the exterior wall of the Welcome Building. Which meant if we were up on the surface, we would now be openly standing inside the Death Strip, somewhere between those two impassable walls of East Berlin's border.

We still had a long way to go — I wasn't kidding myself about that. But if the rest of our digging went as well as today had gone, we would be to the other side in no time. Maybe even farther.

"Why bother stopping once we're in West Berlin?" I said, laughing. "Couldn't we keep tunneling until we reached France?"

"Absolutely," he said with a grin. "I'll make that tunnel come up right beneath the Eiffel Tower and we'll have the most original view of it anyone has ever seen!"

We laughed at that as we stripped off our overalls and hung them over the bench on the other end of the shelter. We set the bucket and shovel beside them, then climbed the ladder and replaced the heavy door over it.

"There's no point in covering this door with dirt," I said. I had done that in past visits, to hide the door in case someone did happen to look in here. But now, if someone looked in, they were bound to see the piles of fresh dirt in the corner. They'd know right away that something was up. We wouldn't be able to hide the evidence of our tunnel. All we could hope was that nobody would look.

Fritz agreed with me and then said it was extra important that we replace the boards over the windows so they looked undisturbed. "Maybe I'll even reinforce them with new boards," he said. "I'll make it impossible for someone to peek inside."

After we got out into the evening light, we realized the overalls might've protected our clothes, but our faces and hands were both smeared with dirt.

"This won't do," Fritz said. "We look like we've been tunneling. Nothing else could explain our appearance."

I pointed to the pond at the far end of the dirt patch and the irrigation river running through it. The problem was that to get there, we'd have to leave the shadow of the wall.

Fritz looked around us. "They'll see our footprints here. Better they see them all over, like a gardener's would be, instead of only near the building. We have to take the risk at some point."

"If they come —"

"If they come, then we'll show them where we want to put the garden."

I straightened up beside him, and though my legs felt numb, we casually walked toward the pond. Once there, we lay on our stomachs and washed our hands, arms, and faces. So far, nobody had come. Maybe this was okay with the guards.

Maybe.

We would've washed more, but dark was coming fast and we knew the guards in the watchtower would have spotted us by now. They didn't seem to mind that we were standing on this land, but their feelings would change after curfew, which was strictly enforced. It was time to go.

"Tomorrow we must bring water to drink," I told him as we hurried home.

"Yes, that and some food."

A smile started in the center of my heart and warmed every inch of me. No matter how hard today had been, how hungry, tired, and thirsty we both were, Fritz planned to tunnel again tomorrow too.

To begin is easy, to persist is art. — *German proverb*

Our progress over the next few days was dreadfully slow. The large clumps of dirt turned into even larger rocks that seemed as impassable as the Berlin Wall itself. Fritz and I spent hours chipping at the edges to pull the rock out, but too often that just led to finding other rocks in our way.

Fritz stood back and examined the dirt wall. "If this is how the rest of tunneling will be, we might as well give up."

"Let's turn sideways and go around it." I brushed my sweaty hair out of my face. "It can't all be rock under here."

"What if it is? It could take months."

"Then let it take months!" I said. "At least we're still moving forward."

"I don't have months," Fritz said. "It's just weeks until they'll expect me for military duty." I was ready to keep arguing, but he only picked up the shovel again. "So there's really no time for complaining, eh?"

He was the one who'd complained, not me, and besides, I was still feeling the surge of energy from our brief argument. I used it to pry my fingers into the dirt and yank out one of the larger rocks. Dirt tumbled over my shoulders when it fell, but I only smiled. I felt better now.

"I should make you angry more often," he teased. "Help me carry this rock up. Then I've got some work to do above."

Earlier that morning, Fritz had removed the hinges from a closet door in our apartment. "While I screw these on the wood boards over the window, maybe you can use the rocks to build us a stairway," he said. "That way it's not such a climb for you to get out."

I did as he suggested, but spent most of that time thinking about how lucky I was to have Fritz here. He was resourceful and good with his hands. So good, in fact, that I sometimes felt like a useless child getting in his way. Sure, I helped him dig and carried buckets of dirt into the basement, and every night I was just as tired as he was when we stumbled back to the apartment. But I had also begun to appreciate how hard this tunnel project was, how much bigger than what I had first imagined.

On one of those walks home, we were stopped on the street by Frau Eberhart, who patrolled the front of our apartment building better than most of the guards in the watchtowers. She saw the dirt on our hands and faces and waddled over to us.

I looked up at Fritz. "Remember, Frau Eberhart thinks we've been gardening."

"Gardening what?" he asked.

I didn't answer because Frau Eberhart was upon us then and he could only smile politely at her.

"What a pleasure to see the two Lowe children." If she felt any pleasure, it was in watching us squirm. "I can tell you've been busy."

Her eyes flicked from me up to Fritz. I wasn't sure which of us was dirtier. We hadn't taken the time to wash off in the pond before leaving tonight. Fritz worried if we did that too often, it would stand out to the guards. Maybe that was a mistake, though. Because sure as anything, we stood out now. We might as well have pasted signs on our chests announcing our plans.

"We have been busy," I said, a bit too defensively. "And we're late for supper, so if you'll excuse us —"

"Late for whose supper?" Frau Eberhart asked. "Your mother isn't there to prepare it. Where has she been? I miss visiting with her."

She didn't miss visiting with Mama because my mother avoided her like she'd dodge a black cat sitting on a crack in the sidewalk. And this woman was far unluckier than any old wives' tale.

"Our mother is helping our grandmother recover from an injury," Fritz said. "We expect her back very soon."

"Maybe tonight!" I offered. "Which is why it would be rude to be late."

Even as the words fell from my mouth, I could've kicked myself for saying them. Why use such a stupid lie to remind her that I had already tried to lie before?

Fritz covered for me. "Gerta means that we are hungry and need to get some supper. We wish our mother was home to share it with us, but if she isn't, we expect her soon."

"Let's hope so." Frau Eberhart pursed her lips and began examining us again. "It's not wise to allow young people too much time on their own. Children will get into trouble."

"I'm not a child anymore," Fritz said. "By the end of this month, I'll join the military."

"And how will you fill your time until then? I heard you're not working as a bricklayer anymore."

"Gardening," I said. "That garden I told you about. We've been working on it."

"Where is it?" Frau Eberhart asked. "I used to love to garden, and I would love to come by and give you some advice."

"We'll take you there sometime." I took Fritz's arm and started to walk forward with him. "Thanks for your help, Frau Eberhart. We'd better go."

Once we were inside, Fritz stared down at me and shook his head. Even before he spoke, I understood his concern. Frau Eberhart wouldn't go away, and she would expect to see evidence of a garden.

"We haven't pulled a single weed," Fritz said. "Nor do we have permission to garden there, or any tools or seeds to get started. This is a big problem, Gerta."

I agreed completely, but after another long day of digging and pulling out rocks, my brain felt as rubbery as my arms and legs. We were running out of food in the apartment, but that was okay too. As tired as I was, I didn't feel all that hungry anyway. I barely took enough time to wash off before I fell onto my bed, already asleep as my head hit the pillow.

TWENTY-TWO

As soon as you trust yourself, you will know how to live.
— *Johann Wolfgang von Goethe, German writer and statesman*

I slept late the next morning, and when I awoke to bright sunshine, I darted from my bed. Why was it so quiet in here? Had Fritz overslept too?

He wasn't in his room, and when I called his name, there was no answer. Now in a panic, I ran into the front room. He was definitely gone, and his shoes were missing from beside the door.

My first thought was that he had gone over to the Welcome Building on his own, but I hoped that wasn't the case. We had agreed that it was always safer for the two of us to go there together.

Still, I went on a hunt for my shoes, wherever I had pulled them off in the fog of last night. While looking for them, I spotted a note on the kitchen table from Fritz. It only said, Be back soon. Stay here.

There was no word about where he had gone, or why, or how long he would be gone other than "soon," which was useless. Was it something dangerous — was that why he chose to go alone, to keep me safe? Because if so, then how could I be sure he would be back soon, or even that he would come back at all?

With my heart threatening to pound out of my chest, I began pacing the floor. He'd said nothing last night about any errands. Claudia had broken off their relationship, so he wasn't sneaking out to spend time with her. Or at least, I thought the relationship was over. If she wanted him back, I knew he'd agree to it in an instant. He talked about her all the time while we were digging. But our conversations about her always ended with him knowing they could never be together. Claudia was fiercely loyal to her father, and her father was no less loyal to the GDR. He wouldn't trust Fritz within a kilometer of her.

Finally, I gave up pacing. Not because my anxiety was any better but because I suspected whoever was on the other end of the hidden microphones might somehow figure out I was pacing and wonder why.

We had dishes in the kitchen sink that hadn't been done in days. I washed those up and then swept the floor of all the dirt we had tracked in. Slowly, I became absorbed in that work, because even if I didn't know what was happening with Fritz, at least I was doing something.

I went to make my bed, but realized the sheets were filthy from the dirt that came in on my hair and clothes at night. It didn't seem right to make up an unclean bed, but I didn't feel like washing the sheets and hanging them to dry either. A quick glance at Fritz's bed showed his was even worse than mine, and I left them both unmade.

It was only then as I slowed down that I realized how hungry I was. I'd missed supper last night and the sandwiches I made for Fritz and me at lunch got thinner every day. Fritz hadn't told me how much money Mama sent in her last letter, but he felt like we ought to save whatever was left for tunneling supplies rather than groceries.

The more I went through our empty cupboards, the more I disagreed. We needed food.

Mama kept a cookie jar on top of the refrigerator. I never went into it because as far as I could tell, it had never held cookies or sweets of any kind. But our food supplies were getting low. If she had stashed anything in there, I wanted it.

I opened the cookie jar and immediately all my hopes deflated. It was empty, of food anyway. An old envelope was at the bottom, though, and I pulled it out, then caught my breath in my throat.

It was a letter from Papa.

The stamp dated it to September 1961, about the time the wall replaced the barbed-wire fence. I pulled out his letter, which began, *To my dear family*. But every line after that was blacked out with thick black marker. Every single line.

No wonder Papa never wrote to us. There was no point in it.

The envelope was addressed with our apartment number and the return address came from West Berlin. If the return address was current, then that was where Papa lived now.

And maybe his letters were blacked out, but if I wrote him, would my words be blacked out too? I couldn't see anything wrong with a daughter writing to her father in the west. No matter who the father was, and no matter what the daughter really wanted, it should be okay. Well, that last part wasn't true. I had to be careful.

The letter I wrote to my father was simple. I said nothing more than what absolutely had to be written and weighed each word carefully, just in case the Stasi intercepted it.

Papa,
    I hope all is well with you. We are all fine, though Mama is out of the city to take care of Oma Gertrude's broken leg. Could you please send some money to help us plant a garden? Fritz is looking for work and we need a little extra.

Love,
Gerta

I debated whether to mention anything about the tunnel, but couldn't figure out a way to word it that wouldn't tip off the Stasi. There were so many questions I wanted to ask, none of them more important than whether Fritz and I were doing what he wanted by digging that tunnel. But I wasn't foolish enough to write a question like that.

Before I could talk myself out of sending the letter, I put a stamp on it and then ran down to the street to drop it in the post-office box. That's where I was when Fritz came running up to me with a paper in one hand and a bag in the other.

"What are you doing out here?" he asked.

"Nothing." I frowned at him. "Where were you? I've been worried!"

Fritz pulled me near the wall of our building and showed me the paper. "They're called *Schrebergärten*, allotted spaces for interested families. The state gives permission to garden in certain areas, legally. I went to ask if we might use that small piece of land near the Welcome Building to make a garden. This paper is our permit, and in this bag I even have some small gardening tools and corn seeds."

"They just gave them to us?"

"The condition is that we don't own the land and we certainly can't live on it. And technically, they'll own everything we grow, though they said we could share in the harvest."

"They don't mind that it's so near the wall?"

"A lot of farmland comes up to the wall, so they're used to it." Fritz's smile was so wide it nearly spread off his face. "Don't you see? We have a reason to be there now, even their permission! We don't have to sneak on and off the property anymore."

My brow furrowed. "We have files, Fritz. Why would they give us permission?"

Fritz shrugged. "The Stasi keep the files — maybe the agriculture office doesn't know about them." He showed me the paper again. "This is good news, Gerta! This could save us!"

I couldn't share his relief or excitement. This only changed one big problem into a different sort of worry. "Yes, but now we'll have to build a garden instead of digging. When are we going to do that?"

Fritz smiled, still pleased with himself. "We'll figure it out, Gerta. Now, c'mon! We've got work to do!"

CHAPTER
TWENTY-THREE

A steady drop will carve the stone. — *German proverb*

As slow as it was to dig out the rock in the tunnel, at least we had been making progress there. The next few days were spent almost entirely in the garden, working hard for no other purpose than as a cover for what we were actually doing — or should have been doing.

I didn't mind the idea of gardening, but the weeds were thick and sometimes thorny and, by the third day, it was hard to care about the dirt out here when I really wanted to be down in the tunnel, working. After an entire afternoon of pointless, sweaty labor, I didn't think the weeds looked any better than when we first began.

When the heat of the day hit us, Fritz and I decided to sneak inside the building to get back to our real work. As before, he went into the tunnel while I removed dirt with the bucket.

But the small basement room was already piling high with dirt, and that bothered me. We had a long way to go before we reached the west. What if we ran out of places to store the dirt? Something needed to be done with it.

I briefly toyed with the idea of returning to the weeding. At least the weeds didn't require me to think so much. Then I smiled as a wonderful idea came to my mind. If it worked, it would solve both my problems.

Rather than dump out the bucket inside the basement, I opened the boarded window and dumped it there. It made a much smaller pile than I expected, so I refilled the bucket from the dirt already in the basement and dumped it outside too. After five or six loads of dirt, I climbed outside and then used the small hand rake from the state to spread the dirt around. It went down smooth and dark and covered up every single weed beneath it.

I didn't need to pull weeds — I could cover them up!

Sure, our vegetable seeds wouldn't grow very well once they hit that hard ground a few centimeters down, but I didn't care about that. I didn't plan to be here that long.

With renewed energy, I began emptying dirt from the basement. The routine was the same, to dump several loads at once and then spread it out. I did it slowly and tried to make it look as if I was pulling weeds rather than covering them. The watchtower was far enough away that unless the guards looked carefully, there wouldn't be any reason to investigate further. Or at least, I *hoped* not. I was always listening for the approaching sounds of one of their vehicles.

After a while, Fritz called up to ask what I was doing, and when I invited him up to see it for himself, he only chuckled and brushed his hand across my head. "Trust you to do so much hard work to get out of other work," he said. "But don't go so fast. If someone is looking for progress, they'll never believe we got all that weeded in a day."

He was right, and I returned to carrying dirt back up the ladder. Over and over, that was my routine.

Climb down to the air-raid shelter. Scoop dirt into the bucket, hook it over my arm, climb up the ladder, dump it out. Repeat. Again and again and again. Rest a little, and then start all over. I'd lost track days ago of how many times I made the climb; I could do this now in my sleep. Who knows? I was so tired, maybe I did.

I usually took my rests in the shelter while I watched Fritz's progress. He was nearly five meters into the tunnel, and kept track of how straight it was with some boards he had nailed together perpendicular to each other. If one end was always kept straight with the shelter's entrance, the other end should point like an arrow in the direction he should dig.

One late afternoon, Fritz said he would lift the buckets for me if I would go and find water to refill his canteen. It required a short walk back to the main part of the city, but I was eager for the change of routine.

I stripped off my overalls and stopped by the pond to wash my face and hands — if I was going to convince a restaurant to give me water, I needed to be presentable enough to walk inside. Then I set off toward a nearby sausage shop where my family used to eat.

When I was almost to the restaurant, my eye roamed across the street to a building that had been bombed during the war and still hadn't been repaired. Attempts had been made to clear it some years ago — I could tell that because of some rusty old machinery and other pieces of equipment left on the site. There was even a long rope with a pulley attached so that the heavier items could be lifted onto trucks.

A pulley!

My mind began racing as I pictured that very item in the basement of the Welcome Building. With a pulley, there would be no more climbing up and down the ladder. Fritz could fill the dirt below and I could pull it up with a rope and then empty it in the basement. We could work twice as fast with half the effort. I needed that pulley!

"Gerta? What are you doing here?"

I swerved around and saw that Anna had come up behind me. Her mother was already seated inside the restaurant where I intended to get water, though I hadn't noticed either of them before now. It shouldn't have surprised me to see them here — this was their neighborhood, after all. But of course she would be surprised to see me, and looking as dirty as I'm sure I did.

I stepped back and forced a smile to my face. "Fritz and I are gardening, like I told you about earlier. I just came to refill our canteens."

"Let me get it for you," she said, and then wrinkled up her nose. "No offense, but you smell like you're up to your eyeballs in gardening."

That was true enough, in a way. I handed her our canteens and she took them inside while I waited, trying as hard as I could not to look at the pulley on the other side of the street. It was only attached by another thick rope. With a good knife, I could cut it free . . . but when? Certainly not on a day as busy as this one. The problem was that in this neighborhood, every day was busy. It was only at night, after curfew, when everything went quiet. After a few minutes, Anna emerged with full canteens of water so cold I could feel it through the metal. I wanted to gulp down an entire one right then.

"Thank you," I said, rather awkwardly.

She called out a "you're welcome" as I walked away, which thoroughly confused me. Were we friends again? Why? Nothing had changed. Unless it had changed on her end. Maybe the Stasi had decided to leave her family alone and she felt safe to be friends with me again. I didn't know if I was ready for that. After all, she had treated me horribly over the last couple of months. And I had much bigger things on my mind than anyone's friendship.

Which included a need to get into her apartment, I reminded myself. For the sake of the tunnel, I would have to make things good between us, and soon.

But in the meantime, I had a pulley to steal.

CHAPTER
TWENTY-FOUR

If you live among wolves, you have to act like a wolf.
— *Nikita Khrushchev, Soviet Union premier, 1958–1964*

I didn't tell Fritz my plan. Not only would he have accused me of every kind of stupidity, but he also would've been right to do it. However, he couldn't feel the aches in my body every night after hauling up those buckets. It wasn't just my arms or shoulders — every part of me was exhausted and sore. Each morning, I started more tired, and ended more drained. I was carrying lighter loads than when we first began, and fewer of them. If something didn't change by the end of the week, Fritz would be doing all the work while I sat aside, useless as the growing piles of dirt.

Police regularly patrolled the streets after curfew. But as young as I was, if they caught me, probably the worst thing to happen would be a ride home in their car with a slapped hand and another page for my file. Probably.

Unless I had already stolen the pulley by then, which would be impossible to explain. It would be reported to the

Stasi, who would wonder what a twelve-year-old girl wanted with such a tool. They would find the tunnel, and we had gone too far for me to pretend Fritz hadn't been involved.

So it was decided, then. I couldn't get caught.

It was very early on a rainy Saturday morning when I snuck out of the apartment. My plan was to get the pulley before anyone else was allowed outside, and to be on my way home immediately after curfew was lifted. That way, I only had to sneak around in one direction. I wore my blandest clothes, which really only required a choice between Communist gray and Communist grayer. They would camouflage me against the walls in the early morning light. I also brought a small burlap sack and our sharpest kitchen knife.

Almost as soon as I got onto the street, a Trabant Kübel drove by, full of police, and I backed into the shadows of our doorway. The officers' rifles reflected from the streetlights and their shared laughter was coarse and louder than it ought to be for this early hour. Louder than it ever ought to be, actually. I wondered what men like them might find funny. Probably we had a different sense of humor, because nothing about our police force ever made me smile.

For several long minutes after they'd left, I fought against my instinct to go back inside. That would've been the smart thing to do. Then I reminded myself that tunneling beneath the Death Strip was hardly a smart act, so at least I was being consistent. After they could no longer be heard, I made myself take the first step onto the sidewalk, and after that I was committed. The streets were quieter than I'd ever seen them and it felt as though the entire city had been abandoned.

This was probably what my neighborhood would've become if the Berlin Wall hadn't gone up. We would've left, and Herr Krause too. A family who lived below us also had plans to leave once. I was sure there were others. Eventually, the whole city would've emptied out except for the most loyal party officials and the Stasi and Grenzer officers. Or what did I know? Maybe they would have left too, given the chance. Russia's new first secretary, Brezhnev, would have rolled through here on a tour from Moscow and found he was the leader of a vast country of empty buildings and overgrown farmland.

I balled up my courage and my fists along with it, rounding the safety of the corner while keeping as close to the shadows and coves as possible. I saw nobody, heard nobody, and, as far as I could tell, I was completely alone out here.

The next part of my walk was the most dangerous — I had to dart across a street that was usually quite busy in the daytime. The rain would help, but it wasn't falling hard enough for a full camouflage, and even at a full sprint, it would take me two or three seconds to cross this wide street. I stayed hidden at the corner for several minutes, steeling my nerves. Even through the heavy clouds, the sky was already growing lighter. I had to run.

If I didn't go now, then curfew would end and I would be stuck here with no hope of getting that pulley. I refused to haul dirt buckets up that ladder again, not when a much better option was within my reach.

That single thought was enough to prompt me into moving. I gave one last look in every direction and then ran. Ran like I never had before. I was blind to everything but the corner in front of me and the protection it would offer. My feet were light upon the street and I jumped the curb so there would be no chance of tripping. Then I lunged for the cove of the nearest building as if fire was at my heels. I landed in there and almost screamed.

A woman was already using that same cove to hide and looked as startled to see me as I was her. Her silky long hair was as dark as her sleek outfit, but pulled behind her in a fashion more elegant than I usually saw. She was beautiful but had clearly tried to play it down by wearing only a bare amount of makeup. I felt clumsy and plain beside her, and would've left right away if I had anywhere better to go.

Her face softened as she looked at me. "I know you. Aldous Lowe's daughter, right?"

It bothered me that she should know that, especially since I was certain I did not know her. She only smiled and said, "It looks like you're no better at staying out of trouble than he was. But your father was a very inspirational man. He meant a lot to those of us who want to see things changed here in the east."

She spoke of him like he was dead, the same way my mother often did, something I always resented. And she hadn't told me anything about herself.

Getting no reaction from me, the woman said, "It's not safe to be out here this time of night." She reached into her pocket and pulled out five *Ostmarks*. "Could you use this?"

Frankly, I was so relieved that she didn't demand a bribe of silence from me, I barely even thought about the fact that I was the one receiving the bribe.

She smiled when I nodded and pressed the money into my hand, then added, "Shall we agree not to have seen each other, then?"

"Agreed," I mumbled. And she ran off the way I had just come, while I darted in the other direction. My mind burned with curiosity for who that woman was and how she knew my father, but there was a much stronger urge for me to get to that pulley. The sun was rising fast. I didn't have much time.

About fifteen minutes later, I reached the neighborhood with the pulley. Since it was a weekend, several of the stores would be closed today, and I had some time before the rest opened. Many of the residents here would have already left for the countryside, drowning their troubles in a bottle of Pilsner. I hoped those who remained were sleeping in late.

I breathed a little easier once I was in the lot with the damaged building. There were plenty of places to hide, and based on the scattered garbage I passed, other people had hidden here before me. I had to stack a couple of cinder blocks on their ends to stand high enough to reach the pulley, but after checking the area carefully to be sure I was still alone, I reached up with my knife, sawed off the rope, and let the pulley drop to the ground.

I jumped down, hid it in my burlap sack, and crouched behind the rubble in the lot until the first signs of traffic grew around me.

It was an easy walk home, but as soon as I rounded the last corner I saw Fritz waiting for me on the street. His face was nearly purple and his breaths were harsh and shallow. He grabbed my shirt collar and yanked me inside the apartment building, then twisted me around.

"What were you thinking?" he hissed.

My chest tightened as I got ready for the argument that clearly was coming. I had known he'd be angry when he learned I was gone, especially that I went alone, but my reasons were good. If he wanted to fight about this, we would. But I would win.

"We needed something and I got it," I said.

"Nothing is worth what you did. How dare you, Gerta?"

I started to retort but quickly lost any interest in arguing. Now that I really looked at him, it wasn't anger in his eyes. It was fear, more than I'd ever seen in my brother before.

I opened the burlap sack just enough for him to see what was inside, and when I did, he nodded and tears streamed down his cheeks. He grabbed me into a hug, his stiff fingers digging into my back to communicate the worries still trapped inside him. He whispered, "That was too stupid to count as bravery. What if we lost you? Never do that again, Gerta. Never do anything like that again."

I gave him an apology, but only for making him so afraid. I could never regret what I'd done. Because now we had a pulley.

Intelligence is not to make no mistakes, but quickly to see how to make them good. — *Bertolt Brecht, German playwright*

Thankfully, the rain had stopped by the time we left for the Welcome Building. On the way there, Fritz and I stopped by a market and bought five Ostmarks' worth of rope, and also a little food we could eat while working on the tunnel. When he asked where the money had come from, I asked my own question instead. "How involved was Papa in the Resistance? Was he only talking to those who were fighting? Or was there more?"

Fritz frowned. "Why are you asking that now?"

Because I already knew the answer and needed him to confirm it. Maybe my father hadn't led any marches or put up protest flyers, but that woman last night knew his name, and knew him well enough to recognize me after at least four years. There had to be reasons for that.

As we walked, Fritz said, "Father promised Mother he wouldn't break any laws, but he bent that promise as far as he could. I know he spent a lot of time next door with Herr Krause, helping him build support against the government. They used to hold meetings there, ones so secret he denied they had ever happened, even after I told him I could hear them through my bedroom wall. Why do you ask?"

"Last night I met someone he used to know," I simply said.

Which reminded him that he hadn't scolded me for a while. But even as angry as he still was, I'd also gotten him to admit the pulley was invaluable. He thought it would only take a few pieces of wood and the rope to get it working.

Fritz grabbed some old wooden slats from the same lot where I'd stolen the pulley and bundled them with our garden tools to carry them into the garden. Once it was safe to bring everything into the basement, he stood the two longest pieces of wood on their ends and attached them at the top with a third piece of wood. He built stands for the base and said I would have to anchor them with my weight while I pulled the bucket up, or else the whole thing would tip over on me.

"I wish I could make it more permanent," he said. "But I think we should lay this down flat each night, so it doesn't draw any attention in case someone does peek in the windows."

I attached the pulley at the top and ran the rope through it. The other end was already tied to the bucket beside me. When I pulled down on the rope, the bucket handle lifted up.

"Let's test it," I said, already anticipating how helpful this was going to be.

Fritz climbed into the shelter and I lowered the bucket beside him. He filled it with dirt and then told me to raise it up.

Even though it was heavier than the buckets I usually hauled up the ladder, the pulley bore most of the weight and took less of my effort than before. I raised the bucket up to eye level, then dumped it on the basement floor beside me and lowered it again.

Fritz and I worked this way until he announced all the extra dirt was gone from the shelter. He suggested he could go to work digging while I got rid of the dirt in the basement.

So I did. I first lowered the pulley system, untied the bucket, and emptied the new dirt from the basement out into the garden patch. The work seemed much easier today, maybe because I wasn't already exhausted from hauling it up and down the ladder. Only an hour of work easily convinced me I had done the right thing by sneaking out to get the pulley.

By midday, the extra dirt was mostly gone from the

basement and spread out in the garden area. Fritz would have more dirt after lunch, but for now, I decided to work outside to make it look as if we were progressing in the garden.

I was accustomed to the constant city noises in Berlin, but here, set off so far from any main roads, it was very quiet. So it was easy to detect the footsteps of someone arriving from the alley, the same way I had come when I first found this building. I took a quick glance back to be sure the boards were covering the window, though I already knew they were. Fritz and I were very careful to always remember that. And I knew he wouldn't come out unless he was sure nobody else was around.

So I turned back to my work and tried not to appear too concerned. Any look of guilt or stress would certainly give me away, because if my only purpose here was gardening, I was allowed to be here. But who I saw emerge from the alley confused me.

It was Anna. Her mother was with her, carrying a basket covered with a cloth.

"Mama thought she saw you working here," Anna said cheerfully. "After seeing you at the restaurant yesterday, we walked this way home and thought something looked different here."

I stopped working and stared up at her while shielding my eyes from the sun at her back. She was smiling and acting as friendly as always, the same Anna as she had been before her brother's death. Or, almost the same. Something seemed different, and I couldn't quite place it. It was like she was too friendly, working too hard to pretend everything was normal. It probably wasn't much different than I had acted on our last day of school together, when I first told her about this garden. Maybe she felt as awkward as I did about repairing our friendship.

"After Peter's . . . accident . . ." Frau Warner chose her words carefully. Maybe she wanted everyone to believe that escaping one's country by hiding out in a specially designed car was an accident. Or more likely, that's how the Stasi had told her to describe it. ". . . you brought us some bread from your mother. That was so kind, and we never thanked her."

I sat back on my heels. "My mother had to leave town to take care of my grandmother."

"Yes, I heard that." Frau Warner casually looked around. "We wondered if there's anything you and your brother might need while she's gone. Where is Fritz, by the way? I thought he was helping you garden."

"He had to run an errand," I said. "He might not be back for a while."

She accepted my lie just as I had told it, without batting an eye. "Ah, well, please tell him hello for me. I know he and Peter were friends, and it would've been nice to see him too. Is there someplace I could set this basket? It has cheese and crackers, and some homemade shortbread. I thought you might like that until your mother is home to cook again."

It all sounded delicious. So good, in fact, that I'd have snatched the basket off her arm and inhaled the food from my filthy fingers if I didn't think it would draw some unwanted attention my way. Instead, I pointed to a flattened rock near the pond. "You could put it there. And thank you." The gratitude I felt could not be expressed enough with words. If only she knew how much the food meant to us.

While her mother walked over with the basket, Anna crouched near me. I returned to working on some weeds, but that didn't stop her from talking. In a low voice, she said, "On the last day of school when you sat by me at lunch, I know you were just trying to be nice and I was horrible in response. I want you to know I'm sorry about that."

I looked up. "I'm sorry too, for not telling you about Peter's plans as soon as I heard. Maybe if I'd told you sooner —"

"That wasn't your fault." Tears filled her eyes, but she blinked them away. "Mama thinks it would be good for me to get out of the apartment more. So if you'd like, I could come by sometime and help here in the garden."

Actually, I didn't like the idea at all. But how could I refuse Anna's polite offer without raising suspicions?

I smiled as kindly as I could manage. "It's hot and you'll get filthy, and it's boring, but if you really want to —"

"Thank you, Gerta!" She seemed genuinely happy about what little I had offered, which made me wish it could've been possible. "I know a lot about gardens, so I can be helpful and we can fix some of your mistakes before you get the seeds planted."

My eyes narrowed. "What mistakes?" Even in my fake garden, I felt slighted by her suggestion that I might have done a poor job.

She chuckled. "Well, you can't just cover the weeds over with dirt, silly. I don't know where you got this dirt from but it won't fix the problem for long. Pretty soon, the weeds will just pop up through the new dirt, stronger than ever."

I didn't answer her. Instead, I glared, which I shouldn't have done. But she had no idea how hard I'd worked, and how important it was that I get rid of our extra dirt. If I couldn't figure out that problem, we would surely be caught. I wasn't angry at her, just frustrated with myself. But all I could do was let her walk away.

After I was sure she and her mother had left, I made my way back inside the building, where Fritz had been watching us.

"I heard it all," he said, even before I could say a word.

"Maybe the next rainstorm will even the fresh dirt out with the old," I suggested.

"We got some rain last night and nothing improved,"

Fritz said. "Whether we cover the weeds or bare ground, it still looks like fresh dirt. We can't use it out here anymore."

He was right. We would have to do the hard work of removing the weeds. Which was bad enough, but the second problem was much harder.

What would we do with all the extra dirt?

One today is better than ten tomorrows. — *German proverb*

The next day was a Sunday, which gave us some much-needed time at home to rest, bathe away at least five layers of caked-on dirt, and gulp down the food from Anna's mother as if we hadn't seen anything edible for weeks.

The tunnel had made us both noticeably thinner, but we were also both more muscular in our arms and shoulders. While I liked feeling stronger, I also knew it was important for us to eat enough to avoid looking like we were in the process of starving. People had begun staring at us lately, and stares invited questions. Questions led to gossip, which surely ended up in the form of reports at Stasi headquarters.

Fritz and I had chosen to dedicate the day to pleasing the hidden microphones. We talked about how grateful we were to have the allotment of land, and how much we were learning about gardening. We spoke of missing our mother, but being proud of her for taking care of Oma Gertrude and not burdening the state. We discussed Fritz's enthusiasm to join the military at the end of the month, and my hopes to get more responsibility from the Pioneers this fall.

Maybe we laid it on a little thick. No doubt some of what we said brought groans from whoever was tasked with listening to us. But these conversations were only a game now. If there were any consequences for our overworked chatter, we didn't care. We wouldn't be around to face them.

Fritz and I worked together to get the apartment cleaned up, but we were both delaying the worst job of all: the laundry. It had piled up over the last week and a half to something on the scale of a small mountain. Our clothes were dirty and smelly and so stiff with sweat that they practically held their shape after we had removed them. The sheets from our beds were even worse. It was bad enough now that I sometimes woke up in the morning with new dirt on my face from having slept on it in the night.

"We have to wash these," I said. "But if we hang them up now, they won't be dry by bedtime, and once we return from the garden tomorrow, they'll only get dirty again."

"It's too bad the washing can't get done for us while we're gardening."

"Yeah, we —" Then I stopped as an idea snapped in my head, like someone had flipped on a light. Suddenly, I knew exactly how we'd get rid of the dirt. I looked over at Fritz and saw a mischievous gleam in his eyes. We had the same solution in mind, I was sure of it.

"The pond next to the garden!" Fritz said.

I grinned. That was exactly my idea.

On our way to the Welcome Building the next morning, Fritz and I stopped by a lumber shop for more wood and rope, and a handful of nails, all for a clothesline. It would take much of the day to build, but it was absolutely worth it.

While Fritz nailed the wood together to make two tall T's, I dug two deep holes in the ground, about ten meters apart. We chose the spot carefully: exactly parallel to the Berlin Wall and in front of the pond. Then we set the posts into the ground and filled it back in with dirt. Our posts weren't quite straight, and Fritz said they'd probably tip over in the next big wind, but I thought they were good enough for our purposes. We ran rope between them. It sagged a little and the longer fabrics might brush against the dirt, but that was fine by me.

It was time for a test. I carried a bucket of dirt from the building with a single bedsheet on top. If the guards were watching, they'd see me wash that sheet in the pond and then hang it on the clothesline to dry. With the sheet blocking their view, I would then empty the dirt into the pond. Then back to the building for another load of dirt, and another sheet to be washed.

With the second sheet on the clothesline, I had even better cover from the guards. There was plenty of laundry to be done, and endless loads of dirt to be emptied.

Fritz and I worked that way throughout the week. By the end of the week, he was ten meters in, but we were also slowing down. It took time to walk the piles of dirt from so deep within the tunnel back out to the air-raid shelter, and it took me more time to empty the dirt because now I had to sneak the dirt out from the building and get it to the pond, then wash and hang sheets on those trips. And we both had to put in time on the garden because it was almost certain that at some point, someone would drive by to check on us. Fritz and I began working longer hours, arriving as early as possible in the mornings and staying as late as we could at night. We were barely sleeping, eating as little as we could to get by, and working. Always working.

Occasionally, on our trips to the Welcome Building, we walked past the platform where I had seen Dominic and Papa, but they were never there anymore. I wished they were. I wanted to let them know we were digging, as Papa wanted.

I tried to remain patient, though, and keep focused on the fact that at least we were moving deeper each day.

The problem was, as Fritz pointed out, that his eighteenth birthday was coming up soon, exactly three weeks from now. That was our absolute deadline to be finished. We weren't sure how much farther we had to dig, but it was a long way. Nor could we just walk away if we didn't finish in time. The tunnel had progressed far enough that eventually it would be discovered. And when the Grenzers found it, figuring out who had dug it would be the simplest of mysteries.

"If we don't finish, we need a backup plan for escape," Fritz said. "The second we began digging this tunnel, we committed ourselves to leaving, one way or another."

"We're not swimming the Spree," I said. That had been a bad idea weeks ago and it was no better now.

Fritz gritted his teeth. "We can tie ourselves together with a rope so we can help each other against the current."

"All the easier for one of us to pull the other underwater. And what about Mama? We're not leaving her behind."

"Then what's our backup plan?" Fritz wasn't as angry as he sounded. It was only the same frustration as I felt too. "Everything else is far more dangerous. We can't jump over the wall. Three of us can't be smuggled across the border at once, and we know how that idea ended for Peter. So what do we do?"

I stood up and dipped the bucket in the dirt again to carry more of it outside. "We'll finish this tunnel, Fritz. We'll finish this tunnel as if our lives depend on it. Because now, they do."

By the beginning of our third week of digging, we had washed every sheet in the apartment at least ten times. And since the pond was constantly being flushed with dirt, the water was hardly clean. The sheets looked worse and worse with each washing. I figured that was good news — it gave me an excuse to pull them down and wash them again, along with more hidden dirt from my bucket, of course. If my mother saw these sheets, which were now only white in the past tense, she would be horrified. But I couldn't have been happier with their lack of progress.

Forget not the tyranny of this wall, horrid place, nor the love of freedom that made it fall. — Written on the Berlin Wall after it came down

A small package arrived the next morning from the post. It was labeled for me and had a return address and writing on it that I didn't recognize. The package was marked as SEEDS.

"Who'd be sending us seeds?" Fritz asked.

The package had been opened already and the Stasi inspection stamp was on the outside. But it didn't look like they had gone through it with anything more than a cursory examination. Seven envelopes of seeds were inside, all of them for squash.

"Squash?" Fritz wrinkled his nose. "Who would ever want so much squash?"

"Papa would," I replied. "It was his favorite vegetable."

Fritz sat beside me. "Did this package come from" —

then he remembered we were bugged and changed his question — "from anyone we know?"

For the benefit of the microphones, I said, "I sent away for some seeds to help with the garden."

Then I poured the envelopes out on the table. Fritz and I tore open each one but they contained only seeds. I felt beyond disappointed. Surely this package had come from my father, but I had expected more from him. When I said we needed money to help with gardening, he should have read more into that note. We didn't need seeds, and certainly not this many seeds for squash! Or worse, maybe he did send money and the Stasi had inspected it straight out of my package.

Frustrated, I picked up the wrapping to crumple it up for the garbage, and then heard something rattle inside. I opened it again and saw one more package of seeds that was stuck in the seal. I pulled it out and made some comment about it being even more stupid squash seeds.

But this envelope was different. It still rattled with the seeds inside but not as easily, and it was thicker than the others. I opened it and saw it stuffed with Ostmarks. I wasn't sure how much was in there, but probably more than we would spend in a month.

My eyes filled with tears, and Fritz's too. But he shook them away and in a cheery voice said, "Well, I suppose we're planting squash, then. That was smart, Gerta, to write and ask for those seeds. By late fall, we'll have plenty of food for as many people as might want it."

As we walked to the Welcome Building that morning, Fritz and I discussed what we should do with the money. I wanted to buy enough food to stock our cupboards again, but Fritz felt we ought to have a wheelbarrow to haul dirt.

"The buckets don't carry enough dirt with each load, and it takes too many trips in and out of the building, which is dangerous. A wheelbarrow would be better."

"Papa sent that money for food," I protested. We were living on so little these days that lately, my hunger won out in any argument.

"No, he sent that money for us. And we need a wheelbarrow more than we need cheese and sausages."

I disagreed. I'd have rather bought a hundred fat sausages with it, or better yet, a fine yellow banana from the black market. I carried my hunger everywhere with me, even into my dreams lately. Mama had said there was a lot of starvation at the end of the Second World War, but I never really understood what that meant. Not until the last few days. Now, every time my stomach rumbled and I had nothing to comfort it, I understood why she always worried about having enough food.

In the end, Fritz won the argument, and we bought a small wheelbarrow on our way there. I'd have still rather had the banana.

At least it made hauling the dirt easier. While he dug, I used the bucket to empty dirt from the basement into the wheelbarrow outside, all blocked from the view of the watchtower. Then I put another sheet on top and walked it over to the pond. With fewer trips, I was removing far more dirt than ever before.

For much of the day, though, Fritz weeded and planted Papa's seeds while I continued removing dirt. It slowed down our work in the tunnel, but if the guards were watching from their tower, they needed to see progress in this garden every day.

Late that afternoon, I was on my way to the pond with another load of dirt, covered over with two sheets from my bed, when a green Trabant Kübel with the word *Volkspolizei* drove up. Two police officers were inside. I froze in place while Fritz's head shot up and he jumped to his feet. I looked at him. Should we run for it? Where would we possibly go?

"Keep working." Fritz's voice was terse. "Wait until they're not looking and then empty the wheelbarrow, but let them see you wash the sheets. Just pretend that everything is normal. We're gardening. That's all."

I put my head down and continued walking toward the pond. I suddenly felt exposed, like spotlights were pointing down at me, revealing to the world every secret I'd ever tried to hide. The secret right in front of me. Why did a girl need a wheelbarrow to haul only two sheets? Why did her muscles strain if the load was only lightweight cotton? Why did she insist on cleaning in a pond that sent the sheets out dirtier than when they went in?

The two officers left their car fully armed, and surveyed the lot like they already knew we were up to something. Truly, how could they miss the glaring signs of what we were really doing here? For as careful as we thought we had been, it all looked so obvious to me now.

Fritz hailed the officers and walked out to meet them as far from the pond as possible. He invited them over to inspect our garden patch and brought them with him to the opposite side of the clothesline, leaving me free to quickly dump the wheelbarrow full of dirt. It plopped into the water far too loudly and soon I heard the footsteps of one of the officers coming my way.

"*Guten Tag.*" I saw white-blond hair and immediately recognized the officer as the one who had put his rifle against my cheek several weeks ago. Müller. That same rifle was still slung over his shoulder, but he also carried a sidearm pistol on his right hip. He had frightened me then, and much as I wanted to hide my fear this time, my legs were already shaking.

"*Guten Tag,*" I answered. My tone wasn't rude, but it wasn't friendly either.

"I know you," he said. "You're the girl who watches the wall on her way to school."

"It's hard to miss the wall, sir."

He chuckled, but for only a brief moment. "Perhaps. But

there are some who glance at the wall and others who seem to study it."

I had no way to answer that, and I panicked for a moment. My eyes darted over to Fritz, wishing he were here to help me.

But Officer Müller didn't seem to notice and only turned to face the garden. "We came to have a look at your Schrebergärten, to see your progress on this land."

"We planted squash and corn this week," I said.

"June is too late for planting. Nothing will grow by the time the frost returns."

"It took us longer than we thought to clear the ground . . . sir." I kept my head down, always at work washing the sheet in my hands.

"Yes, we expected to see more than this."

Müller started to walk away and I leapt from the pond to follow him. Fritz was already showing the other officer around the field, but there wasn't much to see. I worried that Müller might get bored and wander to investigate the building. The window we used to get inside was closed and looked as if it was nailed up just like the others. But of course, it wasn't. A firm push would open it and reveal our two-faced plan.

"Are you a gardener?" I asked, following behind him. "Maybe you can give us some advice."

"How long do you spend in this garden each day?" He ignored my question, which meant he had no interest in polite conversation. And he was walking directly toward the Welcome Building.

"It varies. Often in the heat of the day we rest in the shade."

"You are working this ground on behalf of the state, not for your own pleasure," Müller said. "If you are uncomfortable on warm days, we can find others who want the work."

"The state isn't paying us to be here, sir," I said. "Only allowing us the use of the land."

He turned to me. "The state does not need to pay you. You will expect some of this harvest, I assume. That is your pay."

I lowered my head and held a tone of humility. "Yes, sir." I'd have thrown in a hundred more "sirs" if it helped. When Müller marched on, still walking toward the building, I glanced back at Fritz for assistance. What was I supposed to do if Müller tried to get inside?

But Fritz couldn't do anything to help. He was showing the other officer our permit for the land and answering whatever questions came at him. It was up to me to keep Müller away from the building. But how could I?

Müller wasn't tall enough to see into the long upper windows, and like Fritz, he had to crouch to be low enough for the three windows at ground level. He stopped at the first window — one that was actually boarded up, at least. He pulled out his flashlight and shone it through the cracks in the wood. Luckily, Fritz had filled in the largest gaps with extra wood, and I had gotten rid of most of the dirt that had been in there. The metal door for the air-raid shelter was closed and covered in a scuff of dirt, so he shouldn't be able to see it, and Fritz's pulley system was laid on its end in the far corner of the room. With only a flashlight, I doubted Müller would see anything more than some fallen boards.

"Do you ever go in here?" Müller asked me.

"It doesn't look safe to enter," I said. "The building is old and probably was bombed at one point. It looks like the whole thing might collapse soon."

Actually, I didn't worry a bit about that happening. But I hoped he would believe it might collapse on him and decide to stay out.

"Are there any doors to get inside?"

I shrugged. "We're at the back of the building. The front would be on the other side of that wall. Perhaps you could access a door there, if you're allowed."

"Of course I'm allowed!" he snapped. "But the entrance on that end is bricked over. What is your name?"

If I thought there was any chance to get away with it, I'd have lied to him. But it was too easy to check my story. "Gerta Lowe, sir. I'm twelve years old and live about five blocks away with my mother and brother."

"Does your mother approve of your gardening?"

"She doesn't know. She's out of town caring for my grandmother. We hoped to make this garden a surprise for when she comes home."

He arched an eyebrow. "Gerta Lowe. Is your father Aldous Lowe? I've seen his file."

I hesitated. What else could I do but answer? "Yes, sir. But he lives in the west. We have no contact with him anymore." As soon as I said it, I could've kicked myself for that lie. Only that morning we had received Papa's package. If Müller checked my story, he would return with more questions. Or more officers.

"Your father did not believe in Communism. He felt that it was only a matter of time before the GDR collapsed."

"You'd have to ask my father about his beliefs, sir. I was very young when he left."

Except, of course, that he had taught me everything he believed.

Müller stared down at me and I felt like squirming beneath his gaze. "Only twelve years old? You seem older."

"With my father in the west and my mother at work or with my grandmother, I've had to grow up fast."

"Hmm." Müller's attention returned to the building. "So is there a way inside here or not?"

My eye flicked to the window we used, but I quickly looked anywhere else. "We wouldn't know . . . sir."

Müller walked down and leaned over to tap on the middle window. Then he took another step toward the third window, the one that Fritz and I used. Once he pushed it, he would know. He would see what we were doing, and if I tried to stop him, that would only make things worse. I could try to run, but wouldn't get more than a few steps away before he'd draw his gun.

"Officer Müller," his companion called. "We just got a call to investigate something farther down. It's probably a bird caught in the wires again, but we need to check it out."

"Yes, sir," Müller called back.

"I hope the next time you come, we'll have corn and squash to offer you." He must have detected the fake cheerfulness in my voice.

Müller stared at me again. Was my face as flush as it felt? I could hardly keep two thoughts together and there was so much sweat on my palms that if I brushed them against my clothes, I knew it would leave marks. He frowned at me, then walked on and tapped at the third window with the butt of his rifle.

Müller had pushed the side of the window with the hinges attached. It knocked the boards open only by a hair, but they did open and I was sure if I noticed, he must have too.

"Officer Müller!" his companion called again, more sternly this time.

If Müller had crouched here like he did for the others, he might have seen the boards separate from the wall. But instead he told me to stay ready — the slogan for all young people — and walked away. A minute later, his vehicle vanished down the road.

I collapsed onto the dirt, so full of fear that I could scarcely breathe. Fritz came over and knelt beside me. "Are you all right?"

"No!" I was fighting back hysterics. "He was right here, Fritz! Another second — one more step —"

"Just breathe." Fritz put a hand on my back and rubbed it. "Take some breaths, Gerta, we're all right."

But I still couldn't get enough air. All I wanted was to yell loud enough to get the fear out of my body. "He had to know something was wrong. Our story doesn't make sense! There are too many holes, too much that doesn't come together!"

"But they did believe it, and they did go away. We knew they'd come at some point, and now they're gone. It's over."

"It's not over, Fritz." Down to my bones, I knew it wasn't over. There would be more visits and more questions. Harder questions designed to trap us. Ones we couldn't answer. This would never be over.

CHAPTER
TWENTY-EIGHT

Shut your mouth, then no mosquito flies into it.
— *German proverb*

Fritz and I spent the following morning in the tunnel. He had hit more rock, but he didn't want to move sideways again. "I worry that we're tunneling at an angle," he said. "If we don't stay straight, we'll cost ourselves weeks of extra work."

So we dug out what rock we could and made the path only as wide as it absolutely had to be for a body to squeeze through. I thought about Mama here, whether she would feel comfortable in such a closed-off area. Fritz and I were used to it, but when we brought her down here, she might not like the feeling of being in a dark and narrow tunnel so far below ground.

After several hours' work, we got past the rock, and Fritz helped me haul what we had removed up to the surface. I was reluctant to use the wheelbarrow again — it had been such a close call with Officer Müller yesterday — but I wouldn't be able to get the rocks outside otherwise.

I was on my way to the pond with a load of middle-sized rocks and some dirt, all covered over with one of Mama's sheets, when I stopped. Another visitor was coming. Anna.

She was alone today and wore capri pants and a sturdy button-down shirt. Gardening clothes. Even her brown boots were different from her usual pair. In one hand was a basket that I knew must contain a day's supply of food and water, and in her other hand was a small shovel.

I quietly groaned and set the wheelbarrow down.

"*Guten Tag,*" she called to me. "It looks like you've already had another hard day of work."

"We have," I said. "We're probably going to quit for the day, in fact."

"We?" Anna looked around. "Where is Fritz today?" Her voice turned skeptical. "Another errand?"

"Yes." I knew that didn't reflect well on Fritz, but what choice did I have?

Anna pressed her eyebrows together. "He leaves the hard work for you too often. I don't usually see him working here. Only you."

My mouth suddenly went dry, so much that I had trouble speaking. "You've been watching us?"

She laughed, with no idea of how serious my question had been. "Only when passing by the alley, that's all. Anyway, I told you I would come to help, and my mother said I could stay as long as I wanted. I'm looking forward to it." Her eyes darted to the clothesline. "You started doing your laundry here too? That's odd."

"We have running water and room to hang the clothes when they're cleaned. It's better than our washer back at home."

Anna walked with me over to the sheets to inspect them better. "Are you sure about that? I don't mean to be rude, Gerta. I know you're doing your best with your mother gone, but these aren't that clean."

"I *am* doing my best," I said defensively.

She wasn't being unkind. It's just that she had no idea of how tired I was, how hungry I was, and how frightened I was every minute of the day that we would be discovered. If I were any more tired or hungry or afraid, I would spend every waking minute crying and every moment of sleep racked by nightmares. But as it was, my senses were constantly on alert while we were here, and I fell into such deep sleeps at night that I couldn't remember if I still dreamed anymore.

"I'm sorry," Anna said. "I didn't mean to hurt your feelings. I came to help, really. And I can pull weeds or water the plants or help you with the wash — whatever you want. I brought food we can share, even enough for Fritz if he returns. And I thought we could talk and catch up."

I tried not to look as sad as I felt while I stared at her. Of course I wanted our friendship back. I missed her as much as I missed my parents and Dominic. In some ways, maybe more, because up until a couple of months ago, she had known me better than almost anyone in the world. And it would've been wonderful to have her company here through the long afternoons. Except for the times I was down in the tunnel with Fritz, or he was up here with me, this was lonely work.

But it was impossible to allow Anna to stay. Fritz couldn't leave the building while she was here, and I wouldn't be able to empty the dirt, or even touch the wheelbarrow right behind me. The first thing she'd try to do if I accepted her help would be to peel off the sheet from the wheelbarrow to wash it. And then she'd see what a fraud the entire clothesline really was.

"I appreciate your offer, but Fritz and I want to do this by ourselves." I had to be firm, but tried to be polite as well. More than ever before, I still wanted her as a friend.

"Oh, I did hurt your feelings." Anna frowned. "I truly am sorry. The laundry is fine, Gerta. It's hard to do so much on your own."

"I'm not on my own," I said. "I have my brother with me, and my mother will be home soon. Thank you for asking, but we don't need help." I swallowed hard and added, "We don't want it."

"I'm trying to get our friendship back." Anna's face flushed, as if she were holding back tears. "I'm trying, Gerta!"

But my face had turned to stone, just as hers used to do. "It's too late for that."

"Oh. All right." Anna's eyes darted around as if she wasn't sure what to do next. I had never been so rude, and even if I'd punched her, I couldn't have hurt her worse. She lowered her head and backed off the lot. "Well, good-bye, then."

I stood in place until she disappeared down the alley. Only when I was sure I was alone did I wheel the dirt and sheet to the pond and start the wash again. This time I needed more privacy than ever from the road and from the watchtower and even from Fritz. Because I was certain I had just lost a friend forever, and the sadness of that was more than I could bear.

Lost goods, lost something; lost honor, lost much; lost courage, lost all. — *German proverb*

I spent the early evening back in the tunnel with Fritz. After clearing through the rock, he had made good progress that afternoon.

"It's to the point where we have to know how much farther to go," Fritz said. "You need to get into Anna's apartment and look at the Death Strip."

I had already told him about her visit that afternoon. If only I could go back and redo that moment in a smarter, kinder way. "She won't let me in," I said. "Not now."

"You have to get inside," he insisted. "There is nothing more important with this tunnel than knowing when it's safe to go to the surface. If we come up too early, we'll be in the Death Strip. And if we tunnel longer than necessary, we might run out of time or get caught."

"I'll find a way." Somehow. I exhaled a harsh breath as dread began to fill me. It was bad enough for me to use our friendship for such a dangerous reason. But the friendship was obviously over, and getting into her apartment now would be a product of lies and manipulation. On the few nights when I didn't crash into my bed asleep, I prayed that God would forgive me for all the lies I'd had to tell on our path to freedom.

Fritz said he didn't pray for forgiveness because he didn't consider those lies a sin. He believed it was wrong to lie, but not as wrong as keeping us trapped behind a concrete wall. He said that instead, he prayed for all those people who were forced to serve a country they didn't believe in. Good people who held guns against us through no fault of their own.

"What about the people who want to hold those guns?" I asked.

"I don't pray for them," he said. "I can't."

And I decided in that very same moment that I would. Somebody had to.

Not long before we intended to quit for the evening, Fritz began using the shovel as a wedge to pry out a rock lodged deep into the dirt. We pressed down on the handle together, but the rock was more embedded than we had expected. And now he had pushed the blade so far into the dirt that it was stuck too. Neither would budge.

"Let go," Fritz said. "Let me try something."

He grabbed the handle with both hands, then jumped in the air and let his full weight come down on the wood. Something cracked and Fritz fell to the ground.

"No!" Fritz leapt to his feet again with the broken shovel handle in his hands. I aimed our flashlight at the rock and sure enough, the splinters from the other end of the handle stuck out of the earth like a porcupine's quills.

"We can get another shovel," I said. "They'll have others at the store."

"Shovels are expensive, Gerta." He ran a hand through his hair, then kicked at the wall. "It'll take the rest of the money from Papa."

But it couldn't. We had agreed the rest of the money would be for groceries. In fact, we were quitting early tonight to buy them on our way home. I had spent half the day creating a shopping list in my mind. We'd have bread and sausages and potatoes and maybe a chocolate or two. Even cabbage sounded good.

He wiped his sweaty hair from his face. "We have to make a choice. It's either the food or another shovel."

"Isn't there one we could borrow?" I asked. "There were other shovels in the storage beneath our apartments. Someone will loan one to us."

"Once we're gone, the Stasi will look at everyone who might've been involved. If we borrow someone's shovel, the Stasi will say they helped us escape."

"What if we steal one?" I spoke the words quietly, almost hoping he wouldn't hear them.

But he did. He turned to me with his eyes wide. "Are you suggesting that, Gerta?"

I had stolen the pulley, though I didn't really consider that a crime since it clearly hadn't been used in years and didn't appear to belong to anyone. But to steal a shovel from our own building, that was different. It was wrong and I knew it. The question was whether I could live with it.

"How many laws have we broken already?" I asked him. "We've lied to the state and to the police and to nearly everyone we've spoken to in the last month. You said yourself that isn't wrong, not for this tunnel. We accepted the hand tools and seeds to work on a garden we have no intention of harvesting. Worst of all, we are right now sitting directly below the Death Strip! What does a stolen shovel matter at this point?"

Fritz shrugged. "I suppose it matters to the person who owns it."

I leaned against the wall and listened to the growl of my stomach. If we used the last of our money to buy a shovel, starvation was becoming a very real possibility.

"Some of what the state teaches is important," Fritz said tiredly. "We do have a responsibility to be good citizens. Even if we are rebelling against some of their laws — maybe even their biggest law right now — that doesn't mean we can rebel against everything that is right. They are also telling the truth when they say there are people in the west who will take advantage of others for their own profit. Some people use capitalism to help themselves and let the rest suffer for it. I guess what I'm asking, Gerta, is if that's who you want to be when we're free. Are you willing to sacrifice other people if it means you can get ahead?"

I closed my eyes and let only a single tear escape the corner. "No," I mumbled. "No, of course not."

So we wouldn't steal the shovel. And the rest of Papa's money would buy a new one and we'd pray that it held together until the tunnel was completed.

I was still hungry, though. Really hungry. I just didn't say it.

There we sat for some time, mourning the loss of the shovel and collecting our strength to go home to an empty apartment with empty cupboards. Filthy, exhausted, and alone.

No, not alone. Footsteps had just landed on the floor of the air-raid shelter, I was sure of it.

Fritz had heard it too. We got to our feet and he pressed me behind him, then held out the broken shovel handle as a weapon.

Whoever was on the other end had a flashlight — we saw glimpses of the light as it bounced from one wall to another. Then it turned in our direction and the footsteps came toward us.

I didn't move, I didn't breathe. We both already knew that Fritz's broken handle was useless against the weapons likely heading our way.

Then the light rounded a bend in the tunnel and a man's voice ordered us to raise our hands and to drop the stick.

His light shone directly in our faces, preventing us from seeing who he was.

But it didn't matter. I recognized the voice from yesterday.

"So, the Lowe children are doing something far more than gardening." Officer Müller lowered his flashlight, allowing us to see his face, cast in hard angles of light and dark shadow. In his other hand, a glint of metal was reflected. His gun. "Even this far below ground, I'm sure you know where you are right now."

The Death Strip.

CHAPTER

THIRTY

Caught together, hanged together. — *German proverb*

It felt like hours before any of us spoke. Müller took his time investigating the tunnel, running his hands along the sides and poking at the ceiling to check how solid it was above us. A part of me hoped the ceiling would collapse directly above him, but of course that meant we'd be trapped too, and the Death Strip would cave in on all of us. Not much of a solution.

"You've gone a long way," Müller said. "Farther than I expected."

"You knew we were tunneling?" Fritz asked. "How?"

"I knew there was a reason your sister didn't want me getting close to this building. But I didn't really become suspicious until I looked inside the basement yesterday. I saw the pulley and the bucket and asked myself why so much fresh dirt might be in a building that is supposed to be closed up."

I could've kicked myself, or preferably, kicked him. I knew he'd gotten close to the windows but never thought he'd seen so much. In hindsight, that was plain stupidity on my part, just childish optimism in the face of reality.

Müller ordered us out of the tunnel, but told us not to climb the ladder up to the surface. Fritz dropped the shovel handle, then walked first with his hands held high, and I followed. Müller went last, keeping the gun trained on us. If he shot, I hoped he would get me first. Maybe that was selfish, but I didn't want to go through watching it happen to Fritz, knowing I was next.

Once we were in the shelter, Müller ordered us to sit on the small bench. He stood beside the ladder, and here, under a little more light, I saw the gun all too well. "No trial is required before I shoot you," he said. "You are clearly guilty of attempting to leave the country."

Yes, we were. Not even the best-told lie could get us out of this one.

"I was first alerted to you by a woman who lives in your building, Frau Eberhart. Do you know her?"

I knew her, and suddenly loathed her just as much as I did Officer Müller. Maybe that was unfair — the Stasi would give her much-needed rewards in exchange for information, and after all, she was on the right side of the law, not us. But still, she had betrayed us and nothing was so low as that.

"Frau Eberhart says she first noticed your odd behavior in the week before school got out. Is that how long you've been tunneling?"

"Yes, sir." There was no point in denying that.

"And how long until you expected to cross into the west?"

"There's no way to know," Fritz said. "We're not sure how much farther we have to go, or what conditions we might encounter along the way."

"You're not the first to attempt an escape through tunnels," Müller said. "Why did you think you would succeed when nearly all attempts have failed?"

"We didn't know if we'd get across," I said. "We only knew that we had to try."

"Ah, but now with two shots of my gun you will be nothing but failed escapees. Your bodies will be buried in shame, your mother will be arrested and likely jailed, and your names will be published in every newspaper and throughout all history as traitors and cowards."

"We're neither, sir." Fritz held his head up, clearly determined that if Müller was going to shoot us, it wouldn't be with us acting ashamed for what we had done. "Our country is Germany — one country that should be reunited. We don't belong to Moscow or to the west. We belong to ourselves and I have never betrayed that. This tunnel has taken every ounce of courage we have. We're not cowards."

That seemed to entertain Müller. "And so how would you have yourselves described? As heroes? Are you role models to other young people who are living behind the wall?"

"We're a brother and sister who only want a chance for a better life," Fritz said.

"And to bring our family back together," I added. "Please let us go, forget you've seen us here."

"I am a uniformed officer of the state and could no sooner forget that tunnel than forget my own name." His attention wandered upstairs as a gust of wind blew through the boards in the basement. It provided enough of a distraction that I wondered if Fritz and I could rush at him and overcome him, and then . . . well, I didn't know what. We weren't murderers and we couldn't hold him here. We didn't even have enough money to offer him a respectable bribe.

But we did have a tunnel.

Müller wore a gold wedding band on his left hand. He had a wife. On his left shoulder there was a small milk stain. From a burping baby perhaps?

He looked down into the tunnel again. "Who else is coming with you?"

"No one," I said. Half of East Germany could be lined up to come with us and I'd still deny it. I wouldn't rat them out the way Frau Eberhart had done to us.

"What if others wanted to come?"

Beside me, Fritz looked confused, perhaps wondering if that was a trap to get us to reveal other names. But I didn't think so.

"They'd be welcome," I said. "You could —"

"No, I couldn't!" But from the tone of his voice, I knew Müller had already thought about it, maybe even before he came here. That's why he'd come alone. His eyes flicked back to the tunnel, then over to me. "I'll go up the ladder first. You will follow next, and then your brother. If you try any tricks, I will bury you here."

He turned to leave, but I darted forward to grab his arm, not to fight but only to stop him from leaving. He reacted by shoving me to the ground and aiming his gun directly at me. I raised my hands in the air and closed my eyes tight, waiting for him to squeeze the trigger.

"Would you die for this tunnel?" he yelled. "Risk your lives, your family, for a run to the west?"

"Don't shoot her!" Fritz answered. "This was my idea, not hers."

I opened my eyes again to protest but still felt paralyzed in the sights of his gun. At least he hadn't fired it yet. With a trembling voice, I said, "Bring your family and come with us. Bring them to the west."

Müller's eyes widened. "Escape? How dare you suggest —"

"There is more for your family in the west. It's the life you would want for them, if you could choose."

Fritz caught on to my idea. "You don't have to dig, but you might be able to keep other officers away from this area. Then when we're ready to leave, we can put out a signal, letting you know that the tunnel is completed."

Müller wasn't convinced, but at least he was thinking. "My wife wants to go to America. She has family there."

"We need another couple of weeks," Fritz said. "Maybe more if we run into problems, but I can promise with all my honor to give you the chance to come."

For the first time, Müller lowered his gun. "What's the signal, then?"

I spoke up. "We'll leave a shovel in the dirt outside. A sign that we no longer need it."

A long silence followed. Müller spent most of it staring into the tunnel, and I wondered if he was picturing himself and his family running to freedom. I'd done that myself plenty of times.

Finally, he said, "I will write in my report that I investigated and saw nothing suspicious. But I may return tomorrow to arrest you."

I tried to catch Fritz's eye to see what we should do. Müller's terms were terrible. At best, he would do nothing to help, and at worst, he would get us killed. What other choice did we have, though? We had nothing else to bargain with.

Fritz reached out a hand to shake Müller's. Irritating me even more, he thanked Müller. He actually *thanked* him for agreeing not to kill us . . . yet.

Müller turned to leave and then said, "Whatever I decide, you must hurry. With or without my help, this tunnel will be discovered soon. If I come with the group who discovers you, I will shoot just as quickly as the others, so do not look to me for sympathy in that moment. All I can do is warn you now. Your biggest enemy is time."

I wasn't sure about that. Right now, Müller seemed like a pretty big enemy to me.

Fritz only nodded and said, "We're going to escape, and your family is welcome when we do. Watch for the shovel outside. We'll cross that same night."

THIRTY-ONE

An appeal to fear never finds an echo in German hearts.
— *Otto von Bismarck, creator of the German Empire*

Fritz and I went straight home afterward. Müller's visit had left both of us with legs of jelly, and nothing he had promised was very comforting. As far as I was concerned, wherever we went now his gun was still pointed our way. Another dreaded reality to add to my growing list of worries.

As we walked home, Fritz pointed out the good news that Müller would probably come with us for the escape. Otherwise he could have just shot us there and earned himself a fine promotion for discovering that tunnel. I suppose that was how Fritz's and my thinking had evolved: The fact that we hadn't been shot and left to die was the morbid way in which we cheered ourselves up.

We passed by a bakery offering old bread for a single Ostmark. Fritz said we could spare that much and bought some for each of us, which we munched on as we walked. It was dry and wouldn't go very far in helping our hunger, but it was better than nothing.

Frau Eberhart was in front of our apartments as we approached, so Fritz and I crossed the street and pretended to look in the storefronts there until she went inside. We'd go to any extreme to avoid her in the future.

It was a long night afterward for me. As tired as I felt, too much had happened that day — with Anna and what was surely the final cut in our friendship. The broken shovel. And then Officer Müller. If we had been found by anyone else, Fritz and I might be dead right now. Maybe that was still our fate. If Müller could figure out what we were doing, others could too. It was only a matter of time.

By morning, though, I felt a little better. We shared the last of what little food was in the apartment, and then reminded each other that a new shovel was more important than a full belly. After buying the shovel, we made our way to the Welcome Building. It looked just as it had the night before, but different to me somehow. Because now our secret wasn't ours alone, and any safety I had felt in working on this quiet, unused road was gone.

Fritz rubbed my head. "Today will be better, Gerta. I'm sure of it."

I frowned back at him. "There's a pit in my stomach."

"Well, there's nothing in mine, so consider yourself lucky."

I didn't like his joke, not at all. "I'm serious, Fritz. Something bad is going to happen."

"It's only leftover worries from yesterday." Fritz stared at me a moment too long, as if trying to convince himself of his own words. "Now let's get to work."

Things went fine for a few hours. I was in the garden, clearing more weeds, and had already emptied out a lot of the dirt from the basement. But then I saw Fritz at the basement window, hissing at me to come inside, and to hurry. His eyes were so wide, I could see the whites from here.

The reason for the pit in my gut.

I dropped the spade and hurried for the building, careful not to make it look like anything was unusual, if anyone was watching. But when I ducked inside, Fritz had already returned to the shelter, and I breathlessly raced to follow.

"What's the matter?" I called while descending the ladder.

My answer came as soon as I entered the tunnel. Water trickled beneath my feet and sank into the soil, creating a dense mud. The farther I walked, the more water there was. At the back of the tunnel, Fritz had exposed a pipe that was now spurting out pressurized water like a fireman's hose. The hole in it wasn't large, but it was enough to cause significant damage and was getting worse. The streams of water tore dirt from the walls and sent it in chunks to the ground. Our tunnel was flooding, and if we didn't find a way to stop the water, it would collapse entirely.

"How did this happen?" I cried.

"I nicked it with the shovel. Didn't even know it was there until water shot out at me!"

"What do we do?"

Fritz wrapped his hands around the pipe, which helped, but water leaked down his arms, and we knew it would burst again as soon as he let go. Maybe even break open and flood the entire tunnel before we could escape.

"I have an idea!" he said. "But it'll take some time to get what we need. You have to stay here and hold this pipe!"

"How long? I can't —"

"However long it takes! Come on, Gerta. You can do this!"

So I stood on tiptoes, then reached up and replaced my hands with his. The water pushed at me with a force I didn't expect and it took effort to keep my grip on the pipe.

"Hurry," I told him. "Just hurry!"

He ran from the tunnel and left me in absolute darkness. The flashlight was somewhere at my feet but already buried in mud, and I couldn't let go to search for it. The water dripping down my hands was cold, and the wetter I became, the more I shivered.

Fritz said it would take him some time. How long did that mean? An hour, two hours? Until evening?

I couldn't hold on until evening. With water still dripping from the pipe, I wasn't even sure the tunnel would be here that long. If it collapsed, it'd take me with it.

In the darkness, a chunk of dirt or maybe rock fell somewhere behind me. I instinctively ducked, protecting myself from whatever might fall next. It terrified me to wonder how much had just fallen, and if more was about to come down. The only thing I knew for sure was that the mud at my feet was getting deeper.

Occasionally, when my hold slipped, water would spurt at harsh angles, inevitably bringing down more chunks of dirt. At one point, it loosened a rock overhead. I heard something start to fall and backed away from the sound, but when it came down, it grazed my arm. From the sting, I was sure it gave me a deep cut, though I couldn't remove my hands from the pipe to check it.

It wasn't much longer before I was entirely soaked through. My wet clothes clung to my body, my feet were sinking in mud, and my hair was in my face and over my eyes, but I supposed it didn't matter because there was nothing I could see in here anyway. I was shivering and my fingers and toes were already numb, but I knew if I let go of the pipe, everything we had worked so hard for was finished.

So I held on, doing whatever I could to distract myself. I solved long-division problems, recited poems, and prayed for a stronger willpower, though it'd be the last trait my mother would want me to strengthen. When those didn't work, I sang songs in my head. Ironically, the only ones I could think of were the patriotic songs of the Pioneers. But their rousing tunes didn't help for long. Time was crawling by and I'd lost any sense of how long Fritz had been gone.

Was it an hour? Was it more?

He would come back, I was sure of that. Unless . . . he had been arrested for some reason. Maybe Frau Eberhart had caused us trouble again — she was obviously capable of it. Or what if the tunnel was already collapsing from the outside? Maybe that's why it was so dark in here, and why he hadn't come back. Maybe he couldn't.

That terrified me, and I tried to shake the worst thoughts from my mind. All I knew was that Fritz had said to hold on. So I held to the pipe and to my senses and to my courage, bundling them together and knotting them within my heart. I closed my eyes and repeated his last words to me: "Come on, Gerta. You can do this!"

Fritz did return, eventually. I wasn't sure it was him at first, not until I heard his voice calling for me.

"Where's the flashlight?" he asked.

"Somewhere below me. It fell."

Fritz dug for that first, and when the light finally returned to the tunnel, I began breathing easier. He was fine, and I would be after a while. But for now, I was exhausted and freezing and my numb hands ached from the pressure and the cold. I'd held them up for so long, I doubted any blood was left in them.

"What happened to your arm?" he asked.

With the light on it, I saw the cut was much worse than I had expected. It ran in a long, jagged line that would probably leave a scar and stung like it had been attacked by wasps, but at least it wasn't bleeding anymore. I shrugged it off and asked, "What do you have for the pipe?"

"Not much, but it'll have to do." Fritz held up a clamp and an empty bicycle tube. "Papa once fixed a pipe in our apartment this way. It's not permanent, but it will work for now."

"Where'd you get those?"

"The clamp came from Herr Krause. He had a few people at his place for some sort of meeting, so he told me to go in his back room and take what I needed from his gadget collection. Didn't ask any other questions. The bicycle tube came from Claudia. She has extras in the shop where she works and I hoped she wouldn't ask questions either."

"Claudia? Your girlfriend?"

"*Ex*-girlfriend, remember? Now move your hand. It's going to spurt water, but I've got to wrap this tube around the leak."

I obeyed and caught a powerful spray of water to my face before Fritz got the tube over it. But he pulled it tight and then began wrapping it around the pipe. With every layer, the water sealed up tighter.

"Hand me the clamp," he said. "It's in my back pocket."

I grabbed the clamp and while he worked to get it

pinched around the pipe, I said, "What do you mean you 'hoped' Claudia wouldn't ask questions? Did she?"

He paused for only a moment and then said, "I went into her shop filthy and wet, and you and I are both thinner than we ought to be right now. Yeah, she had questions."

"What did you tell her?"

"Only about the garden. I said I fell into the pond and that we needed the bicycle tube to prop up some plants."

"And did she believe you?"

Fritz finished sealing the clamp and then patted at the pipe. When he was convinced the leak was fixed, he glanced down at me and said, "Probably not. But she used to like me. I hope it'll be okay."

That wasn't good enough, not after all our other close calls. But as things became more dangerous, simply hoping for anything good was probably the best we could do.

CHAPTER
THIRTY-TWO

A nation that is afraid to let its people judge the truth and falsehood in an open market is a nation that is afraid of its people. — John F. Kennedy, US President, 1962

With the mud and standing water, there was nothing more we could do in the tunnel that day. I suggested working on the garden beneath the warming sun, but after we got into the light and each saw how filthy the other was, we abandoned the idea of doing anything useful. We took a quick swim in the pond and let ourselves dry off somewhat before walking home. And we checked for Frau Eberhart around each corner before rounding it. I couldn't even imagine the nosy questions she'd have for us tonight, especially if she noticed the cut on my arm.

Despite our appearances, it was an uneventful walk home. The people who did see us were used to us being dirty and understood we were working a garden, so they barely seemed to notice we were dirtier than usual. But once we got inside our apartment, something was different.

"Fritz and Gerta Lowe! I want explanations!"

Mama had come home.

My first thought was for the hidden microphones. Mama had been gone for a few weeks to a place where she didn't have to think about them. Hopefully she remembered that was always a concern here. Every word we said mattered, and the way we said it mattered just as much.

My second thought was for what Mama must be thinking as she stared at Fritz and me. Nothing about us looked good. Beneath the layers of dirt, we were too thin, and our clothes were soiled and ragged. I had become deeply tanned, and my hands and knees were calloused. In only three weeks, we had gone from being respectable young people to looking more like workhouse orphans.

Fritz smiled warmly, walked forward, and gave Mama a kiss on the cheek. I thought I saw him whisper into her ear when he did, but it was so quiet I couldn't be sure.

I walked forward next and wanted more than anything to hug her, but she was so clean, I only reached up to kiss her too. When I did, she grabbed my arm and saw the long cut from the rock. "What —" she started to ask.

"It's just a scratch," I told her, for the microphones. "From a brambly weed. We've been gardening. It was supposed to be a surprise for you."

Mama was surprised, all right. She pursed her lips together and then told us both to get washed up. Fritz allowed me the first bath and I took my time in it. Better here than anywhere near Mama's temper. When the water got cold enough to force me out, I could've sworn more dirt than water ran down the drain.

When I got into the front room, I expected to see Fritz beside a fire, having written out explanations to Mama. Then everything would be better. But it was too warm outside to justify a fire without creating suspicion. Mama clearly knew we were up to something much bigger than gardening, yet we couldn't freely talk about any of it.

While Fritz went to bathe, I asked Mama about Oma Gertrude. I figured that was safe enough.

"Oma is well enough to get around now, but she'll have a cast for several more weeks. She misses both of you and wondered why you didn't come with me. Where's all our food?"

Mama had been poking around in the kitchen. There were some things — a cup of flour and half a bottle of vinegar in the cupboards, some sausage grease in the refrigerator, and something far in the back of the refrigerator that neither Fritz nor I recognized.

"We haven't had time for the store," I said.

Mama opened her mouth, closed it, and then marched over to the table, where she began unpacking a bag.

"Oma Gertrude insisted on sending me home with food. Some things are easier to buy out in the country and she wanted me to bring them back to you. While I'm cooking, go to your room, Gerta, and get it cleaned up. You could probably garden in there, with how dirty it is."

"Yes, Mama."

Less than an hour later, warm, wonderful smells began coming from the kitchen. Sausage and potatoes and biscuits. Whatever Oma Gertrude had sent back with my mother, I loved them both all the more for it.

Fritz and I didn't need to be called for supper. We were both in our places at the table when Mama served it. Food had never before tasted so good, I was sure of that. I ate greedily and remembered my manners only when I caught a glimpse of Mama's disapproving stare.

"The two of you have turned to savages," she muttered. "And someone had better tell me where all the sheets in this home have gone!" Mama didn't sound terribly angry yet, but then she probably hadn't noticed the missing hinges on our coat closet door either. Fritz and I had a lot of explaining to do.

We invited her for a walk around the neighborhood that night. We kept ourselves as far as possible from any of the crowds, then our story started to unfold.

We started with the picture of the Welcome Building Papa had sent to me. Mama said my father knew it well. During the war, it had been a clothing shop where his mother used to work. As I had suspected, he had sometimes hidden in the air-raid shelter of that basement when the sirens went off.

"We need to tell you about that shelter," Fritz said.

We started with the easier part first, about the garden on the surface, and about the clothesline set up for me to do laundry in the pond.

"You'd wash my sheets in a dirty old pond?" Mother had always prided herself on her white laundry. "Gerta, that will ruin them!"

"They are ruined now, Mama, all of them." I took a deep breath. "But we needed an excuse to be at the pond, so we could dump the dirt."

"Dump what dirt?"

Fritz took her hand, and in that moment I was glad that he was the older brother and that telling her was his responsibility more than mine. He leaned in to her and very quietly said, "The dirt from our tunnel. Beneath the wall."

To her credit, Mama took the news better than we had expected. She didn't yell or faint, neither of which would've surprised me. But it took her a long time to start breathing again, and when she did, it was in loud, shallow gasps. She shook her head in disbelief and let Fritz hold her shoulders to keep her calm.

"What have you done?" she whispered. "Oh, my children, why would you do this?"

As the reality of our confession sank in, she pulled us into a quiet alleyway and faced each of us with horror in her eyes. I hated seeing that expression from my mother. It was one thing to see fear from Fritz, or to feel it myself. But we had handled our fear and were managing our troubles as they came. To see so much worry from Mama was something else entirely. It meant that maybe everything wasn't as safe as we had let ourselves believe.

"What will happen when that tunnel is found?" she whispered. "Because it will be. They always are."

"We'll be gone by then," Fritz said.

"How do you know? You are working in the shadow of the wall! Do you think the guards aren't watching you, aren't curious about what you're doing? A garden is a nice excuse and maybe they'll ignore the laundry. But for how long?"

We hadn't told her about Officer Müller, nor did we intend to. If she knew that one of the Grenzers had already discovered us, it would only strengthen her argument.

"Papa wanted us to dig," I said.

"Your father would never have asked this," Mama said. "No matter how much he misses us, he would never put us at this much risk."

"But he did!" I insisted. "I saw him!"

"Enough of this nonsense. Starting tomorrow, you will bury up that hole and all the tools with it. You will abandon the garden, and, Fritz, you will find a respectable job until you join the military."

"I can't get a respectable job, or any job!" Fritz hissed. "And I won't join their military! What's done is done. Our only choice now is to leave."

"What about Oma Gertrude? Who would take care of her?"

I felt awful for having forgotten about my grandmother. We couldn't leave her behind, of course. And with a broken leg, she couldn't make the walk through the uneven and narrow tunnel.

"I never understood the way your father thought, and I don't understand it in you two either." Mama was shaking her head again. "We have a good life here."

"No, Mama," I said. "We don't. So much of what we tolerate is just wrong, even if nobody wants to think about it. We can't keep living this way!"

"But at least we will live! It's what your father would've wanted."

"Don't talk about him as if he's dead!" My words came out just as sharp as if I'd yelled them. "I know what Papa wanted, for all of us to come to the west with him that night. You said no! If it weren't for you, we wouldn't have to build a tunnel, and we'd be safe and all together. This is your fault!"

"Gerta, that's enough!" For a moment, Fritz's tone had sounded the way I remembered my father's voice. And I thought about how disappointed Papa would be if he had heard me speak so rudely to my mother.

"I'm sorry," I whispered to her. "That wasn't true."

"Some of it is," she said quietly. "I'm sorry for that too, that I wasn't brave when I needed to be."

Mama's face seemed to have aged years during our conversation in that alleyway. I felt older too, as if the things I spent so much time thinking about were light-years away from what other girls my age were doing. I no longer cared about dolls or dresses or even smuggled Beatles records. What a silly rebellion that was compared to my actions now, near treason in the eyes of my government.

"We'll take you to the tunnel tomorrow," I said. "You'll see."

"Only if it's dried out by then," Fritz reminded me. "It got a lot of water today."

He shouldn't have said that. Mama's back stiffened and I knew she was picturing Fritz and me swimming for our lives. That hardly helped our cause.

"Let's go." Mama shook off a shiver that ran through the length of her. "I feel too exposed out here. We're safer at home."

But as we neared our apartment, I doubted that was true. Stasi vehicles were in front of our building with armed officers on the street. Mama instinctively got us behind her while Fritz and I looked at each other. My heart lurched into my throat. Were they there for us?

"Oma Gertrude gave me her car," Mama said cautiously. "There's not much gas left, but we'll go as far as we can. I parked it in a lot behind us. You and Fritz go get inside the car and hide on the floor. I left the keys on the table upstairs. I'll come back for you soon."

"No, Mother." Fritz put a hand on her shoulder to guide her away with us. "If they're here to arrest Gerta and me, then they'll arrest you too."

Before we could act, a woman's screams caught our attention. Stasi officers were leading her outside in handcuffs. I immediately recognized her as the beautiful woman I had seen the night I stole the pulley. She was trying to fight the officers, but once she got onto the street and saw the crowd, she yelled, "It's no crime to think, or to speak, or to be me."

They were nearly the same words that had been on Herr Krause's handmade stamped papers.

Even after being arrested, Herr Krause must've found another way to get his message out. Maybe with small meetings in his apartment, like those he used to hold with my father.

Herr Krause was brought out again, but this time his body was on a gurney and perfectly still. And since Stasi officers were carrying him out, I figured it was safe to assume his death wasn't an accident. Herr Krause had received his punishment for daring to think, and for getting others to think too.

Sadness stabbed at my gut for how wrong this was, how

unfair. Yet I couldn't cry. I wanted to, but in that moment, fear was overwhelming every other sense in me.

Whatever crimes Herr Krause had committed, it was safe to assume that Fritz and I had done far worse. If we couldn't get Mama to change her mind, soon we would face Herr Krause's punishment too.

THIRTY-THREE

God preserve me from my friends, I can deal with my enemies. — *German proverb*

Mama wouldn't allow Fritz and me to go back to the tunnel the next day, not even to garden. But Officer Müller had warned us that time was our enemy, and so I decided even if there was something small I could do to help, I would.

We needed to know how wide the Death Strip was, and the only place I could get a decent view of it was from Anna's bedroom window. Somehow, I had to beg, swindle, or steal my way inside.

Fritz drew me a picture that explained how to estimate the distance of the strip. The Berlin Wall was three and a half meters high. I had to look at it and pretend it was laid out flat on the ground. Then I had to imagine another wall behind it, and so on across the entire Death Strip.

"Try to be as accurate as you can," he whispered in my ear. "But if you are going to make any errors, estimate a distance wider than we need. The worst possible mistake is for us to come to the surface inside the Death Strip."

Since Mama didn't know about Anna's and my dissolved friendship, she gladly gave permission for me to visit her. I knew she believed seeing Anna would weaken my resolve to leave East Berlin, but if anything, it would be just the opposite.

My pulse was racing when I knocked on Anna's door. Despite the great number of laws I had broken over the past few weeks, none of them caused me anywhere near the guilt that I felt now.

I had nothing to offer Anna as either a gift or an apology. And although I was bathed and my hair was combed and I was in one of my few remaining nice outfits, I felt unnatural, as if the sweat and dirt I earned each day in the tunnel had become the real me.

Anna's mother answered the door and at first didn't seem at all pleased to see me. But she called for Anna, and then with a voice like an icicle, she invited me in.

There, I was in her apartment, though I had only been allowed in as far as the front door. I could see Anna's bedroom from here, but that wasn't good enough. And once in there, I needed time to look out the window. That would require several uninterrupted minutes.

"Hello." Anna entered the front room and stopped far short of where I stood. She looked as uncomfortable as I felt, but since I had come to her home, it was my job to repair things.

"Can we talk somewhere?" I asked. In her room would've been nice, but I couldn't ask for too much too fast. Besides, now that I was here with her, I really did want us to talk.

Anna awkwardly motioned me toward her couch. I followed her there and we sat on either end, so close and yet it felt as though an ocean divided us. Or a wall.

I started. "You came to help on the garden and I wouldn't let you. I've thought about that a lot since then. I'm sorry."

"You've changed, Gerta," Anna said. "You're frustrated or angry all the time. You're jumpy around others, and distant. It's almost like you're —"

"Like I'm what?" I hoped she wouldn't accuse me of trying to escape, because I'd have to deny it and I really didn't want to lie to her anymore. But I had to ask.

Anna frowned. "Like you're unhappy, I suppose."

"I miss being your friend," I said softly. That wasn't a lie.

"Do you?" she asked. "Because sometimes I think you do, and then other times it's like you don't want me anywhere near you."

"I'm sorry," I said. "I wish you could understand."

"I want that too." Anna looked sideways at me. "Is there anything you can say to me, to explain *anything*?"

The way she emphasized the final word worried me. Was she asking me to explain my odd behavior over the last several weeks? Because the answer involved telling her the biggest secret of my life, and I could never reveal that.

Anna's mother came into the room to dust and Anna quietly rolled her eyes at me. I understood. This was a tough conversation and having an adult in the room didn't make things any easier. She stood and motioned for me to follow her. My heart jumped. We were going to her room.

I would've been more excited, except that I couldn't help but feel like a traitor in the face of her trusting attitude. She wanted a chance to repair our friendship. But I was only here as a clumsy sort of spy.

Anna's room was the same as it had always been: simple and sparse, and painted in a cream color that somehow reflected gray. I'd always thought of it as boring, even depressing, but Anna seemed to like the simplicity. As soon as I entered, my eyes went directly to her window, but the curtains were closed.

"It feels dark in here." It was a ridiculous thing to say, considering that her curtains were white and plenty of light shone through, but I was committed to it now. I sat at the head of her bed, where I'd have the best view. She took my hint and widened the curtains, though from my current angle, I couldn't see as much as I wanted.

"How do you enjoy gardening?" she asked.

Pulling my attention from the window, I shrugged. "It's not as fun as I thought it'd be. It could be a long time before we see if anything grows."

"If you ever see it." I did a double take, but Anna only smoothed out her bed cover. "I mean, since you planted so late in the year."

"Right." I was becoming increasingly uncomfortable with this conversation. Our friendship was hanging on by threads, and there was nothing I could do to change that. I was here for one reason only. First, I had to get Anna out of the room.

It required me to abandon my pride, but it had to be done. "The problem is we haven't had much to eat for a while."

Anna responded just as I knew she would. "Do you want something to eat now? We have plenty of food."

"Maybe a sandwich?" I suggested. That would take some time to make. It also sounded truly wonderful.

"Okay." As Anna slid off her bed and left, I went to work.

I made sure her door was shut and then crossed to her window. I could see the top corner of the Welcome Building from here, but not all the way to the ground. That was a relief. It meant she couldn't be spying on us, if that was ever her intention. If I stood at just the right angle, my view of the Death Strip was better than what I'd expected. In fact, there was a dark area inside the Death Strip that was probably very close to where we were tunneling. That made it easier to know where to measure.

Fritz said the wall was three and a half meters high, about one and a half times his height. In my mind, I laid it out flat. That was three and a half meters into the Death Strip. I imagined another one behind it, and then another and another. I'd glanced at this area several times before but never really considered how much wider it was than I thought. When I stood in the tunnel, I imagined us being at least halfway across, and maybe even more. But we weren't anywhere near that far.

Another length of wall went down in my mind, and another. The farther I went, the harder it was to be sure of my distances. So much of the open area looked the same as everywhere around it, and no matter where I stood, I was still at an odd angle. In fact, I might've lost track altogether if I didn't have that dark patch of ground to keep me oriented.

"Gerta?"

I swerved away from the window, so startled that I jumped, which must have looked very odd to Anna. Her eyebrows pressed low. "What are you doing?"

"Nothing important." I shut the curtain and walked over to take the sandwich from her. My mouth was full with the first bite when I added, "Thank you for the food."

"There's more I can do to help," Anna said. "My mother talked to me just now. We know a lot of your clothes have been ruined in the garden this summer, and there's some things I've outgrown." She walked over and opened her small closet. "Would it offend you to take any of the things I can't use?"

She started to pull some outfits from her closet, but my focus was on a pair of her boots on the floor. Not the brown pair she had worn when she visited me in the garden patch before, but her usual black ones. Clumps of mud still clung to the soles and what was dry had flaked off onto the floor. I had seen so much dirt in the last few weeks that if there was anything I could recognize, it was the dark soil we had tunneled out from beneath the Welcome Building.

Anna had been to the garden patch recently. Maybe she had gone farther than that.

I forgot about the clothes Anna was laying out on the bed, and even about the sandwich in my hand.

"I need to go," I announced, already halfway to her door. "I forgot . . . something."

"Gerta, don't — where are you going?" Anna called after me.

"Home."

"I'm sorry. Was it the clothes? Did I do something wrong?"

Oh yes, she certainly had. But behind her innocent facade she had to know this wasn't about the clothes. I'd always known there was a risk of someone I knew becoming a spy against us. But never in a million years would I have expected it to be Anna. There was no longer any question of our friendship. All that remained was to wonder just how much of an enemy she had become.

A disaster seldom comes alone. — *German proverb*

My tears had dried by the time I told Fritz the story shortly afterward. Which was a good thing because he wasn't showing much sympathy for whether I held on to a friend I was going to abandon soon anyway.

His larger concern was for the dirt on Anna's boots. "Are you sure the mud was on different boots than when she came to see us before?"

"Positive. The mud wasn't that old. Not over a day, I'd bet."

"You should've asked her about it."

"Asked her what, exactly?" I retorted. "If she knows about the tunnel? If she's going to turn us in to the Stasi? Because I didn't need to say a word. The answer to both questions is pretty obvious!"

"Okay, calm down." Fritz and I were in the basement of our own apartment building. This was our new sanctuary since Frau Eberhart patrolled the sidewalks and since we weren't yet sure which was more dangerous inside our own apartment: the microphones or Mama. "We have to assume that Anna knows, and that sooner or later, she's going to tell someone. Whether it's the Stasi or not, it'll eventually get back to them."

"Müller will come with them." My voice wavered, revealing too much of my fear of him. "He already told us what he'll do when that happens."

"Then we have to finish. Fast." Fritz paced a moment, then finally sighed and shook his head. "Did you get a chance to measure the Death Strip?"

"Sort of. Anna came in before I'd finished, but I got a good start. It was hard because I got distracted a couple of times, and I thought —"

"How wide?"

"One hundred meters."

Fritz let out a low whistle and almost staggered to a nearby crate where he could sit down. "We're not even half-way." He cursed and kicked at another box next to him.

Hoping to keep his spirits up, I said, "Let's dig it smaller, then. We can walk that distance hunched over, or even crawl through."

"That'll help," Fritz said. "But we need to take weeks off our time, not days. What if we ask Officer Müller to dig with us?"

"We can't trust him — he told us that himself!" I shook my head fiercely. "With a shovel in one hand and a gun in the other, which will he use when Anna calls the other officers to check out the tunnel?"

"You told me that you got distracted," Fritz said. "Maybe you were off on your count."

"I might be off by a few meters, but not twenty or thirty! And I know I was accurate almost to the halfway point because there was this dark spot in the strip, almost where our tunnel ended." For the first time, I thought about the chance of that, of a dark spot so close to the tunnel. That couldn't be a coincidence.

Fritz had caught on as well. "What do you mean, a dark spot?"

"I saw it from far away, and that's just what it looked like at the time." My breaths became shallow as I realized what I must have seen. "But I don't think it's a spot. It might be a shadow. I think the ground is sinking where we've dug it."

Fritz leapt to his feet. "C'mon. We've got to go and see it for ourselves!"

Even as I followed him, I said, "We're not allowed to go there. Mama doesn't —"

"There's no time to explain!"

"If the tunnel collapses while we're inside, or if the Grenzers notice the dark spot and come to investigate" — I shuddered — "either way, we're dead."

The only exception that I could see was if Mama figured out we had gone to the tunnel in defiance of her orders. Then we wouldn't have to worry about the Grenzers. She'd get to us first and do worse than the police ever could.

Fritz and I hurried along the street, got to the block that emptied into the back lot for the Welcome Building, and then crept along the wall to get inside. I wished we could just peek through the wall from here. Carve out a hole big enough to see if we had left our own "X marks the spot" for our secret beneath that ground.

But we would have to content ourselves with entering the tunnel and looking for any sign that the ground was sinking. My biggest worry was that from within the tunnel, the collapse wouldn't be noticeable. If we couldn't find it, then we couldn't fix it.

I scanned the roof of the tunnel. Instantly, everything became suspicious to me. Why was one area lower than elsewhere? Exposed rock jutted out overhead and to my left. Was it new? So far, everything looked how it had when he dug this section, Fritz assured me. But that didn't make me feel any better.

We finally found the sunken area at the end of the tunnel, around where the pipe had been nicked. Endless liters of water had sprayed so powerfully here, we probably should've expected it to affect the ground's stability overhead.

"We'll be caught for sure," Fritz said.

"Maybe Officer Müller can explain it away." I didn't

necessarily believe he would, but maybe it was the best of the few horrible options we still had.

"How deep did the dark spot look?"

"I dunno," I answered. "Not very. But it does look different from the area around it."

"Maybe we can brace it up. Or at least do something to keep it from falling any farther."

"How?"

Fritz already had the answer. "I'm a bricklayer. I can build supports overhead, maybe even raise some places if the ground is still soft enough. But the brick will be expensive and too suspicious to purchase."

"There's brick upstairs!" I said. "Maybe even a bag of mortar too."

"Then I'll get started right away," Fritz said. "Help me get it carried downstairs."

I was already on my way.

THIRTY-FIVE

The only way to deal with an unfree world is to become so absolutely free that your very existence is an act of rebellion. — Albert Camus, French author

Dinnertime was coming soon and Fritz and I were debating what to do. Mama would be expecting us for supper. If we didn't show up, her initial worries would turn to anger when she realized why we were late.

On the other hand, her anger was inevitable now. The instant we came home, she would know we had disobeyed her. And even if we tried to explain why, neither of us was sure the reasons would matter to her. Nothing we'd already said mattered anyway. Besides that, we had spent the last several hours at a mad pace getting brick loaded into the tunnel, mortar mixed up, and finding tools and supports that we could use. To avoid having to build frames overhead, Fritz was mortaring together larger sections of brick on the ground. He said it'd be several hours before they were dry enough that he could lift them into place, but we had plenty of work to do until then.

"I'll go home and explain to Mama," I offered. It was the last thing in the world I wanted to do. I'd rather have faced an angry bear right now, but Mama needed to know where we were, and Fritz had to stay here and keep working.

He looked down at me and nodded. "She's only doing what she thinks is right for us, Gerta. Try to remember that."

"One of her children is on the other side. And her husband!"

"Yes, and he would be the first to agree with her. Papa will be happy if we make it to the other side, but Mother is right — he would never want us taking this risk."

Fritz reached out for another brick in his stack and I handed it to him. "What do I tell Mama, then?"

Fritz sighed. "Tell her that we love her, and that it'll break our hearts if she doesn't come with us. But you and I are going to finish this tunnel."

It had never occurred to me that Mama might not come with us. Tears burned my eyes at the possibility. I couldn't be happy without her in the west any more than I could be happy in the east without my father. Somehow, I had to make her come.

Fritz dug away at the wall and inserted a brick deep into the dirt. That would hold up the wider stacks he'd already mortared. Fritz figured they would brace the dirt until we were able to finish the tunnel.

My thoughts drifted back to Anna. How long had she known our secret? And how much longer until she finally decided to tell? Time was running out for us. I could feel it, probably the same way my father had felt it days before the wall went up.

"This might help support the dirt," Fritz said as he examined the sunken area again. "But I don't see how we can lift it so it doesn't get worse. That dark patch on the Death Strip is going to remain there. If they run a patrol through there, they'll figure out what caused it."

"You can slide wood planks above the bricks to lift it," someone behind us said.

Startled, both Fritz and I turned. It was my mother's voice, firm and commanding. I couldn't quite read the expression on her face. It wasn't anger or fear or even disappointment — thank goodness for that, because I could withstand my mother's anger and knew how to calm her fears. But the times in my life when I had disappointed her still felt like unhealed wounds. Now Mama held a flashlight aimed toward the ceiling. Over her arm was a sack filled with food. My recent days of hunger had fine-tuned my sense of smell, and I always knew now when food was nearby.

I stared at her, completely unsure of what to do next. I hated to disobey her but I would if I had to. Nothing was more important than keeping this tunnel from caving in.

Mama seemed almost rigid, making every effort not to touch the walls or look up at the dirt ceiling. "I didn't bring you much to eat because we don't have much." Her voice was as near to stone as her body. "And I thought it would be all right once I started back to work today. But when I got there, they demoted me."

"Because of us?" I asked.

Mama sniffed and shook her head. "While I was with Oma Gertrude, they started looking into some letters I'd written to your father years ago. They said it was evidence that I was still divided in my loyalties. I told them that he was my husband and of course I was loyal to him. They offered to help me divorce him, but I won't do that. So I was given a much lower job as a consequence. What they'll pay me now won't begin to cover our rent, or our food, or anything else."

Fritz started forward. "Mama —"

But she held up a hand. "How much farther do you have to go?"

"A long way," Fritz said. "We're not halfway yet."

"How deep below the surface are we?"

Fritz shrugged. "We started at the level of the air-raid shelter. I've tried to keep it flat, but the farther we've gone, the harder it's been to keep track of that."

I stepped forward. "Mama, we know you don't like this idea, but now that we've started, we have to finish it."

"I know." Mama finally patted at the tunnel walls, then looked back toward the entrance. "Fritz, you will not join their military, and, Gerta, you must grow up where you can read any book you want, think any idea you want. And we will be together again as a family. We will finish this tunnel."

With that, she set the food on the ground and pushed past me, pausing only long enough to gently brush a hand across my cheek. Then she stood beside Fritz and pointed to the sunken area.

"Those bricks will give us support," she said. "But if we can find a sheet of wood, we can force everything upward. It might work."

"But where can we get the wood?" Fritz asked.

"There's a door on the upper floor of this building," I said. "It fell off its hinges so it's just lying there on the floor. It's the perfect size!"

"How do you know about that?" Fritz asked. "We only went up to the main floor for the brick."

"On one of the trips, I checked upstairs to see if there was more," I said. "But I hurried back down because most of the roof is exposed to the sky. At the right angle, the guards could look down from the watchtower and see inside."

Mama pressed her mouth tightly together and Fritz only shook his head. "We'll have to get the wood from somewhere else," he said. "Not upstairs, where we're exposed."

"Then from where?" I asked. "Unless we dismantle our own doors at home, where would we get something like that? And even if we did, can we just carry a big door through town? What'd be our excuse for having it?"

"I bumped into Frau Eberhart when I was bringing you this supper," Mama said. "The woman wouldn't let me go until she asked a hundred questions about you two and this garden. I can't imagine her letting us get past with a perfectly usable door."

Fritz exhaled slowly. "Okay, then we'll get the door from upstairs, but tonight, after it's dark. I'll do it."

"It'll be me," Mama said. "You two have taken enough risks."

"No, I'll go," I said. "Neither of you knows where it is and we obviously can't bring a light to look for it. I'm strong enough, and I'm the smallest. If they turn their spotlights onto the building, I'll fit in the shadows the best."

Mama and Fritz looked at each other. Neither wanted to admit it, but they knew I was right. And so without another word, it was decided. After dark, I would go under the noses of the guards.

THIRTY-SIX

I learned that courage was not the absence of fear, but the triumph over it. — *Nelson Mandela, South African activist*

We spent the remainder of the evening working in the tunnel. With Mama's help, we made far more progress than ever before. She suggested we concentrate our efforts on deepening the tunnel and not to worry about spreading out the dirt anymore.

"It was a good plan while you needed it," she said. "But if the Grenzers come back for another investigation, they'll find the tunnel anyway."

So we piled the dirt up in the basement, similar to how we had done it at first. Mama showed me how to pack it down with the bucket so that more would fit into the same space, and so that it wouldn't fall all over. While Fritz continued to build supports for the sunken area, Mama dug and I hauled dirt. I hadn't thought she'd be as strong as Fritz, but she dug with a ferocity I'd never seen before.

"This is the strength of a mother fighting for her children," she said. "When you have children of your own, you will understand. I should've been here with you from the first day."

"We should've told you from the first day," I said. For the first time, possibly ever, my mother and I were on the same side of an argument.

When we took a rest shortly before curfew, Fritz suggested Mama should return to the apartment and make noises to cover for our absence. "If someone is listening, they need to think we're all home."

"I won't leave you both here overnight."

"We'll get the door, then sleep here in the tunnel," Fritz said. "That'll mean Gerta and I can start working first thing in the morning. Besides, we're in no greater danger here than we would be at home."

I doubted that was true. If they came for us at home, we'd probably be arrested. But if they found us here . . . well, we knew where we were.

Still, Fritz was right about satisfying the microphones, so Mama reluctantly kissed each of us good-bye and said she would return in the morning. She also promised to bring us enough food for another day's work, which cheered me up considerably. Even though I knew we had almost nothing in the apartment, she was my mother, and if she said she would bring food, then food was coming.

Fritz and I continued working until long past dark. Mama had run into a sandy patch of dirt, so it came apart easily and wasn't as heavy to haul away. When it was very late, we at last made the decision to go upstairs.

"Are you sure you want to go?" Fritz asked.

I was sure I didn't. If there was anything I had ever been so certain of in my life, it was that I didn't want to drag a door off the exposed top floor of this building. But it couldn't be Fritz who went. He was taller, and there was more of him to get caught in their searchlights.

We went first to the main floor. I wasn't comfortable here since we could be seen from the back windows if someone happened by. But we'd spent enough time here earlier today to know where it was safe to stand.

It was the upper floor that worried me. From my view out Anna's window, I knew she could see this level if she happened to look, which meant any number of other people could too. It would be a bright moon tonight, but the moon hadn't yet risen. All the more reason to hurry and get this over with while I still had some darkness on my side.

Obviously, the main thing to avoid was being in the view of the watchtower guards. There were always lights on the tower at night, but I figured if I couldn't see the lights, then the guards shouldn't be able to see me.

"Be careful." It was a completely unnecessary thing for Fritz to say, but I was glad he said it anyway.

I nodded and then started up the stairway to the upper floor. If I stayed against the far wall, I was in total shadow cast by the watchtower lights. A few glowing stars would help me see, but mostly I hoped my eyes would adjust soon. Dirt and small rocks littered the stairs. That meant they could be slippery, and we'd have to carry the door down when we were finished. Dragging would make too much noise, especially if it pushed rocks down with it. At the top of the stairs, a wide hole in the roof gave clear sight to the watchtower. Since the hole was much closer to me than to them, I figured it was easier for me to see out than for them to see in, and I prayed I was right. My urge was to hurry and get this over with, but I forced myself to move slowly. Slow would be harder for them to see. Slow kept me carefully thinking through every choice I made up here.

The door was in the opposite corner from where I was crouched. Half of it remained in shadow and the other half sat beneath the light of the stars.

I patiently crept on all fours toward the door, instantly aware of how still and quiet the night was. Every creak in the floor seemed magnified, so I was sure they could hear me. My breath seemed to echo in the air. Even the pounding of my heart was a drum that their dogs could surely hear, if not the guards themselves. Despite all that, I soon reached the door and lifted it to test its weight. It was made of solid wood — very good news because it could withstand the weight of the dirt when we tried to stabilize the tunnel. But bad news for moving it. I would have to drag it to the stairs.

I wasn't worried about my strength in moving the door — day after day of hauling dirt had made me much stronger than I used to be. But a heavy door would make more noise along the floor and probably leave a noticeable trail of dirt behind, one I couldn't clear without getting out into the open.

I tugged at the door, but it didn't budge. I couldn't figure out what the problem might be. It should've moved in my hands.

Then, with a high-pitched whine, the watchtower light powered on and I froze. There was no reason to panic yet — the lights always swooped around in the night, much like the paths of birds of prey, patrolling for anything on the ground that could be devoured. The light washed across the Death Strip and then up in the air. It shone through the broken-out windows above me, stealing too much of my shadow, but also revealing the problem with the door.

A broken beam from the roof had fallen on the door, pinning it to the ground. I had to remove that beam.

The watchtower light swung in a pattern. Two swoops over the ground to the south, where I was, then once through the air as it moved to the right. Then two swoops to the ground on the north. While the light went north, the darkness returned. That was my chance to get the door.

I used that moment now to dart forward, keeping my body low. By the time the light returned, I was closer to the broken beam, but safely back in the shadows. With the next round of darkness, I pushed at the beam, but only gave it one nudge before I had to withdraw again. When my next opportunity came, the beam wouldn't roll at first, and every shove caused a cracking sound that echoed through the quiet night. Determined to get it free, I pushed with every ounce of strength within me. Finally, it turned just enough to release the door. It took another several slow-motion minutes to get back into my original shadow. Then, one centimeter at a time, I began pulling the door again. I dragged it through the darkness and hid while the light swept past.

How ironic that I had been so critical of East Berlin for feeling darker than the west. Now, that very darkness was my only hope to complete this task.

After I got the door into total shadow, Fritz was there to help me carry it the rest of the way down the stairs. Only then did I feel safe enough to breathe again. With his help, we were soon back on the second level. I wanted to return to the upper floor and brush over the drag marks, but Fritz insisted it wasn't worth the risk. I agreed without protesting, not because I thought he was right, but because the idea of returning there turned my insides to jelly. That was as close as I ever wanted to come to being in the lights of the Death Strip.

THIRTY-SEVEN

*He only earns his freedom and his life who takes them
every day by storm.* — *Johann Wolfgang von Goethe, German
writer and statesman*

Fritz and I had a surprise waiting for Mama when she
returned the next morning. The door was already in place
in the tunnel. It must have been a closet door once, we
decided, because the narrow width was perfect for this
space. And after we lifted it onto the dirt ceiling and added
Fritz's mortared bricks to hold it up, we started pushing
in other bricks to force the door upward. That part was
incredibly hard, but Fritz was smart. He figured out how to
raise the door little bits at a time with smaller wedges, then
work the brick in to push the dirt upward.

"Did the door do any good?" Mama asked.

We didn't know. But the ground wouldn't sink any further and Fritz said he would keep a better eye on the ceiling
from then on.

After her inspection was complete, Mama pulled out the food she had promised us. Several times during the night, I had wondered what she might bring, but never imagined anything this wonderful. There were meat patties, honey and crackers, some fruit, and even a few candies.

"Where did this come from?" I asked gleefully.

Mama frowned. "Will you promise not to think too badly of me?"

Fritz and I agreed, and then she said, "It was in Herr Krause's apartment. I figured he had lived there alone and nobody had cleaned his place out yet. The food should go to somebody, why not us? But still, this is stolen food, and that was wrong."

To make her feel better, I told Mama about taking the pulley. She scolded me properly for that, not only for stealing but for the risks I'd taken. I didn't mind. Knowing that her crime wasn't as bad as mine seemed to make her feel better, and that was good enough for me.

While we were eating, Mama also pulled out a letter addressed to Fritz. He turned it over once in his hands, then frowned and tore it open. He had to hold up a flashlight to read it, and when he did, I saw the military stamp show through the paper.

"What is it?" Mama asked.

Fritz's eyes drifted from her over to me. "They changed the date for me to report for the military," he muttered.

"I'm expected to begin serving on Monday. That's only two days away."

I nearly exploded. "You had until the end of the month! You're not even eighteen for another two weeks!"

"I worried about this." Mama's hands began shaking. "Orders change sometimes."

I put my hands over hers to steady them, but instead, it made mine shake too. We had so far to go, and still no idea of how we'd get back to the surface in the west. "We'll never finish the tunnel by then. We were barely going to make it by next week."

Fritz crumpled up the letter and threw it on the ground. "Yes, we will." He stood up and grabbed the shovel, then began tearing into the wall. Without a word, I picked up the bucket to continue working while Mama quickly packed up the food. If we weren't finished in two days, then nobody could've finished it, because we would dig harder than anyone ever had before.

When Fritz got tired, Mama took over for him, and while the one worked, the other helped me haul dirt up to the basement. Meter by meter, our tunnel grew and expanded. It was no wider than it had to be, and the work wasn't as neat as Fritz and I had done in the beginning. But we were going forward.

By early afternoon, Fritz and I were so tired that Mama insisted we sleep while she continued working. So we returned to the air-raid shelter and my eyes closed before my head even hit the ground. I wasn't sure how long she let us sleep, but it felt like hours. I only knew that when she called for us, we both sat up groggy and disoriented. Then Mama called again and I raced into the tunnel with Fritz at my heels.

Mama held up a hand for us to stop, then motioned for us to be silent. With urgency in her voice, she whispered, "Listen," and pointed to the end of the tunnel.

I couldn't hear anything at first, but when I walked forward and pressed my ear against the dirt, a sort of sound did come through. Thumping. Digging.

Something not far from us was hitting against rock. Someone else was tunneling!

Panicked, the three of us retreated to the shelter to discuss the matter.

"There must be other East Germans trying to escape!" Fritz said. "Somehow our tunnels have intersected. If we connect with them, we can join our efforts."

"If you're right, that's too risky!" Mama said. "We don't know these other people and we shouldn't tie our fate in with theirs. If they are found out, then we are found out."

"But we could move so much faster then," Fritz said. "Besides, they didn't sound that far away. They'll probably connect with us at some point anyway. We might as well try to get to them and see how we can help each other."

"I think the sounds came from ahead, toward us," Mama said. "Could it be Stasi, building a tunnel along the length of the Death Strip? That way, anyone who tries to cross underground will have to run into them."

That was possible, maybe even likely. And if she was right, then it meant we were only another meter or so away from walking directly into their hands.

"There's a third option," I said. "Maybe the tunnel is coming from the west. What if it's Papa?"

I hadn't believed it until the words emptied from my mouth, but once they did, I knew I was right. Papa would never have asked us to dig — Fritz and Mama both told me that. But maybe he wasn't asking me to dig. Maybe the dance was telling me that *he* was already digging.

Mama didn't seem convinced but Fritz nodded his head and said, "He sent Gerta the picture of the building. But it wasn't about where our tunnel should start — he was telling her where his tunnel would end. He wanted us to be ready for the time when he broke through."

"What if you're wrong?" Mama asked. "How can we know it isn't the Stasi?"

We couldn't know, not for sure. But we couldn't stop digging either. Maybe when we broke through to the other tunnel, there might be other East Berliners, or the Stasi. Or, as I was sure must be the case, we would find my father.

Everything that is done in the world is done by hope.
— *Martin Luther, German priest*

Curfew was approaching, which brought on another fight with Mama. Fritz and I wanted to keep working. With only two days left before he would be expected to report for military duty, our time crunch was worse than ever. If my father was on the other side, then we could connect with him tonight and be free.

"And what if it's not him?" Mama asked.

I didn't dare to think about that. If it wasn't him, then our efforts here were doomed. No, *we* were doomed.

"We won't get much farther tonight," Mama said. "We're all exhausted, and it's important for whoever is listening in our apartment to hear your voices. Besides, if there's bad news coming our way, I'd rather they find our tunnel while we're not here."

Mama was right about everything, especially that we were exhausted. Too tired, in fact, to put up any reasonable protest for staying. So we put down our tools and followed her home. In my bedroom that night, I was so excited about what might be in the other tunnel that I was sure I would never get to sleep. But within only seconds, sleep found me anyway.

I awoke early, and deliberately made plenty of noise so that everyone else could wake up too. We had a quick breakfast, chatting cheerfully the entire time about how excited we were for Fritz to report to military service the next day, and about our confidence that once the state saw how well he served, Mama would surely be restored to her former job. Lies. I was tired of always having to lie.

As soon as we felt it was appropriate, we ventured back onto the street. In our anticipation to reach the tunnel, we started down the sidewalk too quickly and bumped straight into Frau Eberhart.

The dour woman clearly wasn't in a good mood this morning. She scowled when she saw us in work clothes and brushed herself off, even though I was sure we hadn't gotten any dirt on her.

"I excused their poor manners while you were out of town," Frau Eberhart told my mother. "But I thought they'd have improved again when you returned, not worsened."

"You bumped into them," my mother snapped. "You should be the one apologizing!"

Frau Eberhart straightened herself up and evaluated my

mother's appearance. "I thought you were a church-going lady. But it seems you have more important plans today."

Mama and I looked at each other. With so much else to think about, none of us had remembered today was a Sunday.

Mama attempted to excuse it with a joke. "Well, Frau Eberhart, I suppose some days the Lord wants us in his house, and some days he wants us going about his work. Which are *you* choosing?"

Frau Eberhart reacted by wrinkling her nose, as if we smelled. Maybe we did. "And the Lord's work is gardening? Did your daughter mention that she promised me some of the harvest from that garden? She seemed to think it might encourage me to keep quiet, in case I saw anything suspicious."

Mama smiled at Fritz and me. "Why don't you two go on ahead? We have to talk, mother to mother."

Fritz grabbed my arm and pulled me off with him. By the time I looked back, they were already engaged in what looked like a very tense conversation. Something had changed in Mama over the last few days. She looked tired and worried, just as we all did. But she seemed younger, and stronger too, as if digging the tunnel had reclaimed the spirit of who she used to be.

"Frau Eberhart was right," I said. "I did sort of bribe her."

"Let Mother work it out," Fritz said. "Our job is to dig."

After we made it into the shelter, Fritz and I had the luxury of deciding what to do about the second tunnel without Mama getting a vote. We knew what she'd have wanted, and that once she made up her mind, the decision would be final. For Mama, any risk was too much risk.

But Fritz thought Mama had made some good points last night. "Other families have escaped through tunnels," he said. "If the Stasi have gone to such efforts to barricade the ground above us, why not below as well?"

I disagreed. "Why didn't Officer Müller warn us, then?"

"Officer Müller never said he was on our side."

Fritz was right about that. If anything, Müller had promised just the opposite — that if we were discovered he would be there for our arrest.

I listened again with my ear pressed against the tunnel wall, but this time there were no sounds. Either the other tunnel had moved farther away from us, or else nobody was digging right now.

I grabbed the shovel and began digging in that direction. "Whatever is ahead of us, we can't quit now," I said. "Maybe it's Stasi, but what I fear even more is missing Papa's tunnel."

So Fritz relented and worked with me. We had to move carefully because of other pipes overhead, and there were large rocks in front of us. But at least we were digging again.

Mama joined us soon after. When we asked what had taken so long, she said, "Frau Eberhart believes you two are up to something. I tried to convince her otherwise, but she insisted I was in denial. 'Children today are more slippery than they used to be. A lazy mother can miss the signs.'" Mama huffed. "She sits outside all day like a lump and then accuses *me* of laziness?"

I shrugged. "You're not lazy, but in all this mud, I can believe that I'm quite slippery!"

Mama laughed, then grew serious again when she said, "Our conversation moved to Herr Krause's death. She's upset about it, just like the rest of us. She admitted that she was the one who had turned him in, but also insists she had no idea what they would do to him. I told her to go inside and stop asking so many questions, or there would be more deaths."

"Does she suspect about the tunnel?" Fritz asked.

"I don't think so. But she didn't go inside either."

"Shh! Quiet down!" I hissed. "Shh!" I paused from digging and pressed my ear against the dirt. The sounds in the other tunnel had begun and they were closer than ever. It was impossible to know exactly, but I was sure whoever was on the other side must be within an arm's length of us.

Then, very high up, a stick poked sideways through the dirt. It was no rounder than an earthworm, but there was lantern light on the other side, far more light than what we allowed ourselves here. None of us breathed.

The stick went forward and wiggled as if the person on the other end was feeling for more dirt or some rock. Feeling nothing, it was withdrawn, and then the more focused beam of a flashlight came through.

Still, we said nothing and didn't even move. We had been discovered, but by whom?

Then, in a low voice I well remembered from my childhood, someone sang an even more familiar tune. *"They dig and they rake and they sing a song."*

Papa.

I was aware that it could all go horribly wrong.
— Günter Wetzel, *escaped East Germany with his family in a hot-air balloon, 1979*

Fritz immediately started to widen the hole, but after a quick greeting, Papa warned him to stop.

"Why?" It took real effort to keep from kicking the dirt wall down entirely, and my tone showed it.

"Sweet Gerta, how I've missed you." Papa's voice wavered a bit, then became serious again as he said, "We're too shallow. We've been measuring this morning and we're certain that we've been slowly tunneling uphill. Last night we heard the dogs over us; they might even be able to detect us below. We heard barking and maybe we're the reason why."

"Then let's dig lower!" The impatience I felt streamed through me like raw energy. The fact that we were just sitting here, so close and yet conversing through a tiny hole in the dirt, was impossibly frustrating.

Mama stepped forward and put her hand on my shoulder. "Patience, Gerta. This must be done right."

There was silence and then my father's voice broke as if he was crying. "Katharina? My dear wife, is that you?"

I looked up at my mother and in the low light saw tears on her cheeks. "It's me, I'm here," she answered. "Aldous —"

"I tried to get back to you, my love. All this time —"

Mama pressed her hand against the wall, as if touching it brought her closer to my father. Suddenly, I felt shame for my anger toward her these past four years, when my father seemed to have held on to nothing but his love for her. Who was I to judge her when he had not? In apology, I wrapped an arm around her and nestled closer as she brought me against her side.

Then another voice came through. "Mama?" I didn't recognize it, but only one other person would have said that word.

"Dominic?" Mama pressed even closer against the dirt. She folded a little, and for the first time I began to understand how painful it must have been to be separated from one of her children. Tears filled my eyes, but with such a filthy hand I could only let them fall. Behind me, even Fritz sniffed with emotion.

"You never should've dug this tunnel, Fritz," Papa said. "The danger of it —"

"Careful who you blame," Fritz said. "It was Gerta who started this."

"Gerta?" He stopped and chuckled lightly. "I see that she is no less headstrong than the night I left. My wonderful, brave girl, I should've known." Even from here, I heard his sigh.

"You suggested it, Papa," I said. "I saw you."

"I only wanted you to know we were coming," he said. "So you could be ready."

Fritz gave me a look. That was exactly what he had told me.

Then Papa continued, "But now that we're this close, I'm glad you did. We'd have been another couple of weeks to get over to you."

"Let us keep digging," Fritz said. "We could open this tunnel in the next few hours."

"Then we must dig deeper," Papa said. "I don't like the way the dirt looks above us."

"It's like clay beneath our feet," Fritz said. "It'll take a month to bridge the tunnels if we have to go lower." But he started anyway.

The tunnel wasn't wide enough here for Mama and I to help, and Fritz wasn't emptying enough of the dense, packed soil to require us to remove it. Papa said he had to go back to help carry out some dirt. We promised him that we would wait there.

Hour after hour passed with very slow progress on our end. The dirt on Papa's side was collapsing and sealed up the hole he had made with the stick and even the little gap Fritz had made. Then Fritz suggested he and Mama should better fortify our end of the tunnel for when the entire gap was broken open.

"We need more bricks," Fritz said, eying the dirt above him. "If it starts to collapse when we join these tunnels, I want to be ready."

"There're still some bricks left upstairs," I offered. "Not many, but maybe one more pile on the main floor."

"Be careful," Mama said. "Send them down in the bucket when you're ready and I'll unload them into the tunnel."

I hurried out of the shelter, up the ladder into the basement, and then up the stairs onto the main floor. The bricks were indeed there as I had thought, but it occurred to me that in this daytime light, I could possibly see into the Death Strip and confirm that our propped-up door had repaired the dark patch on the ground. It was a terrible risk to be up there with no shadows to keep me in the safe zones. But I was also becoming used to risks, and this one had to be taken.

I crept to the upper floor, aware of each step I took and of even the smallest movements I made. I went slowly and kept my body pressed to the wall as if I were part of it.

The window in front of me was missing its glass, but if I stayed low, that would be the best place for a view. All it would take was for a watchtower guard to look at this building while my head was visible and it would be over. Alarms would sound, dogs would be called, and shots would be fired. Nobody would be quicker to acknowledge the stupidity of me being up here on the very same day as we would surely break through to my father.

But I thought about what Papa had said, that they had gone too shallow. And that worried me.

I would look very quickly. No hesitations. No stares. Just the quickest glance into the center of the Death Strip. So fast that if I happened to catch the corner of a guard's eye, when he looked again I would be gone and he would assume it was a trick of the light.

The best news would be to see the dark spot was entirely gone. There wasn't much chance of that, but I hoped at least it was no worse. And then I would look a little farther on, to Papa's side of the tunnel.

After brushing away the sweat from my palms, I peeked through the window, but suddenly couldn't tear myself away. I had heard the phrase "frozen in fear," but never understood it before, not like I did in that moment. When I finally forced myself back against the wall, my heart was racing so much that I could barely breathe. Nobody had seen me, or at least, no alarms were sounding. But our problem was just as awful.

A line seemed to be caving in on Papa's side. It wasn't just one little sunken area, like with ours. Papa's entire tunnel was going to collapse!

"Stop!" I cried once I reentered the tunnel. I flew past my mother in the shelter, ignored her question about what had taken me so long, and grabbed Fritz's arm. "Papa's tunnel is collapsing, just like ours. I saw it. Just now, I went to the upper floor and saw it."

Fritz's mouth opened, then shut. And then he used the handle of the shovel to push another hole through to Papa's side.

Papa wasn't there, but Dominic was, and Fritz relayed our panicked message. Instantly, we heard Dom run off, calling for our father. When Papa returned to talk with us, Fritz told him the danger signs we had noticed earlier on our end.

"I see it here!" Papa said. "There are fissures in the earth where it's begun to separate. How have I missed it?"

"Gerta said the problems run through most of the length of your tunnel. You have to prop it up now," Fritz cried. "Use anything you have, brick or wood, or anything that will hold it up."

"Get out of your end," Papa said. "If our tunnel collapses, yours will go down too."

"We can't!" Fritz said. "We have to finish tonight. If I don't report for military service tomorrow, they'll arrest me."

"Do not report there," Papa said. "Do you hear me? If they get hold of you, we'll never get you out again. Come back early in the morning. If I haven't stabilized this tunnel by then, it'll be too late anyway. I want you all to make preparations to leave. Either you pass through this tunnel tomorrow, or you'll all have to leave the city and hide until we can figure out another way."

"Aldous!" Mama cried. "If it collapses and you're in there —"

"Get out," Papa said. "Now that I'm looking, the failure is worse than I thought."

"We can help!" Mama said.

Papa's voice was firm, just the way I remembered it on the night he said good-bye four years ago. "Please, Katharina, get my children out of that tunnel. I can't work if I have to worry about you too."

We had no choice. We ran from the tunnel without knowing whether we would ever see it again. Whether we would ever see our father again. Or ever again have a chance at freedom.

CHAPTER
FORTY

No one knows where the shoe pinches, but he who wears it. — *German proverb*

As we walked home, Mama made us wipe our tears and told us to smile and properly greet everyone we passed.

"People get caught when they look like people who should be caught," she said. "Smile."

"What about Papa?" I mumbled.

"You will see him tomorrow. Save a hug and kiss for him until then, because he will want it." Mama spoke with confidence, but I didn't know whether that was because she believed it, or because she wanted me to believe it.

There was a time in my childhood when I accepted as fact everything my parents said simply because it never occurred to me they could be wrong. But Papa had said he would return from his visit to the west, and he was wrong. Mama had said the wall wouldn't last and we'd all be together again. That was wrong too. So wrong that to make things right again, we had now put everything at stake, including our lives. I wished I could return to that time of my childhood just long enough to believe my father would be okay simply because my mother had pronounced it so. But I had seen too much reality to ever go back. As it was, the best I could do was to pretend to believe her, so she would worry less about me.

Mama assumed she had cheered me up and went on to say, "Until we're all together tomorrow, we are going to pack our clothes and wash ourselves and clean the apartment."

"Clean?" I asked. "Why, if we're only going to leave it?"

"When we're gone, Stasi will be everywhere in our home." It was Mama's German pride speaking now. "I won't have them saying the Lowe family are pigs. We are going to clean it."

Fritz and I didn't argue. There was no point in it.

We returned home with only a passing comment from Frau Eberhart that we were back earlier than usual. Mama walked past as if she hadn't heard her, but I curtsied politely and we hurried back to our apartment.

None of us needed reminding this time about the microphones. Mama only announced that the gardening could wait for a day. Today, we would clean and get Fritz packed to leave for the military tomorrow. It was a perfect cover story for our real purposes.

I was given the job of cleaning the front room, which I still thought was ridiculous, but I didn't say anything. I couldn't, because any complaint would be overheard, flagged, and reported. So I pretended to be cheery, but compensated by giving my mother irritated looks whenever she passed by.

Mama prepared an early supper for us, more of Herr Krause's food, and Fritz and I ate as if it was our last meal. Fritz said my constant hunger was all in my mind, but I noticed he acted the same way, always eating whatever was available in case no food came to us tomorrow.

"I'm supposed to be at work tomorrow for my new job," Mama announced. "But I need to go back to Oma Gertrude this evening and make sure she's okay. I might not make it home by curfew, in which case I'll return first thing in the morning."

Fritz and I looked back at her and nodded our understanding. The visit wasn't to be sure Oma Gertrude was okay. Mama was going to say good-bye. It would be her last chance to see her mother, ever. As guilty as I had felt for starting the tunnel without Mama's knowledge, I couldn't imagine how she must feel for leaving without being able to bring Oma Gertrude with us. The fact that they were being pulled apart was my fault, and I hoped Mama could one day forgive me for that.

Partially to compensate for my guilt, I offered to clean up the kitchen so my mother could get on the road as soon as possible. Besides, I felt more worried than ever because we were so close now, and because I couldn't be at the tunnel tonight. Even if my father survived a collapse of his tunnel, Grenzer officers with their long rifles in hand would be there to greet him at the surface.

Mama left as soon as she finished eating. Afterward, Fritz helped me finish in the kitchen and then said he had his own errand to run. It shouldn't have been any of my business where he was going, but I needed to know. It had to be something good to justify leaving me alone on such a dangerous night.

"Claudia," he said. "She's often at the clubs in the evening. I just want to say hello."

Or good-bye. That would probably be a hard conversation, especially since she would never know how final his farewell was. I nodded and he darted out the door.

After he left, it was a very long evening for me. There was nothing more to pack, or to clean, and nothing I could concentrate on for more than a few seconds. I thought it might be nice if I had someone to say good-bye to. Anna. But I'd sooner talk to Frau Eberhart than my former friend.

Curfew began when it was dark out, and it was only a few minutes after that when Fritz came trudging into the apartment, with his head held low. He looked up at me with heavy eyes and started toward his room.

"How did it go?" I was hopeful, though from his appearance, I already had my answer.

He only muttered, "I really did love her, Gerta. More than she ever loved me back, apparently."

Only then did I understand his full purpose in going. It wasn't to say good-bye to Claudia. It was to ask her to come with us. I wasn't sure how much Fritz had said or what promises he possibly could have offered her about their life together — they were both so young. But I knew he still loved her.

So that was it, then. He had gone to beg Claudia to come with us where they would be free to be together.

And she had refused him.

FORTY-ONE

Postponement brings danger. — *German proverb*

Those joining the military were supposed to report for service first thing on the morning of their appointed day. However, since some boys throughout East Germany had to travel into Berlin, they would be accepted at the intake station throughout the day. Fritz hoped the extra hours would buy him time for one final walk to the tunnel.

He seemed in better spirits today, or at least, he was covering well enough. During the night I had listened at his door for any sign that he was upset, but if he was, I didn't hear it. That was how we became in the east, never too happy and certainly never too sad. Compared to most others, I wasn't as good at reining in my feelings. Lately, I was a split of two strong emotions, each fighting the other to control my mood. Today might be the day of our escape. Or the day of our arrest. I wasn't sure exactly how to feel: intensely excited, or intensely afraid.

Mama came home shortly after Fritz and I finished breakfast and announced to the microphones that she was ill. Despite the weak tone of her voice, just one look at her assured me she was fine.

She turned up the radio and then whispered in my ear that she would have to stay inside, at least for the morning. Of course, this was only her excuse to delay going in to work. However, it did create one problem. If she was sick, she could not risk being seen on the streets.

"Did you talk to Oma Gertrude?" I hated to ask, but I wanted to know.

Mama whispered, "She only wondered why we waited so long. I will see her again, Gerta. Somehow."

Mama instructed Fritz and me to go to the tunnel to be sure things were okay, and then to do whatever was necessary to connect them. When that was finished, we were to come home and get her. We would have supper tonight in the west.

It was everything I could do not to run to the Welcome Building. Fritz reminded me more than once to walk slower and to wipe such an eager expression from my face.

"You're like a beacon right now," he said. "All someone has to do is look at you to know you're up to something."

"How do you do it?" I asked. "How can you look so casual on a day like this?"

"Because I know what's at stake if I don't. Now relax. Be calm."

I was calm as a blizzard, but tried hard not to show it. That became extra important as we approached the wall. Even from a distance we heard noise on the other side, barking dogs and the angry voices of the Grenzers. The last thing we needed was to get their attention.

"Why are they there?" I hissed. Had the tunnel already collapsed? Were they just waiting for us to show up, walking like fools into the lion's den?

Fritz hushed me and then we pressed against the wall to listen. To be heard above their dogs, the officers were shouting at one another, and every so often we caught their words.

". . . water pipes . . . leak . . ."

". . . West German incompetence . . ."

". . . investigate . . ."

They said nothing about a suspected tunnel, or about anyone's arrest or death. From the little we could gather, they knew water pipes ran through this corridor and blamed the sinking soil on a leak somewhere underground. Perhaps any digging noises they'd heard was also credited to the leaking pipe. But we also caught the word "investigate." They were going to dig down, and when they did, they would discover far more than a broken pipe.

Fritz grabbed my arm to reassure me. "We're leaving this afternoon, Gerta. They probably won't go looking before then."

Maybe not. But it wasn't impossible either.

At least the tunnel hadn't collapsed. That was my first thought once we entered. It may have unnerved me the first time I went underground, but now this small dirt corridor was the only place I felt truly secure. The world outside was the dangerous place. That's where the Stasi and Grenzer officers hunted night and day, where gossips and tattlers could destroy lives, and where conversations in the privacy of a home were anything but private. But in this tunnel, nothing bad would happen, not unless the world figured out we were here.

As we got deeper into the tunnel, better news awaited us. Dominic was already over on his side, quietly digging. A small hole had opened up in the clay soil between us, nothing that any creature larger than a rabbit could squeeze through, but it was a start. If I went all the way down on my stomach, I could see his feet.

"Where's Papa?" I asked Dom in a voice no louder than was necessary.

"Still securing the braces. We worked all night."

"There are Grenzers overhead," Fritz said. "They found the sunken area and want to investigate."

"We know," Dom answered. "We can hear their dogs."

"So let's dig," I said, getting to my knees. "Let's dig and be out of here before they find us."

"We can't go much farther," Dom said. "Papa thinks this last connection is holding the tunnel up, like the bearing wall of a home."

"Then we can't open it?" It was impossible, that we should have come so far just to be stopped now. "Let's just try it and see what happens."

Dom was always more of a tease, and he was back in that role now. "Sheesh, Fritz, has she really gotten that pushy in the last four years? How have you managed?"

I sat back and folded my arms. Pushiness was a necessary side effect of being the youngest, and I felt like throwing a full-scale tantrum right then to remind them of it.

Fritz only chuckled and brushed his hand across the top of my head. "She's worse than you can imagine, Dom. But if it wasn't for her, we wouldn't be here." He was quiet, then said, "I missed you."

There was silence on the other end. Then Dom's voice came in little more than a whisper. "And I missed both of you. Mama too. Papa's cooking is terrible."

I knelt forward again. "So what can we do?"

"Papa said we have to be patient for another couple of days, until the dirt settles."

"No, the settling *is* the problem!" I protested. "Fritz is supposed to join the military today. If he doesn't —"

"We can't open this until we know it will hold." Fritz sounded certain, but just from looking at him, I knew he was every bit as worried as me. He didn't have two days left — not even one.

Dom continued, "Papa wants you to brace your side of the tunnel. Do anything you can to secure the dirt overhead.

Once we're sure both sides are strong, then we'll finish chipping away at the middle."

"I'll make mortar for the bricks," Fritz said. "Gerta, to make it, I need water from the pond."

I was already on my way with the bucket in hand.

FORTY-TWO

Never say there is nothing beautiful in the world anymore.
There is always something to make you wonder . . .
— *Albert Schweitzer, German theologian, physician, and*
philanthropist

This time when I ducked through the boarded-up windows, I needed to be more careful than ever before. If the ground was being studied on the other side of this wall, I couldn't do anything that would make the watchtower guards take notice of me here. If they hadn't done so already, it wouldn't be hard for them to connect my actions with their sinking ground.

So I stuck to my routine when I entered their sights. I loaded the bucket with dirt and then stuffed the sheet over it. My buckets were heavier than they used to be, and I was carrying them better. It was a small thing, but I was proud of it.

I glanced back once at the watchtower, as I always did more often than I should. I couldn't see anyone there this time, so maybe they were inside, or maybe they were part of the ground investigation. If so, I hoped that was a good thing.

When I turned forward again, I jumped with surprise and almost cried out. Anna was standing there, nearly in front of me. I wasn't sure where she had come from — the only way she could have arrived so suddenly was if she had already been here hiding. And watching. Anna had surely seen me come from inside the building just now.

She looked as nervous as I felt, with a rigid posture and licking her lips as if we lived in the driest of deserts, but I couldn't understand why. I had everything to lose in this moment, while she only risked losing her clean dress if I decided to push her into the pond. Which I was seriously considering.

"Can we talk?" she asked.

"You can talk to me, but I'm not sure who I'm talking back to." My words were bitter and angry. "Am I talking to the Stasi right now? Or the Grenzers? The only thing for sure is I'm not talking to a friend. Maybe I never was."

"If you won't talk, then will you listen?" Anna asked. "Because I have things to say. If I don't tell them to you, I will have to tell somebody. Which would you prefer?"

Reluctantly, I nodded for her to follow me and then continued on to the pond. After all, I still had work to do.

Anna sat on a rock near the pond and clasped her hands together. "The Stasi visited us after Peter died," she said.

"They searched our house and found things from the west — innocent things that everyone has. Some black-market perfume for my mother, a television with its station tuned to the west, and some forbidden books — nothing we'd purchased, just ones my family still had from the old days. I don't think my parents even remembered we had them, to be honest. The Stasi used those things to blame us for Peter's escape attempt, and said my parents would be arrested for encouraging subversive behavior, and I would be taken away."

I dumped the bucket into the pond. It didn't matter that she saw dirt wash into it along with the sheet. As I did, I said, "You told me that in his note, Peter took responsibility for his own actions. Didn't they care about that?" I already knew the answer, and felt naïve for even asking. Of course they didn't care. The Stasi always hunted for the biggest game they could catch. The rest of us were simply their bait.

"We begged them for mercy," Anna said. "We promised if they let us go, we'd do anything they wanted."

"How could you make a promise like that?"

"What choice did we have? Gerta, tell me honestly, wouldn't you have done the same thing to save your family?"

Maybe. Probably. Of course I would have. But there was another part to her story. The part I wasn't sure I could stomach.

"The Stasi offered us a trade," she said. "For the right kind of information, they would erase any files on our family, give us a fresh start. We agreed — we had no choice but to agree. So we started looking and listening and trying to find something suspicious. We told ourselves we were doing the right thing, because whoever was breaking the law deserved to be caught." Then Anna's eyes filled with tears. "I didn't know it would be you, Gerta. Why did it have to be you?"

I tried a bluff. "Whatever you think —"

"I know about the tunnel. I've been there. You saw the dried mud still on my boots when you were in my room."

Something had become lodged in my throat by then and speaking took effort. "Your parents?"

"They only know about the gardening. They think you're terrible at it."

"But you've told the Stasi?"

"Not yet. My parents haven't learned anything useful on their own and so we keep delaying, but the Stasi are getting impatient. They want names; they want arrests. I've already lost my brother. If I don't say something soon, I'll lose my parents too."

"So you'll sacrifice my family to save yours?" My tone was icy, even though it shouldn't have been. I was no saint and couldn't pretend my choices would be any nobler if I were in her situation. And she was right: Her family was innocent of any crimes against the state. Mine was not.

But Anna shook her head. "Gerta, to save my parents, I am going to tell the Stasi . . . tomorrow. I need you to be gone tonight."

My heart pounded with the impossibility of that. "The tunnel isn't finished yet!"

But Anna replied, "I gave you as much time as I could. Don't you see that all this time I've been trying to protect you? I could've run to them a month ago with my suspicions, but I didn't. I wanted you to give up this crazy plan or turn yourself in and beg for mercy. What do you suppose the Stasi will say when they realize how long I waited to tell them? I'm already going to be in trouble."

I didn't want Anna in any trouble, and the thought of her facing consequences for my crime made me cringe.

"I never thought about that," I said. "Anna, if you're in danger . . ."

"Just go, but do it today. Be free, Gerta, the way you want to be free."

"Come with us," I said. "Be free with us."

"My family would never leave," she said. "They wouldn't dare . . . not after the way Peter died."

"Tell them it's what Peter would've wanted." I took her hand and gave it a squeeze. "In his honor, you should live the life he wanted to have."

But Anna pulled her hand free. "Even behind a wall, this is our home. And the wall can't last forever. It will come down one day and then I want you to be the first to greet me."

"I'll be there," I promised her. "And every day until then, I will miss you." Hot tears filled my eyes. "You are my friend, Anna."

"I always was," she said. "And always will be."

I wanted to hug her good-bye, but she refused it. At first I thought that was because of how dirty I was, but then she cast an eye toward the watchtowers and said, "We don't say good-bye when they're watching. We only say 'see you soon.'"

So I waved at her as she walked away, but instead of a farewell, I said, "Ask yourself why Peter left. Please, Anna, promise me that you will find that answer."

She didn't respond or turn around. As she faded into the alley, I wasn't even sure that she had heard me at all.

Back in the tunnel, I told Fritz and Dominic about my encounter with Anna. Dominic had plenty to say about her decision to talk to the Stasi tomorrow, but he didn't understand the intimidation of the secret police, not like Fritz, who merely nodded and said we would find a way out in time.

After Fritz mortared the brick we had already brought down, there wasn't much more we could do from our end. It would be several hours before the mortar was dry enough to lift overhead. I offered to dig, just a little, but Dominic said Papa had insisted we not weaken the wall.

Neither of us wanted to go home either. Mama must've been pacing the floor to wonder how things were going here, but I hoped she'd know bad news would carry to her. If there was no news, it meant things were still okay.

Dominic spent some of our wait telling us about his life in the west. "Things between our two countries are much more tense than you probably hear about," he said. "They call it a Cold War between East and West. Nobody is firing shots, but each side wants to make the other believe they're ready for World War Three if necessary."

"We get some news reports," Fritz said. "We know about the Cold War."

Dominic chuckled. "Yeah, but until you see it from this side of the wall, you can't appreciate how much of the battle is about show. Berlin is like this microscope for the rest of the world, because anyone can look at the two halves of the city and so easily compare our lives. Papa says both sides are like two insecure men on a beach, flexing their muscles to prove who's strongest."

I smiled and asked, "Who is the strongest, then?"

Dominic paused. "It's hard to say at this point. School is harder in the east, and the Communist newspapers always show lots of happy crowds. If you only read their papers, your lives look really good. But I stand on the platforms to see into the east and then turn back to the west and think, where do I want to live? There's nothing, *nothing* that would take me back there again. We have more things here, and fancier buildings and music that will knock your socks off. But the difference isn't about any of that. It's just —"

"The wall," I whispered. "If our lives are so good, we wouldn't need the wall."

"Yeah."

Fritz tapped my shoulder. "Go get Mama. We're leaving tonight."

I sat up. "Really? We'll be able to open this tunnel?"

"We have to open it. Even if we have to run for our lives as the tunnel collapses behind us, we're going to open it tonight." Fritz turned to where Dominic would be. "Go tell Father what we're doing. It must be tonight."

We heard Dominic scramble off, and then I said, "Mama can't leave yet. If she's spotted by someone who knows she called in sick —"

"Then stay with her until this evening. She should be all right to leave then. But be careful. There'll be police hunting for me and if I'm seen on the streets I'll be arrested. So you and Mama will have to get yourselves here. Can you do that?"

I swallowed hard. "Yes."

Fritz handed me the shovel. "Go stick this in the dirt outside. If Müller is watching, we need to give him the signal to come."

I pushed it back to him. "We don't owe Müller anything. Besides, we still need the shovel in here."

He gave the shovel to me again. "We made him a promise, Gerta. And as far as we can tell, he's kept his end of our bargain. Besides, I have the hand shovel."

I nodded and took it out with me. I stuck it square in the center of our garden patch, where for the first time I noticed sprouts from young squash plants. Maybe they would grow and provide food for some families here. I hoped so.

Even at those times when you want to say good-bye, it's still sad when the moment comes. I thought about that as I walked home, how odd it was to realize I might never see this side of the wall again. Wherever I looked before, I had only seen the bland, Communist gray, but this time I noticed spurts of color on our trees and in decorations that occasionally hung from windows. The approved Communist art on the sides of buildings inevitably depicted strength and power. I didn't much care for it, but I realized that it had encouraged me to be a stronger person, a lesson that ironically had carried me through the hardest moments of digging out the tunnel. I was proud of the person I had become over the last month, and all that I had withstood. And no matter where I went in the future, a part of me would always belong to the east.

Mama clutched at me when I came home, but said nothing. I had already planned out the words I would say to her, something to make our situation clear without betraying us. "Are you feeling better?" I asked. "Because Fritz is definitely joining the military tonight and he wants us there to see him off."

She smiled with tears in her eyes and then hugged me tight.

Just a few more hours to wait, and we would be gone.

*There is no such thing as a little freedom. Either you are
all free, or you are not free.* — Walter Cronkite, American
journalist, 1965

I stared at the clock over our stove, willing the hands to
move faster and then feeling frustrated because they didn't.
Everything had been cleaned and packed up, so now there
was nothing left but to wait and to think, and then to think
about waiting. It was unbearable, and I didn't understand
how Mama could sit so calmly on the couch and knit a blan-
ket she knew full well would never be finished.

I did have one particular thought that continued to nag
at me. As silly as it might have been to care about something
so trivial, I wished I had offered Anna the harvest from our
garden.

I looked back on all she had done for me since we started
on the tunnel. What I had thought was her cruel rejection of
our friendship was only her way of creating distance between
us, so that she wouldn't have to know anything I might be

up to. Then, when the Stasi began putting more pressure on her, she had warmed to me again. By my cold responses she must have known I was keeping secrets. But when she discovered them, and would have been entirely justified in revealing everything she knew, she held back to protect me, risking herself and everyone she loved.

And in return, I couldn't even offer her family our harvest.

But there was something I could do. I sat at the small desk in my room that afternoon and began to write a letter. Her name was at the top, but the letter wasn't for her. It was for the Stasi who would search my apartment tomorrow.

Dear Anna,

I'm writing this letter to apologize for my rude behavior over the last couple of months. You were brokenhearted when your brother tried to escape and never guessed he would try such a thing. But I wasn't there for you like I should have been. I wasn't the friend you deserved.

What I couldn't tell you was that I came to understand why Peter left. You don't know, so I'm telling you now. He was right.

We are not animals who can be corralled behind a cement wall. And although the state might listen to our words and watch our actions, they will never know my thoughts, which means they will never truly

control me. And if I am my own person, then it's
time for me to leave this prison.

   Somewhere in his growing up, Peter saw the sun
in the west, and couldn't live through another dark
night. Nor will I. If you had known my plans, I know
you would've tried to stop me, so please forgive me
for keeping you ... in the dark.

Your truest friend,
Gerta

I read the letter over and over again, erasing parts that didn't seem quite right and replacing them with words that better communicated my feelings. Everything I wrote in there was true, except for the last couple of lines. Those were meant to protect Anna from any accusations of helping us escape. Then I left the letter on my desk, where it would easily be found tomorrow.

Once I left my room, Mama had returned to cleaning. I suppose that kept her mind busy, but at the moment she was polishing the brass knobs on an old rocker in the corner of the room. She was as anxious as I was.

In the center of the room was a pile of the things she wanted to bring with us to the west. It was far more than she and I could carry together and I knelt beside it to weed out what could be left behind. Mama let me do it without protesting. Maybe she figured that would keep me busy too.

I didn't want any of my clothes, not one piece. They were bland and orderly and represented a life I intended to leave behind. Besides, I'd seen the magazines and knew how girls my age were dressing elsewhere. Fritz wouldn't want his clothes either, and I promised myself that I would make Mama change her fashions too. It was for her own good.

In the center of the pile was a box of china that had been passed down to my mother when she was married. It had been in her family for generations, which meant it had come through two world wars, the Allied bombings, the Hunger Winter of 1947, and somehow had even survived the tennis balls my brothers swore they never tossed around our apartment. Mama loved those dishes and so did I — they were supposed to come to me one day. But how would we ever carry them so far? I shook my head at her and pushed the box aside. Mama must've known I was right because her only protest was a weak sigh and passing frown. She knelt down and wrote on a paper, *For Frau Eberhart. I forgive you.*

I set her note on top of the box more gently than Frau Eberhart deserved. If my mother was trying to teach me a lesson, then the point of it escaped me. I hoped to understand forgiveness better one day.

Moving my attention back to the pile, I found my old stuffed bear near the bottom. One eye was missing and the stitching had come loose along his back, but I never cared that he wasn't perfect. For weeks after the barbed-wire fence went up, and Papa and Dominic didn't come home, I wrapped this bear in my arms every night and cried into its fur. It had comforted me then, but within a few hours, I would have my father back again. I didn't need the bear anymore.

Mama also had her Bible in the stack. I shook my head and started to move it aside, but Mama pulled it back, insisting it must come with us. I took another paper and on it wrote, *For the Stasi, who need it more than we do.*

Then I set it on the Bible and handed it over to her. She read the note, silently mouthed words I couldn't read, and then set the Bible aside.

As part of her insistence that we leave everything cleaner than the day it was new, Mama suggested we put away the items that couldn't come with us. Afterward, we shared a small supper together. I wished there was more, but told myself I could have as big a supper as I wanted tomorrow. We didn't say much to each other. Our hearts and minds had already flown to the tunnel, so nothing was left to talk about here.

Once we were cleaned up, Mama announced it was time to go and meet Fritz, to take him to the military station. I literally dropped everything and dove into a sweater to leave. After so many long days of back-aching work, our time had finally come. But even as we reached for the knob to leave, a knock came at our door.

Mama quickly motioned for me to remove my sweater and clear everything from the front room that might look suspicious. Maybe it was only a neighbor coming to borrow an egg, or something equally innocent, but even the simplest visitor could present a major problem. We had only a few sacks, mostly old photos and family records and a personal treasure for each person in the family, but I grabbed them and stuffed everything into an empty cupboard in the kitchen. Then she answered the door.

"Frau Lowe, *guten Abend*," a man's voice said. "May we come in?"

The door was just wide enough for me to see who was on the other side. When I did, my breath caught in my throat. This was no visiting neighbor. The Grenzers had come for us at last.

FORTY-FOUR

Many kiss the hand they wish to cut off. — *German proverb*

Mama stood at the door, wedging a foot behind it to prevent them from pushing past her. It was a nice idea, though I knew it'd do little good if they wanted to get inside.

"How can I help you?" Her tone was just as it ought to have been: polite, firm, and innocent.

"We just got word that your son, Fritz, has failed to report for military service today."

I tilted my head, curious about why they came before the day was over. Surely other boys had also failed to report in. Why did they take all this trouble to check on Fritz? Then I answered my own question. Fritz's file. The GDR already considered Fritz a potential enemy to the state. Above nearly anyone else, they would make sure Fritz was in their custody.

"He still intends to go," Mama said. "In fact, my daughter and I were going to join him on his way, very soon."

"Where is he?" the officer asked. "Perhaps we can bring him to meet you."

Mama hesitated. I could see her mind working for the exact words that might technically allow her to avoid telling a lie. I rarely went to so much effort. "He can't be far away right now. His things are here, so I know we'll see him soon."

"Of course." He said that as if he didn't believe her. "Well, Frau Lowe, we will wait outside the apartment for him to come. As you said, I'm sure we'll see him . . . soon."

Mama nodded, then shut and locked the door behind him. She didn't need to tell me what to do next.

As quietly as possible, we raced through the apartment, destroying anything that made it look as if we were packing to leave. I tousled my bed, Mama put dishes in the sink, and we put away anything that had been left out as intended gifts or to take with us. The notes on the china and Bible were ripped up and flushed down the toilet. So was my note to clear Anna of any suspicion. That left an ache inside me, but I promised myself to find a way to help her once I was on the other side. *If* I reached the other side. None of that was certain now.

From the front room window, we could see onto the street where two Grenzer cars were waiting, almost acting as barricades to our building. Curfew began in less than an hour. Afterward, getting to the tunnel would be very difficult, if not impossible. Worse still, I knew it wouldn't be long before the Grenzers would demand answers for where Fritz was. And what could we possibly say when their questions came?

Mama said things for the microphones about how Fritz would be back soon and about how silly the officers would feel for ever wondering about him. But fear clutched at my throat like a noose, and I could barely answer. It seemed senseless now to pretend.

With every tick of the clock, the Grenzers would become increasingly convinced that Fritz wasn't going to show up. Which would lead them to one of two conclusions. Either he was escaping the country on his own, or else we were helping him hide somewhere. Whatever they decided, the Stasi would be here soon with questions we absolutely could not answer, no matter how they threatened us. Or worse. If we talked, it would cost Fritz's life, and Papa's and Dominic's. Even Officer Müller and his family, if they came.

When I looked, there didn't appear to be any officers out the back window. Maybe we could use a rope or something to lower ourselves down. But it would take us past the windows of apartments below ours, and someone was bound to see and report us. Besides, we had no rope here, and the sheets we might've tied together for an escape were hanging from a clothesline at the Welcome Building.

Mama cheerfully suggested we might go for a walk, offering the microphones an excuse that we'd find Fritz ourselves. But we both dismissed that idea without further conversation. The Grenzers wouldn't just let us walk away, and even if they did, we'd certainly be followed.

One more thought came to my mind, something so awful it made my toes curl inside my shoes. But I couldn't ignore it anymore. Expecting that Mama and I would arrive soon, Fritz and Papa would open that tunnel tonight. They would wait as long as possible for us to come, hoping for the best, and silently wondering if the worst might have happened. At some point, it would become obvious that we weren't coming. They would see the instability of the tunnel, discuss the Grenzers' investigation directly overhead, and conclude the only logical thing they could: Tonight was our last chance. Fritz would be forced to cross into the west without us. By morning, Mama and I would be in a Stasi prison.

The thought of that terrified me, but I had always known things might end this way, and I had to be strong. Or at least, pretend that I was for Mama's sake, since she looked as afraid as I was. She'd probably been thinking the same thing, though neither of us could freely discuss it here.

Another knock came to the door and Mama went to answer it. This time the Grenzers didn't wait for courtesies before they barged in to search our home. There was nothing to find — Mama and I had made sure of that. And in full view we had left Fritz's bags packed for the military, hoping it would look like that was still his plan.

They were thorough in their search, looking in closets,

under beds, and behind doors, even in places where no human body could fit. When they began opening drawers and rifling through papers, I realized they were looking for more than just Fritz. They wanted grounds for arrest. His arrest, and ours.

For the first time, I was grateful that Mama had made us clean so thoroughly. Nothing in our apartment led to the tunnel or to any sign of us planning an escape.

We stood in the center of the front room, Mama and me holding hands. My clutch on her was fierce, but she whispered that we must remain calm. Finally, one officer approached us. I recognized him as Viktor, Fritz's old friend. If Viktor remembered me, he gave no sign of it. Viktor was with the Stasi. I remembered that all too well.

"Our apologies for any inconvenience to you and your daughter," Viktor said. "You understand that at this point, it is clear that your son is not planning to report tonight?"

"I can't give you any explanation," Mama said.

"Nor am I asking for one," Viktor replied. "But if he is not here by curfew, we will bring you and your daughter in for a conversation with my superiors. They will demand an explanation and you will provide one to *them*."

The way he ended his sentence turned my stomach into knots. Mama couldn't say a word in response, and I only gripped her hand tighter.

Viktor frowned down at me. "You and your brother are very close, no? Where do you think he is?"

I shrugged lamely. From his expression, he obviously knew that I was holding something back, something big, but he wasn't authorized to pry those secrets from me. That was for the interrogators to do. And they would pry, or dig, or tear those secrets from me using methods I couldn't begin to think about without feeling sick. I wouldn't pretend to be strong enough to resist them. I only hoped I could hold out long enough for Fritz to get away.

They do not have the courage to say it was a wall of disgrace. — Helmut Kohl, chancellor of West Germany when the wall came down

Once they had determined that Fritz wasn't here, the other officers said they would conduct a search of every apartment in this building, in case Fritz had gone into one of the others to hide. Viktor was ordered to wait here with us.

Mama released my hand and casually went into the kitchen to prepare some tea. Why would she care about that with everything else happening? I couldn't even think straight, and she wanted a cup of tea?

But my mother surprised me again. Because when the tea was ready, she offered it to Viktor.

"Thank you, Frau Lowe, but no," he said.

Mama insisted. "You must be thirsty from such a long evening, and it's my family's fault that you've been so inconvenienced. It's only some tea."

I'd known for a long time that when my mother wanted her way, it was impossible to refuse her. Now Viktor understood that too. After she held out the tea long enough, he slung his rifle over his shoulder, then took the teacup. As if this had suddenly become a social visit, Mama sat down on our couch and patted the cushion for me. She gestured for Viktor to sit as well, but he would not.

It didn't seem to matter to her. "I remember when you were no taller than my knee," Mama said to him. "You and Fritz were in nursery school together so long ago and have remained friends since, I believe."

"We were friends as children, yes," Viktor said stiffly.

"But look at you now, so strong, so grown-up. You're young to have so much responsibility."

"I'm just a junior officer," Viktor said. "But perhaps in time, I will earn my way up."

"I'm sure you will." Mama stood again. "But part of becoming a man is knowing what's important in life. Would you agree?"

Viktor stiffened his spine. "I know what's important. Your son would do well to learn the same things."

"Absolutely. Things like family are what matter most. You have a family too, Viktor, you have a mother. If you were in trouble, how far would your mother go to help you?"

Viktor faced forward without answering. But I knew he was listening.

Mama took my hand and brought me to my feet. She reached into her pocket and pulled out the keys to the Trabant from Oma Gertrude, then left them on the kitchen table. He eyed the keys and looked away again. But he understood what was happening as well as I did.

Trabant cars weren't grand in any way, but even the most run-down car often took months to find. A new Trabant might take a decade or more, if someone as young as Viktor could even afford one.

Viktor and my mother were locked in a stare, and I wondered if they were coming to a sort of unspoken agreement. I didn't know, I couldn't tell. I had trouble looking at anything but the gun over his shoulder and thinking about anything other than the way he'd dumped Herr Krause on the sidewalk not so many days ago.

Viktor belonged to the state. His friendship with Fritz meant nothing to him, and we mattered even less. Though he continued staring at Mama, his hand slid to the stock of his gun. He didn't need to shoot. All he had to do was call in the other officers and they would do it for him.

Finally, Mama raised all ten of her fingers and nodded at him, but he didn't respond. Then she started backing us toward the door, one small step at a time. How far would he let us go before he grabbed the trigger? Or were the ten fingers part of their silent agreement? I squeezed Mama's hand like I'd never held on to anything before. What if she was wrong?

Finally, Viktor stole a glance at the Trabant keys, and then I knew we had him. Bribery was a form of currency in the GDR, and we finally had something valuable enough to offer.

He looked forward again and said, "I hear a sound in the back room. Don't either of you go anywhere while I check it out." He grabbed the keys, and then started to walk toward Fritz's room. As soon as he was gone, Mama opened our door.

There was a back exit in case of fire and Mama and I took that way down as silently as the metal stairs would allow. To me, our footsteps sounded like booming echoes, forcing both of us to our tiptoes to dull the noise.

I didn't dare ask Mama about her ten fingers, not even in a whisper. If it was a signal for time, was that ten minutes, or did we only have ten seconds? I didn't know and only hurried faster. Once we reached the main floor, we inched the back door open, leading us into a dark alley so quiet that it sent shivers up my spine.

"I expected someone to be waiting here," Mama whispered.

Which made me wonder what her plan had been if there was. We were out of money, had given up the only valuable thing we still owned, and carried nothing with us but the clothes on our backs. I only answered, "There aren't enough officers for every exit."

"This is God's hand at work, helping us," Mama said, clutching my hand to leave. "Say a prayer of thanks as we walk."

I intended to obey her, but only after we were safe, and that wasn't yet. We were barely out of the alley when whistles blew from inside our building. Our absence had been discovered.

This time, I took the lead. Over the past few weeks, to avoid Frau Eberhart and any other curious eyes, I had found every possible back route to the Welcome Building. I knew where to go now. We heard Grenzer sirens on the main road, searching for us, but we didn't need the main roads to get there. At least, not until our last dash into the alley.

The problem was that curfew had already begun. Nobody should've been on the streets, so if the officers saw anyone at all, it would be us.

We went as carefully as spies, through dark back alleys, walkways too narrow to be used as roads, and even through unlocked doors of other people's apartment buildings. The final crossing into the alley was our most difficult, with a long run from one hiding place to another. I wanted to split up, so that if I didn't make it, perhaps my mother would have a chance, but she only grabbed my hand and pushed me into the street as she hurried along at my side. I saw a woman in the window of an apartment overhead reading a book. When we were in the center of the street she looked down right at us. I froze for a fraction of a moment, wondering what she might do, but she only pulled the shade for her window and then switched off the light. I thought of the proverb "to see no evil" and hoped it would follow with the woman also refusing to speak any evil. Before I knew it, we were inside the alley.

From there, we ran until my garden came into view just ahead. How beautiful it seemed to me then, how deadly. The irrigation ditch that bordered the garden patch would get in our way, slowing us, but I hoped it wouldn't have much water this late at night.

"You have to jump the ditch," I explained to Mama. "And we collected a stack of rocks to the right of it. So just follow me, exactly where I go."

Her hand pressed against my back. "Whatever happens, you keep running, Gerta. Keep running and don't look back for me." Then she pushed me forward.

There was nothing more to say. We ran.

By now, I knew the land so well I could've run it with my eyes closed, and on this dark night, I might as well have done just that. The ditch was narrowest to my left, and I took that way. I jumped it easily, but Mama missed the bank and splashed in with one foot that became lodged in the mud. No matter what she had said, nothing would make me leave her behind, so I came back and grabbed her hand to help her back onto hard ground. We continued running, and suddenly lights blazed on in the watchtower ahead of us.

Mama and I dropped to the earth like falling timbers. Even without being aimed our way, the lights still brightened the garden considerably, casting everything in long shadows. They swooped up and down the Death Strip in their usual path and then began to turn our way. I knew this routine. I'd seen it before. Along with other areas east of the wall, the lights would survey this garden patch next. We'd be spotted and our position called out to the Grenzers, still searching for us on the streets. We had less than a minute to get all the way to the building.

We ran, so fast that my lungs ached and my head pounded. Rocks had gathered in my shoes, but I barely felt them. We dove against the bricks while the watchtower light swept down onto our field. It stayed there for a long time, highlighting the shovel I had placed in the dirt earlier that day. That shovel was our monument to freedom, even if nobody else knew it.

We weren't there to see where the light went after that. For we had already climbed inside the Welcome Building and shut the boards tight behind us. Mama leaned against the wall to catch her breath, but I whispered, "No, Mama, please. We're not there yet." She nodded at me and followed.

Fritz was waiting for us down in the shelter, and looked so relieved that I thought he might almost deflate right in front of us.

"What took so long?" he asked.

Mama's response was simple. "We had some trouble."

He looked at us, with red faces and sweat along our foreheads. "Are you both all right?"

I only beamed back at him. "We are if that tunnel is open."

"It isn't yet," he said. "Papa wanted to give the bricks as long as possible to dry and so we haven't removed the final load of dirt yet. He figured once we did, even with our fortifications, it's only a matter of time before it collapses."

"Then let's get in and remove it," Mama said.

"Officer Müller?" I asked.

"He's already in the tunnel with his wife and baby. He said when his wife heard about the plan she insisted they go. They got here an hour ago."

We followed Fritz inside. A woman I assumed must be Frau Müller was seated on the ground with a young baby in her arms who, at least so far, was asleep. She smiled up at me and I thought she was a rather pretty woman. Officer Müller stood over them, in full uniform and armed. He greeted me with a solemn nod that seemed more respectful than in our first meeting. I nodded back, but said nothing. It bothered me that he had his gun, because we certainly weren't safe yet, and I remembered his promise if we were caught.

Still, when he saw that we had come, he walked over to Fritz and whispered, "We waited for them, as you asked."

"The tunnels must be connected immediately," Mama said. "It won't take the Grenzers long to figure out where Gerta and I have gone."

"Katharina?" my father's relieved voice called from the other side. "You've finally come?"

"We're here," she said. "Though I wouldn't have made it without Gerta's help."

"I expected nothing less from my daughter," Papa said. "Let's open the tunnel, but dig carefully. I don't like the cracks I'm seeing on this side."

"I bought you some time," Officer Müller said. "My last call in to the central command tonight was to tell them that I checked this area out and nobody was here. But it won't work for long. When they can't find you on the streets, the senior officers will bring out their dogs, who will follow your trail here."

"If only we had some rain," Mama said. "That would erase our trail and mask any noise of us clearing this barrier."

"Or it could make the ground so wet that we flood," Fritz reminded her.

"Enough talk!" I said. "Let's dig!"

Müller and Fritz went to work at our end, and from the other side I heard Papa and Dominic chiseling away at their dirt and rock. We decided to dig low, to maintain as much dirt over our heads as possible. We would have to crouch down to pass through this space, or even crawl, but if necessary I would've squeezed through the eye of a needle. All I wanted was to be on the other side of this wall.

The rabbit-sized hole widened. I could see Papa's boots from here, the same sturdy boots he had worn the night he left, only now with a hole in one side. With another chip, I saw the cuff of his pants and I begged them to go faster. It was torture to have my father revealed to me one centimeter at a time.

The dirt was beginning to pile up around Fritz and Müller, so I offered to go back to the shelter for the bucket and remove what I could. I planned to empty all the spare dirt into a large pile at the entrance to slow the Grenzers if they came.

But I was only halfway there before I heard noises above us, in the basement of the Welcome Building. It wasn't voices, or at least none I could detect from here. But there were footsteps, several of them.

I ran back into the tunnel. "Someone's here!" I hissed. "We must go now!"

The gap had opened enough that I could fit through and maybe Frau Müller, but none of the rest could. And there was a jagged rock jutting out from the center that would probably keep us from getting all the way through. They had been working to gently pry it free.

There was no time left to be gentle. It had to be now! I'd

rather have had the tunnel collapse than be arrested or shot. Officer Müller withdrew his gun and ran back down the tunnel. I wasn't sure what to do. Did he plan on shooting whoever had come? Or shooting us?

Then he said, "I'll hold off whoever's there as long as I can." He looked over to Fritz. "Get my wife and baby out first — you owe me that."

If Müller intended to protect us, he needed help. With everyone else busy, I grabbed a couple of rocks from the tunnel floor. If someone got past Müller, I could throw hard enough to slow him down until the others escaped.

Müller shouted out a warning that he was armed and for whoever was approaching to stop. Then a voice called, "Where's Gerta? Is she here?" That was Anna!

I dropped the rocks and ran past Müller to the mouth of the tunnel. "Lower your gun," I hissed at him. "Don't shoot!"

Anna was waiting in the shelter with her mother while her father finished climbing down the ladder. Seeing my curiosity, she only shrugged and said, "You asked me to figure out why Peter wanted to leave. Well . . . we did."

My mother appeared right behind me. "And we're glad to have your family here."

Anna's father nodded at us in return, but said, "Then let's go now. I'm afraid we were noticed being out after curfew and may have put some officers on our trail. They're not far behind us."

Flashlights were already showing in the garden patch. It wouldn't take the Grenzers long to follow us inside. They were coming.

FORTY-SIX

Freedom is never voluntarily given by the oppressor. It must be demanded by the oppressed. — *Dr. Martin Luther King, Jr., American civil rights activist, 1963*

Once we were close enough to see him, Fritz motioned that the gap was open and to hurry. Women and children were to go through first, which was fine by me, but Anna didn't seem to be adjusting as well to the closed-in tunnel. I took her clammy hand and half dragged her to the very end, then whispered that everything would be all right, even if I wasn't convinced of that yet. Frau Müller was there too and Fritz told her to lie on her stomach and crawl through the low opening. She thrust her baby into my arms while she went through.

I hadn't expected that and took her child somewhat clumsily. The baby reacted to the awkward change of position and began fussing in my arms. I bounced him and tried to coo at him, but he must've sensed my own anxiety and started crying louder.

"Stop him," Fritz hissed.

But I didn't know how. I was certain that somehow, this baby could sense the panic inside me, and so everything I tried only made him more upset. Then without even asking, Anna took the baby from me and cradled him in her arms as comfortably as his own mother had. He instantly quieted down until Frau Müller said she was through, and then Anna crouched down to pass the baby through the opening into her hands.

Anna had saved the moment but, just as important, the baby had forced her to gather her own courage enough to go through the gap, an opening so small that it didn't look like it should be able to accommodate her body, much less any of the rest of us. Fritz told Mama to go next, and Anna's mother would be next after that.

I got in place for my turn and watched my mother easily slide through the gap. I heard her brief reunion with my father and could only imagine what it must have taken for her to push away from him as he begged her to keep running to the end.

Anna's mother went next, but she was too close to one edge and got stuck. She panicked and began squirming and kicking, trying to roll over to her back. In the process, she kicked out and her foot struck the wall of dirt. Instantly, a large chunk crashed down on her upper legs. She gave a cry, though I didn't think she was seriously hurt.

"Give me your hands," my father said. Just like that, Anna's mother was pulled through.

"I don't like this," Fritz said, feeling the wall above the collapsed chunk. "This whole thing is going to come down. Hurry, Gerta. It's your turn now."

I went down to my stomach and put my cheek against the cold ground. With my hands in front of me, I clawed at the dirt, wiggling forward like a worm or a snake. Dirt crumbled down onto my back, more of it than I liked. Fritz was right. This wall was going to come down, and maybe the rest of the tunnel with it.

Papa grabbed my hands when I was halfway through and yanked me forward just as he had done for Anna's mother.

Once on the other side, I was immediately caught in my father's tear-stained embrace. Even through the dirt and sweat, he smelled to me just as he had when I was young. Over the last four years, I had tried so many times to re-create in my mind that combination of strong cheese and stronger coffee, just to hold on to his memory, but now everything about him rushed back at me, as if we had never been separated at all. It was too dark to see much of his face, but I did see a tender smile and the whites of his eyes when he said, "Run, Gerta. Go."

But I wouldn't leave without Fritz. Not after everything he and I had been through together. Anna's father came through next and needed no urging to run past us toward his family.

Then a voice from far on the eastern end shouted, "Whoever is in this tunnel, you are ordered to stop!" I didn't need to see them. I already knew the Grenzers were here.

Shots fired into the tunnel, their echo so loud that even from this end it rang in my ears. Officer Müller came through after that and when his eyes met mine I wanted to hurt him. Why had he come through next? Where was Fritz? I nearly screamed with terror. I fell to my knees to slide back to the other side of the gap. If he was injured, I could still drag him through. And if he was worse than injured — I couldn't even think about that. Papa grabbed my arms and pulled me back to my feet. I started to protest, but he wrapped his arms around me, put a hand over my mouth, and hushed me.

"They know Fritz is there," he whispered. "They don't have to know you're here too."

He tried to make me run again, but I wormed free and went back to my knees. Where was Fritz?

Then I saw his head poke through. He was alive, but wasn't wiggling through as quickly as he should have. Working together, Papa and Officer Müller pulled him through.

"I'm shot," he said through clenched teeth. "A bullet got my leg."

Papa helped him to his feet, then motioned for me to come over. "Get him out of this tunnel," Papa said. "Bear up his weight."

"I will." I wasn't sure *how*, but I would get him out.

Fritz wrapped one arm around me and used the other to brace himself through the tunnel. He couldn't use his injured leg at all, and whenever we moved too fast or it bumped against a rock, he grunted with pain and clutched my shoulder so tight that we both nearly collapsed. Still, we kept going forward. I had the strength to support him, but not the height, and he had to lean over too far. Papa would've done better. Where was he? What about Müller? What were they waiting for?

After several meters, more gunfire echoed in the tunnel. With a strange cracking sound, the bridge between our two tunnels collapsed. That's what Papa was doing, then. Shots still rang, but they wouldn't pass through the dirt. The Grenzers were trapped behind us. But a lot of tunnel remained ahead.

In the dim light, I could see where Papa had put in supports to hold up the dirt roof, but they weren't as strong as Fritz's bricks, and dirt rained down on us, some of it in large chunks that signaled a bigger collapse was coming. Suddenly, several meters ahead, shovels pounded in the ground. Their crunch and plunking sounds were all too familiar to me now. Maybe we'd left officers behind in the tunnel, but more of them were in the Death Strip directly above us. The layers of dirt to the surface weren't nearly thick enough to hold them out for long.

I wondered where the outer wall was, when we would

pass beneath it. Wherever it was, I knew we hadn't crossed it yet. Not with the length of tunnel still remaining.

"Agh!" Fritz's leg bumped into some protruding rock and his hand pinched my shoulder so tight that I wanted to cry out too.

"I'm sorry," I mumbled.

"I'm slowing you down." Fritz leaned heavier on me and swayed as if he was dizzy. "Leave me here."

"That's the dumbest idea you've ever had," I told him. "Stay with me, Fritz. We're going to make it."

Then Papa and Officer Müller ran up behind us. Papa picked up Fritz in his arms, drawing strength I never imagined he had to run with a body nearly as large as his own. And Müller grabbed my hand to pull me along with him. I yanked it free and dug my feet into the ground. Maybe he was on our side, but just barely. My family had taken all the risks to get us this far, while he had stayed in the safe zone just in case things turned bad. I didn't want his help now and certainly didn't need it.

But Müller didn't seem to care. He grabbed my arm again and this time his grip had no forgiveness. I would run at his side or get dragged behind him.

Papa and Fritz weren't far ahead of us, but they rounded a short bend out of our sight and I held my breath. Müller probably didn't think of himself as a Grenzer anymore, but I still did.

Then right above our heads, one of the holes being dug crashed through from the surface. Dirt cascaded over us, and a large rock fell at my feet, momentarily forcing Müller and me back. I looked up, expecting to see starlight, but saw only shadows of several Grenzers standing over the hole. There were foul curses and orders being shouted to widen the hole, but Müller steered me around the rock so we could keep running. Then a hand reached down into the tunnel with a gun at the end of it. It aimed directly at me, so that even in this dim light I thought I could see directly down the barrel. I froze, as if every part of me had just turned to ice.

All that remained was for someone to order him to fire.

CHAPTER
FORTY-SEVEN

All free men, wherever they may live, are citizens of
Berlin. I take pride in saying, "Ich bin ein Berliner!"
— *John F. Kennedy, US President, 1963*

Müller gave me a hard shove, forcing me toward the bend, then turned back and reached for the gun, evidently hoping to grab it before any damage was done. I rounded the bend in time to hear the echo of gunshots inside the tunnel and a body's collapse onto the ground.

I wanted to keep running; I couldn't be more than a minute away from safety. But I also couldn't ignore that Müller had just saved my life, putting himself between the gun and me. I had to help him.

I crept back to the bend. The hand with the gun was gone, but shovels were digging back into the dirt, widening the hole. Müller was on the ground directly below them. There was enough moonlight now that I could see the blood on his chest.

Only a few nights ago, I had grabbed a heavy door and

dragged it beneath the eyes of the watchtower. This wasn't much different. The same eyes were above me now, and I had escaped their guns once before.

I pried my arms beneath Müller's shoulders and locked my hands together across his chest. I felt his blood there, warm and sticky, and it took all my courage to stay with him. Then I heaved a deep breath and dragged him, so slowly that I wasn't sure if I was moving at all. Dirt rained down over us as the gap widened. It wouldn't be much longer before it was wide enough for an entire body to fit through, or before they weakened the roof and collapsed the tunnel. I wasn't sure which would be worse.

Müller mumbled something to me about letting him go, but I ignored him and kept dragging.

"I'm sorry," I told him as we went. "I wouldn't trust you and I'm sorry about that. You saved my life."

"Get my wife to freedom," he mumbled. "My son."

He was heavier than the door, but I knew I was strong enough. We rounded the bend with his boots dragging along the tunnel floor, slowing me down. Worse still was that Müller's body was steadily becoming heavier. Both his arms had fallen into the dirt and his head was slumped off to one side. I couldn't explain why, it just was.

"Gerta, set him down."

I felt my father's hand on my shoulder and looked up to face him. "I can't. He's hurt."

Papa pressed between me and Officer Müller, removing my arms and gently laying him on the ground. "He's not hurting anymore."

Oh.

I backed against the dirt while my father felt for a pulse at the base of Müller's neck. He turned to me and shook his head.

"I was wrong about him." That was all I could say, and it didn't seem like nearly enough.

Papa took my hand. "Let's go, Gerta."

I started to protest, but we heard orders aboveground for a man to be lowered into our tunnel. Wordlessly, I let my father lead me away.

The officer who had dropped into the tunnel behind us ordered us to halt, but by that time, we were too far away for his gun to be fired at the right angle. And then, suddenly, he stopped calling for us and I knew why. Just ahead of us in the dirt, Papa had stuck the striped flag of West Germany as a place marker. After three more steps, we passed beneath the Berlin Wall. We might not be out of the tunnel, but we were in the west.

We were in the west.

I could scarcely believe it. I felt like I was moving in a dream, one I hoped would never end.

Only a few meters ahead, I saw the end of the tunnel. I first mistook the dim light for sunrise and then realized it was a nearby streetlight. A single star in a sea of darkness.

I emerged from the tunnel in a small graveyard, blocked from the watchtower's view by the caretaker's shop. And from a hole disguised as a grave, I rose up to greet the coming morning. West German soldiers were here with their weapons drawn, making it clear that the Grenzers had missed their chance at us. They would not be allowed to step even a single toe into this half of the city.

I filled my lungs with the fresh air, too exhausted to even sit down.

Papa squeezed my shoulder and then went over to talk to Frau Müller. I couldn't hear what they said but I did see her tears as she cradled her baby close to her. Anna's parents went over to help comfort her.

From there, my eyes drifted to the Berlin Wall, the side of it we had never seen before in the east. It was covered in graffiti and signs protesting its very existence. The sight of it startled me, that people would dare to express themselves so boldly, so publicly. Beside me, Dominic leaned his elbow on my shoulder. "There's a lot more that you'll have to get used to," he said.

"I look forward to it," I mumbled, then jabbed him in the side, the first time in four years I'd been able to tease him back.

Mama hugged me and then we all walked over to Fritz, who was being cared for by one of the West German officers. The smile on his face was so wide that nobody would've suspected the injury to his leg.

"You did the impossible," Mama said, cradling each of our faces with her hands one at a time. "I could only sit back and hope. But you three children made it happen."

I hugged Anna next. "I can't believe you came," I said to her.

"You made me think about Peter, about what he would want us to do." Then her smile fell. "But I'm sorry about one thing. I promised you that I wouldn't tell anyone about the tunnel until tomorrow. I didn't even get halfway home before I knew I'd be breaking that promise with my parents."

I only hugged her even tighter. "You can break those kinds of promises to me any time you want!"

My father was there to hug me last of all. I had never seen him weep before, but now his tears flowed freely and he smiled through them. He held me back so he could look at me better and brushed his hand over my hair and across my shoulders. I knew how I must've looked: filthy, bone-tired, and even bloodstained, but he only gazed at me like he might look upon an angel. "My precious daughter," he said. "So brave. So bold."

"Officer Müller's family —"

"They are part of our family now." He looked at all of us, then back to me. "How should we celebrate our freedom?"

I smiled back at him. "Maybe we could all sleep for a few hours," I said. "And then I thought we'd go to the market together, to get something to eat."

He chuckled. "And what might you want from the market?"

"A banana." I'd been planning to ask for one since the first day of digging.

He hugged me again. "You shall have one today."

Only a few short hours later, I felt sunlight on my face. The sun never rises in the west, but that day it did. For me, and for my family, the long, dark night was over.

Geschichte wiederholt sich.

History repeats itself.

— *German proverb*

ACKNOWLEDGMENTS

There was nothing logical about my decision to write this book. The timing was too tight, I was already contracted for a different trilogy, and, as was pointed out to me more than once, I wasn't a historical writer.

But Gerta was insistent, constantly interrupting my thoughts the way I'm sure she often pestered her family. Eventually, I gave in and wrote the first few words, which led to a story that refused to let me go. Although I didn't know if I could do Gerta justice, I was determined to try.

This could not have been written without the support of my family. While I holed up in a quiet room to complete this project, they assured me that clean laundry was a bonus rather than a necessity, and that they were perfectly good cooks (or better, as it turned out). They are a finer family than I deserve. Most of all, I am grateful to my husband, Jeff, who is unfailingly good to me. I cannot imagine a day without him.

Warmest thanks to those whose input and advice came at the most crucial times: especially my agent of awesomeness,

Ammi-Joan Paquette, and my friends and fellow authors, Joanne Levy and Lisa McMann.

I am eternally grateful to the Scholastic family. It is their combined expertise and brilliance that sends this book out into the world.

Speaking of brilliance, thanks also to my editor, Lisa Sandell. It is the highest privilege to work with her, and with every book, I continue to learn from her wisdom. (If anyone wants a laugh, ask her what else she was doing the day this project went to acquisitions.)

Finally, my thanks to Dr. Cristina Cuevas-Wolf, Manager of the Collections Department at the Wende Museum in Culver City, California. With her help and expertise, I was able to see firsthand the objects and images of Cold War East Germany, of daily life behind the wall, and the invasive reach of the Stasi into its citizens' lives. I learned so much more there than I could have anticipated. Any factual errors in these pages are mine.

Above all, with this book, I send my respect and honor to the people of Germany. *Ich bin ein Berliner!*

AFTER WORDS™

JENNIFER A. NIELSEN'S
A Night Divided

CONTENTS

After Words™ guide by Olivia Valcarce

About the Author

Jennifer was born and raised in Northern Utah to parents who couldn't possibly know what they were getting into. She rode bicycles no-handed, climbed trees with power lines running through them, played the outfield on her three-person baseball team, and found many other activities that shall remain unnamed (i.e., stuff her mom still doesn't know about, and she's not about to find out here).

She also grew up with a love for books and an imagination that often interested her far more than the real world. Stories and characters and fictional worlds were constantly in her head.

However, it never occurred to Jennifer that becoming an author was a real career option. That changed in sixth grade when she discovered that S. E. Hinton, the author of her then-favorite book, *The Outsiders*, had written that story while she was a teenager. Inspired to try writing her own book, Jennifer began a story about a girl with a wild imagination (sound familiar?) whose daydreams come alive one day and get her in heaps of trouble. The writing was going fine until this girl became locked in a closet and needed to pick the lock. Jennifer had no idea how to pick the lock, but now that she was a serious author like S. E. Hinton, it was no problem to call a locksmith and ask.

The locksmith disagreed. Believing that Jennifer was misbehaving, he yelled at her on the phone. She hung up and found a place to hide. Eventually, she left the hiding place, but her character never did. Jennifer never wrote another word of the story.

In fact, Jennifer didn't begin seriously writing again until she was an adult. Her first few manuscripts were catastrophic attempts at storytelling that are now mandated in her will as items that must be buried with her one day. Seriously.

After much failure—followed by the requisite consumption of ice cream—her tenacity and study of writing began to pay off. In 2012, Jennifer released *The False Prince* with Scholastic. Since then, she has published thirteen novels—and counting.

Jennifer is married to an awesome guy whom she met in her senior year of high school when they played husband and wife on stage (stage kiss!). She has three children and a dog that won't play fetch, and she has recently acquired a cat that hallucinates. She lives in the mountains of Northern Utah and there enjoys spending time with her family, watching movies, and writing snarky biographies of her life.

Q&A with Jennifer A. Nielsen

Q: *What inspired you to choose divided Berlin and the construction of the Berlin Wall as your setting?*

A: I never set out to write a Berlin Wall story. But one day, I was thinking of a family friend who had been born into East Germany and her harrowing story of escape. This friend, at age five, was drugged and hidden beneath a pile of hay in the baggage car of a train. Her family knew if she so much as rolled over in her sleep while that baggage car was being searched, it was all over. When I remembered the story, my first thought was that I simply wanted to read a Berlin Wall–era fiction book for middle-grade readers. As it turned out, I couldn't find any—not one! So I decided that I would write it.

Q: *What aspect of the story came to you first?*

A: The point at which I knew I would have to write this story is when I heard Gerta's voice in my head, saying, "They built a prison around us as we slept." I knew nothing about Gerta at that point, but her voice was so strong, so desperate, I wanted to learn more about her. I admired her as a character from the beginning, and it was amazing to see her come alive on the page with each new chapter.

Q: *Can you describe your research process?*

A: I knew that I'd be writing about a real time and place, and that there were many people still alive who had lived in or visited East Germany, so it was particularly vital for me to get the details correct. For that reason, I focused heavily on first-person research—on any articles, testimonies, or videos that came directly from a person who had lived it. That meant a lot of my research came from interviews and YouTube videos. For example, I watched a man talk about how he had escaped from East Germany, standing on the very street where he had done it. Some of what he described directly influenced a scene in *A Night Divided*.

The other place that heavily influenced the writing of the book was the Wende Museum in Culver City, California. There are some fabulous displays in this museum, but they also have an enormous collection of East German Cold War memorabilia available for study. I was fortunate enough to be taken through the museum and shown firsthand the everyday items that Gerta and her family would have had access to, as well as equipment that would have been used by the Stasi (State Security Service of the German Democratic Republic) and police officials to spy on and catch people like Gerta.

Q: *Were families really divided by the wall?*
A: The Berlin Wall began as a barbed-wire fence that was erected overnight on August 13, 1961. It was done without warning, and after government officials had denied it would happen. Because it was so unexpected, certainly there were cases where immediate family members might have been caught in the west, now unable to return home. Over time, those displacements would have been corrected, with one exception: if the family member in the west was considered a dissident, as Gerta's father was. Dissidents were not allowed to return, regardless of family circumstance.

For extended family members, the governments made no effort to keep everyone on the same side of the wall. So there were many cases where brides waved at their grandmothers from across the wall, where new parents held up an infant for family on the other side to see the child from a distance, and where expressions of sympathy over the passing of a loved one had to be expressed through mail, because they could not be made in person.

Q: *What did you learn about real escapes from East Berlin?*
A: As part of my research, I studied the escapes very carefully; not only what succeeded, but what failed and why. It is difficult to assess exactly how many successful escapes there were, because often, a person who made it to the west said little to anyone about where they had come from, not wanting to put at risk friends and family still in the east. And many failed attempts were reported to the family as accidental drownings and heart attacks, so those numbers are equally vague.

Escapes were attempted in as many ways as people could create: hidden inside rebuilt car engines, flown over the wall in hot-air balloons or homemade airplanes, tunnels, swims across the Spree River, being smuggled out with false papers, desperate runs across the Forbidden Zones, and many more plans.

Q: *Was East Germany as controlled a place as it seems to be in the book?*
A: To understand how controlled the environment was, consider this: At the height of power for the KGB, the Soviet

secret police, there was one agent for every 5,830 citizens. At their most powerful, the Nazi police, the Gestapo, had one officer for every 2,000 citizens. For the Stasi, the secret police of the East German government, there was one agent for every 166 citizens. If one takes into account their snoops and secret informants (every apartment building had one, and someone's mailman, bus driver, or teacher could be one), the ratio condenses to one for every 6.5 citizens. In any gathering or group, it was safe to assume that at least one person was there to spy on the others.

Q: *What would you like readers to take away from Gerta's story?*
A: I believe that readers will take from Gerta's story the theme that means the most to them at the time. But as I delved deeper into her life, I gained a respect for the price of freedom, how those who are free often take it very much for granted. There are many places in the world that are still fighting for even basic freedoms, and I hope they will be remembered.

Q: *Do you remember when the wall came down?*
A: The Berlin Wall fell on November 9, 1989. I distinctly remember sitting with my mother at the kitchen table as we watched the events unfold on the television, both of us absolutely incredulous. What has always amazed me most about the way the Berlin Wall story ends is that it was not brought down by treaties or war or by military arrangements. In the end, the Berlin Wall was taken down by the people of East Germany who decided they would not live one day more within barriers

that had been built for them. That was inspiring to me then, and continues to influence me today.

Q: *Can you describe your writing routine?*
A: Once I get the hook for a story, I spend a lot of time searching for my main character. I need to know enough about them to begin forming the story around their strengths and weaknesses, their fears and challenges. Once I have my hero, I build the other characters around him or her; some characters are there to help and the rest are there to get in the way. The story forms within that process.

I write a quick first draft that is abysmal, at best. But I'm a firm believer in the power of rewriting, so I will return to the manuscript again and again until it starts to become something I don't entirely hate, and then something I sort of like, and when I think I've got a good story, it goes to my editor. Then the real work begins!

I often think of my writing like starting with a rough lump of clay and gradually forming it into the approximate shape I want, then molding it, and finally adding the details that make it come alive.

Q: *You also write fantasy novels; how is writing historical fiction different and how is it similar?*
A: The differences are probably obvious to most readers. Whereas fantasy is limited only by my imagination, with historical novels, I have to remain true to actual events, people, and places. That challenge is actually one of my favorite things

about writing a historical book, because it forces me to stretch myself as a writer.

Despite that, I find there are more similarities than differences. I'm drawn to stories in which ordinary people discover themselves in extraordinary circumstances and are forced to find their heroism. That sort of story is not limited by genre. And my goal with anything I write is for the reader to say that it "felt real" to them, so I'd hope a fantasy world I create would be one the reader could walk into with the same authenticity as a world that once existed in our history. And finally, no matter what genre I am writing in, I hope to create a story that will be loved and have meaning for the reader's life.

Q: *Would you want to write more historical fiction?*
A: I love to study history! I believe that when we tell the stories of history, it's one of the best subjects anyone could learn, so I'm always looking to the past for inspiration. A few years ago, I was traveling in Poland and walked through the former Krakow Ghetto. I happened to notice a sign that referenced a resistance movement that had happened there. That same night, I began looking for more details and eventually came upon the true story of some Jewish teenagers, both girls and boys, who decided to fight back against the Nazis in defense of their people. Many stories of the Holocaust have been told, and all of them *should be* told. But this is one that I believe offers something new to young readers today. That story is what inspired *Resistance*, which I'm so excited to share with my readers!

IMAGES OF DIVIDED BERLIN

The Death Strip.

In September 1961, a woman talks to her relatives through the barbed-wire fence separating East and West Berlin.

East Berlin border guards add barbed wire to the Wall in November 1961.

A map showing the boundaries of the Berlin Wall and the sectors into which the city was divided by the victors of World War II.

A Time Line of the Berlin Wall

MAY 8, 1945 — Following Germany's surrender in World War II, Berlin is divided into four sectors: American, British, French, and Russian. Germany as a whole is also divided by June 1946.

JUNE 15, 1961 — More and more East Germans stream into West Berlin as conditions in the east worsen. Walter Ulbricht, East German Communist Party leader, declares: "Nobody intends to build a wall." But the exodus from east to west continues.

AUGUST 13, 1961 — After midnight, East German soldiers begin erecting a barbed-wire barrier along the border, which East German leaders call an "anti-fascist protection barrier."

AUGUST 22, 1961 — Ida Siekmann becomes the first known victim of the Berlin Wall, after jumping through the window of her 4th-floor apartment in East Berlin into West Berlin, just nine days after the wall's construction began.

AUGUST 24, 1961 — The first killing following the wall's construction occurs: Twenty-four-year-old Günter Litfin was shot dead by East German border guards as he swam across the river Spree.

JUNE 26, 1963 — US President John F. Kennedy declares, "Ich bin ein Berliner" (I am a Berliner), in a pledge of solidarity during a visit to West Berlin.

MARCH 30, 1970 — Four-Power talks on the status of West Berlin begin.

SEPTEMBER 3, 1971 — The Quadripartite Agreement is signed in Berlin by representatives from France, Great Britain, the United States, and the USSR, marking a relaxation of tensions in east-west relations, allowing West Germans to enter East Berlin in order to visit family, and permitting traffic between West Berlin and the rest of West Germany to move unimpeded.

MARCH 11, 1985 — Mikhail Gorbachev becomes the leader of Soviet Union and initiates cautious reforms.

JUNE 12, 1987 — US President Ronald Reagan challenges Mikhail Gorbachev, leader of the Soviet Union, to "tear down this wall."

JANUARY 1989 — Protests against the East German government spread and grow more audacious, but leader Erich Honecker insists: "The wall will stand in 50, even 100 years."

SEPTEMBER 10, 1989 — Hungary opens its border with Austria to East Germans, creating the first crack in the Iron Curtain. Thousands of East German "tourists" travel west.

OCTOBER 18, 1989 — Erich Honecker resigns as head of the German Democratic Republic while unrest continues to grow.

NOVEMBER 4, 1989 — More than half a million people gather in East Berlin to demonstrate for democracy.

NOVEMBER 9, 1989 — The Berlin Wall falls. After an announcement that East Germans can travel to the west, hundreds of people descend on crossing points and pour into the west. Crowds climb the wall and begin to bring down parts of it, and over the course of months, remove it entirely.

READ ON FOR A SNEAK PEEK AT *RESISTANCE*
BY JENNIFER A. NIELSEN!

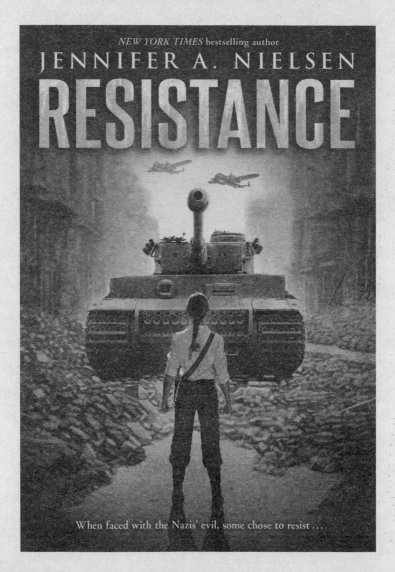

October 5, 1942
Tarnow Ghetto, Southern Poland

Two minutes. That's how long I had to get past this Nazi.

He needed time to check my papers, inquire about my business inside the ghetto. Maybe he wanted a few seconds to flirt with a pretty Polish girl. Or for her to flirt back.

But no more than two minutes. Any longer and he might realize my papers are forged. That it's Jewish blood in my veins, no matter how Aryan I look.

"Guten morgen." This one greeted me with a smile and a hand on my arm. I learned early not to smuggle anything inside the sleeves of my coat. You only had to be stupid once, and the game was over.

This officer was younger than most, which I once believed would give me an advantage. I'd thought the younger ones would be more naïve, and maybe they were. But they were also ambitious, eager to prove themselves, and fully aware that capturing someone like me could earn them an early promotion.

"Guten morgen," I replied in German, but with a perfect Polish accent. I smiled again, like we were old friends. Like I wasn't as willing to kill him as he was my people. *"Wie geht's?*" I didn't care how he was doing, on this morning or any other, but I asked because it kept his attention on my face rather than my bag.

Like other ghettos throughout Poland, Tarnow Ghetto had been sealed since nearly the beginning of the war, cut off from the outside world. Cut off from Jews in other ghettos. This isolation gave total power to the German invaders. Power to control, to lie, and to kill.

For the past three months, I'd worked as a courier for a resistance movement known as Akiva. My job was to break through that isolation, to warn the people, and to help them survive, if I could. But we were increasingly aware that time was running out. We'd seen people being lured onto the trains with promises of bread and jam, pacified into thinking they were being relocated to labor camps. Then they were crammed into cattle cars without water or space to move. And their destination was never to a labor camp.

They were headed for death camps, designed to kill hundreds or even thousands of people a day. I'd seen them. Been sickened by them. Had my heart shattered by them.

The Nazis called these camps their solution to the so-called "Jewish problem."

Yes, I very much intended to be their problem.

MOTIVES WILL SHIFT, SECRETS WILL EMERGE...

An electrifying new series from *New York Times* bestselling author JENNIFER A. NIELSEN!

Nothing is as it seems in the kingdom of Antora. Kestra Dallisor has spent three years in exile in the Lava Fields, but that won't stop her from being drawn back into her father's palace politics, or snatched by a group of rebels. As motives shift and secrets emerge, she will have to decide what and who it is she is fighting for in this epic tale of treachery and intrigue, love and deceit.

DISCOVER AN EPIC TALE OF POWER, MAGIC, AND DESTINY.

From the *New York Times* bestselling author of *The False Prince*

The Mark of the Thief Trilogy
by Jennifer A. Nielsen

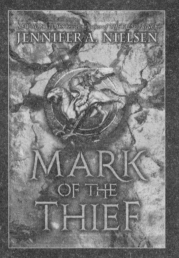

LOSE THE GAME, LOSE YOUR LIFE.

A *New York Times* bestseller

THE RUNAWAY KING

THE FALSE PRINCE

THE SHADOW THRONE

The Ascendance Trilogy
by Jennifer A. Nielsen

"Should appeal to fans of…Suzanne Collins…. [A] surefire mix of adventure, mystery, and suspense."—*The Horn Book*

"A page-turner."—*The New York Times Book Review*

"The twists keep coming."—*San Diego Union Tribune*